The Primrose Hill murder

The Primrose Hill murder is a novel set among the treason trials of the Popish Plot.

On October the seventeenth 1678 the body of a London magistrate was found at the foot of Primrose Hill. Was he murdered by Catholic plotters – or by Protestant fanatics? Had the underworld taken its revenge – or was it suicide? The death of Sir Edmund Berry Godfrey has remained an unsolved mystery for more than three hundred years.

The characters portrayed are real people. Charles II is seen at his most devious in politics, and in the arms of the most seductive of his mistresses. Mr Pepys is seen fighting for the navy and his life. Here are the rival Catholic and Protestant dukes (York and Monmouth), the little Earl of Shaftesbury and the giant Earl of Pembroke, together with humble clerks and maid-servants and sundry unsavoury persons, not least among them the Reverend Titus Oates.

The trials too are real. This was an age when the law was far removed from justice. Informing was lucrative, and perjury rife. Those charged with plotting treason or murdering a magistrate had little hope of acquittal, however innocent.

Through the detective work of its young hero, this historical whodunit offers a solution to the questions asked at the time and still asked today: How and where did Mr Justice Godfrey die? Who really killed him, and why?

Also by Jeremy Potter

Fiction

Hazard Chase (1964, reprinted 1989)
Death in office (1965)
Foul play (1967)
The dance of death (1968)
A trail of blood (1970)
Going west (1972)
Disgrace and favour (1975)
Death in the forest (1977)

History

Good King Richard? (1983)
Pretenders (1986)
Independent Television in Britain, volume 3:
Politics and Control, 1968–80 (1989)
Independent Television in Britain, volume 4:
Companies and Programmes, 1968–80 (1990)

THE PRIMROSE HILL MURDER

Jeremy Potter

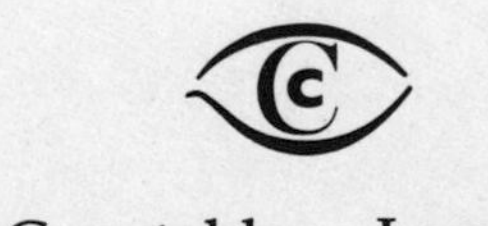

Constable · London

First published in Great Britain 1992
by Constable & Company Ltd
3 The Lanchesters, 162 Fulham Palace Road
London W6 9ER

ISBN 0 09 471650 1
Set in Linotron Palatino 10pt
and printed in Great Britain
by Redwood Press Ltd
Melksham, Wiltshire

A CIP catalogue record for this book
is available from the British Library

AUTHOR'S NOTE AND ACKNOWLEDGMENTS

This is a work of fiction in which all the characters are real people, and all the public events described are actual occurrences, but the story and the interpretation of the characters' actions and motives are my own.

In previous novels in this genre I have attempted plausible explanations for some of the other mysteries in English history: the killing of William Rufus in the New Forest; the disappearance of the Princes in the Tower; and the poisoning of Sir Thomas Overbury. But the violent death of the metropolitan magistrate, Sir Edmund Berry Godfrey, who vanished in unknown circumstances in the midst of the Popish Plot, is perhaps the most puzzling of all.

The murder (if murder it was) represents both a turning point in history and a landmark in the failure of crime detection. Thomas De Quincy in his satirical essay, *On Murder, Considered as One of the Fine Arts* (published in 1827), hailed it as a masterpiece: 'The finest work of the seventeenth century is, unquestionably, the murder of Sir Edmundbury Godfrey . . . In the grand feature of *mystery,* which in some shape or other ought to colour every judicious attempt at murder, it is excellent; for the mystery is not yet dispersed.'

Down the years since 1678 the reason for, and facts behind, Sir Edmund's untimely demise have been argued and disputed in innumerable books and pamphlets, whose accusations and counter-accusations have resulted in a medley of enlightenment and confusion. Those works which I gratefully acknowledge to have been the most helpful to my researches are Sir John Pollock's *The Popish Plot* (1903), John Dickson Carr's *The Murder of Sir Edmund Godfrey* (1936), John Kenyon's *The Popish Plot* (1972) and Stephen Knight's *The Killing of Justice Godfrey* (1984).

PROLOGUE

It was truly said to be an age given over to all vice; an age of whores and harlots, pimps and panders, rogues and rascals; an age of lechery, treachery and perjury. It was the year of Our Lord 1678, and in Westminster Hall on the fourth day of April a peer of the realm was on trial for his life, arraigned on a charge of murder most foul and brutal.

The majesty of the law had become debauched by corruption. It was wont to pronounce the innocent guilty and the guilty innocent with awesome solemnity. About today's proceedings there were but two certainties: first, that Philip Herbert, seventh Earl of Pembroke and Montgomery, had killed a man; and, secondly, that he would not be punished for it.

An august procession of the highest and mightiest in the land emerged from the House of Lords, and the spectacle of their lordships, the judges and their retinues entering the hall two by two in full regalia drew gasps from the crowd thronging the hall. It was not every day that common folk could savour the sight of an earl on trial before his peers.

On the appearance of the presiding dignitary, the venerable Earl of Nottingham – appointed Lord High Steward for the occasion – a hush fell. Four maces were borne before him, and he was escorted by his sergeant and purse-bearer. These were followed by Garter King of Arms in heraldic splendour and Black Rod bearing his white staff of office. To the goggling mob it was as good as a pageant.

All made obeisance in front of the vacant throne before taking their places; only to rise again and stand uncovered for a proclamation by the Sergeant at Arms, who read His Majesty's commission to the Lord High Steward. The Constable of the Tower was then commanded to produce the prisoner, and at the first glimpse of him the spell was broken. A babble broke out which all the ushers' threats of eviction failed to quell.

The accused was an evil-looking giant: broad-chested, burly as a prize-fighter and more than six feet tall. Towering above his guards and strolling between them as though taking a carefree walk through his own estates, he greeted the company with a supercilious stare. All other eyes were fixed on the axe which was carried only a few inches from his ear, but the blade was pointing away and he paid it not the slightest heed.

'My Lord of Pembroke,' the Lord High Steward addressed him when he stood at the bar, 'you are now brought before this great assembly to undergo a trial wherein all that can concern you in this world – your estate, your honour and your life itself – is at stake. There is no less a crime charged on you than the murder of one of His Majesty's subjects, and this charge is made not by common fame or rumour but by a grand inquest composed of gentlemen of quality and consideration. The king will have a strict account of the blood of the meanest of his subjects, by whomsoever it is shed, and by his command your lordship is to be tried not by a select number of lords but by the whole house of peers here assembled.'

The response to this homily was a glare of intense malevolence which swept across the entire hall. Its force caused those on whom it rested to cower with fright, but the Lord High Steward continued unperturbed, lecturing the defiant prisoner on the shame of his situation, the indignity of his becoming a public exhibit and the disgrace of a nobleman's appearance as a felon at the bar.

When told that he might think this penance worse than death itself, 'for he that outlives his own honour can have little joy in whatever else he lives to possess', he exchanged his scowl for an expression of disbelief. This deepened into a sneer, and he cast a mocking glance at the rafters as though calling on God to be his witness, when the Lord High Steward ended his peroration with the promise of a fair trial.

The reading of the indictment was a formality which the Clerk of the Court chose to dispose of at speed in a singsong voice, as though chanting a prayer: 'That you, not having the fear of God before your eyes but being moved and seduced by the instigation of the devil, on the fourth day of February in the thirtieth year of the reign of our sovereign lord, Charles II, by the grace of God King of England, Scotland, France and Ireland, Defender of the Faith et cetera, et cetera, did with force and arms in the parish of St Martin's in the Fields in the county of Middlesex feloniously and with malice aforethought assault one Nathaniel Coney, gentleman, did strike and bruise him, beat him to the ground and kick him on the head, neck, breast, belly, sides and back so that he on the tenth day of February following did languish and die.'

When asked how he pleaded, the earl shrugged his shoulders indifferently. When pressed for an answer, he took a coin from his pocket, slapped it on to the back of his hand, glanced at it casually and replied: 'Not guilty'. When asked whether he elected to be tried by his peers, he nodded curtly.

The Attorney-General then told the court that to sustain an indictment of murder there must be proof of malice, and that malice could be either expressed or implied. In this case, he declared, there was no evidence of hatred or ill-will expressed beforehand, but malice was implicit when a man caused the death of another by violence without provocation.

The facts according to the prosecution were as follows. On Sunday, the third of February last, the Earl of Pembroke was drinking with some friends in Long's alehouse in the Haymarket (and Mr Attorney-General was sorry that the Lord's Day was not better employed by them) when Mr Coney entered the house with the intention of drinking a bottle of wine with a companion, Mr Goring. The prisoner, knowing Mr Coney, invited them to join his company, but Mr Coney declined, stating that he had business to discuss with his friend. The earl, however, would brook no denial and after some argument they consented to go into his private room, where they all drank together.

At an hour after midnight (or thereabouts) a quarrel broke out between the earl and Mr Goring. Angered by some words used by Mr Coney's friend, the earl threw a glass of wine in his face, and Mr Goring had to be restrained from drawing his sword to avenge the insult. He was put out of the room, but when Mr Coney attempted to follow he was prevented and set upon by the earl, who struck him to the ground and kicked and trampled on him until he became senseless. After some attempts to revive him the victim was carried away in a sedan chair to his lodgings, where he passed a week in bed in unbearable pain, complaining that the earl's bruising had brought him to that condition; of which he thereupon died.

The prosecution's witnesses were then called, and it soon became apparent that most had been bribed or intimidated by the earl's minions. Mr Goring gave evidence of the quarrel, but claimed that before being thrust from the room he had seen no more than the earl making towards his friend. Certainly, when he visited Coney at his lodgings the next day, the unhappy victim had told him that it was the earl who had knocked him down, but because he had then fainted he was unable to say whether it was the earl himself or one of his drinking companions who had assaulted him on the ground.

According to the next witness, Richard Savage, who was one of those companions, Goring had used impertinent language towards the earl. Savage had evicted him to prevent a fight. While so doing, he had heard the noise of a scuffle behind him and had turned to see the earl strike Coney and give him a kick as he fell – but only one kick, and that not with any great force.

Under examination Savage admitted that Coney had been rendered unconscious, that his temples had had to be chafed before he opened his eyes, and that he could then neither speak nor recognise anyone. On the earl's orders he had been hoisted on to a row of chairs and consigned to the care of a servant of the house. Savage had visited him two days later and found him in 'a pretty good condition'.

John Shelley, another of the earl's cronies, told the court that the quarrel had begun when Goring suggested playing at dice but changed his mind and declined because the earl sent out for £500 to set the stakes higher than he could afford. The earl then told him that he was an idle fellow to propose something and not pursue it, and Goring responded with the taunt that being an earl did not make a man a gentleman.

It was for this affront that he received the glass of wine in his face and was thrown out. Coney was then ordered to leave too, and when he refused the earl boxed him on the ear and he fell. But, according to Shelley's testimony, it was drunkenness, not the blow, which had laid him insensible.

Captain Fitz-Patrick, the third of the earl's men, confirmed the evidence of the others, adding for good measure that when they picked him up false dice fell out of one of Coney's pockets. No one would wish to speak ill of the dead, declared the captain, but it had to be said that Nathaniel Coney was both a drunkard and a cheat.

Next into the witness box was William Viner, the servant from the alehouse, who knew which side his bread was buttered and swore, as God was his witness, that the earl never laid a hand upon the poor drunken gentleman, who had fallen down of his own accord. He recalled an evening a few weeks earlier when Mr Coney had been so far gone in wine and small beer that when he tried to sit down he had missed the chair and fallen to the floor in the same manner.

Charles Coney then told the court how, on the following day, he had found his brother in bed at death's door.

An apothecary and a physician summoned to the victim's bedside gave evidence of injuries to his belly consistent with what might be expected from 'the Pembroke kick'.

Two surgeons reported on the inquest. A post-mortem had revealed an extraordinary quantity of extravasated blood, blackened and congealed, in the lower part of the belly. There were bruises and great black spots on the body, which was black and blue in diverse places. The diaphragm was contused and swollen, and the right breast marked by a very large and very black bruise. Both men gave it as their professional opinion that such injuries could come only from violence.

Most damning of all was the evidence of Coney's nurse, one Alice Avery, who was straightly charged by the Attorney-General to 'tell your whole knowledge'. Her patient had told her, she said, that he had never been so beaten, kicked and abused in all his life. These were the last words he had uttered before he died: 'I wish to God that I had never been in Lord Pembroke's company, for I do believe, in my conscience, that my lord hath been the death of me.'

'Speak those words again,' the Attorney-General demanded, and every whisper was silenced while she repeated them, looking the prisoner full in the face. Then a sigh of belief ran through the great hall, followed by cries of 'The axe! The axe!'

All eyes were turned on the prisoner, searching for some sign of guilt or contrition; but the earl stood impassive as though deaf. He had disdained to cross-examine any of the prosecution witnesses, but now, with an ill grace, he deigned to accept the Lord High Steward's invitation to produce his own. His demeanour made it plain that he was not responding to the demands for his head; merely resigned to the need to show some trifling interest in these tiresome proceedings.

His first witness was a Dr Conquest, who said that he had treated Mr Coney for fainting fits in December. His patient had been a very hard drinker of wine and strong spirits, which caused stagnation of the blood and had led to the fits. When called in again in February after the attack, he had found Mr Coney's condition attributable to the consumption of a great quantity of small beer, and Coney had confessed to him that he had been too drunk to have any recollection of what had happened that night at Long's.

Dr Lower, the second witness for the defence, was yet another medical man who had attended the victim. He testified to having found no symptoms of fever on the day before death.

'Can any man be mortally hurt and bruised, whereof he may languish, and yet not have a fever?' inquired the Lord High Steward.

'According to my knowledge and experience, my lord,' replied the physician, 'usually and most commonly upon a mortal bruise an inflammation follows and that inflammation causes a fever, which will be evident in the patient's pulse or tongue or water. But none of those I found so affected in Mr Coney.'

At this the prisoner smiled for the first time and called his next witness with an airy flourish.

Another surgeon who had examined the body after death next came forward to contradict his colleagues for the prosecution. He testified to having noticed no external blackness or blueness caused by bruising. Internally, the blood was clotted, the pericardium withered, the heart loose as a rag, the lungs adhering to the ribs. The organs were those of a sick man, but not of one mortally injured. Whatever harm had been done to the body had been self-inflicted.

The three medical men had earned their doubtless handsome fees from the earl, and he thanked them sweetly before bowing to the Lord High Steward to signify that there he rested his defence.

Mr Solicitor-General, the king's second law officer, summed up for the prosecution at some length. He told their lordships that this was a clear case of wilful murder. They had heard evidence from four witnesses that the Earl of Pembroke had invited Mr Coney into his room at Long's alehouse. They had heard evidence from four witnesses that, although the earl and Mr Goring had quarrelled, no provocation to strike him had been given to the earl by Mr Coney. Yet all – save one manifestly untrustworthy pot-man – were agreed that the prisoner had indeed struck him. It was also common ground that before leaving he had ordered a servant to light a fire and watch over Mr Coney, and their lordships were invited to consider why he would have issued such an order if he were not conscious of having inflicted some grievous injury upon the unfortunate gentleman.

In conclusion, the Solicitor-General made much of the nurse's evidence that Coney had blamed the prisoner for his mortal sickness, and of the professional diagnosis of two witnesses that his condition was attributable to 'the Pembroke kick'. To the question whether Coney's drinking habits hastened his end the answer had to be 'no': 'For from the instant he did receive the earl's blow he never had any ease till he died.'

Finally came a reminder of the penalty for such a crime. 'The king's justice in this prosecution conforms to the law given by the Almighty in the infancy of the world, namely, that whosoever sheddeth man's blood, by man shall his own blood be shed. Now will your lordships please withdraw to consider the evidence?'

Stiff-jointed after so full a sitting, they trooped out of the hall, leaving the onlookers to speculate how long their deliberations would last. Determined not to miss the final act in the drama, the mob settled down to chatter and bring in its own verdict of guilty.

Some argued that, on the evidence they had heard, the lords could not avoid convicting the earl, who was well-known for his evil reputation and ungovernable temper and widely reported to have committed other murders in a drunken rage. Others claimed that the law officers of the Crown had made a hash of an open-and-shut case. But was this due merely to incompetence or were they (as some suspected) acting under orders not to cross-examine the earl's suborned witnesses and expose their perjury? And if they had been so instructed, who had issued the instruction? One held the king's ministers responsible; another his former ministers – out of office but still powerful – amongst whom the earl was known to have influential friends. The boldest blamed the king himself, for if earls were to be punished for their misdeeds, why not kings?

It was two hours before the prisoner was led back to learn his fate and the lords returned to cast their votes before him in open court. 'The order of your lordships' opinions is to be delivered beginning with the puisne barons and so on upwards,' announced the Lord High Steward. 'My Lord Butler, how say you?'

The named junior peer rose and answered in a loud voice: 'Not guilty of murder,' adding, when the hubbub which greeted these words had died down, 'but guilty of manslaughter.'

Peer after peer followed suit, and when all their verdicts were delivered, only six had found the prisoner guilty of the charge; eighteen not guilty. The remaining forty had concluded that the killing was without intent and brought in the same verdict: 'Guilty of manslaughter'. Manslaughter was a lesser offence than murder, but one incurring the same penalty.

'My Lord of Pembroke,' the Lord High Steward addressed him, 'it is but two months and a few days since, by the king's mercy, you were released from the Tower of London where you were held for uttering such horrid and blasphemous words as are not fit to be repeated in any Christian assembly.

'Since your release a complaint has been laid against you that you did, one Saturday evening in the Strand, assault an innocent gentleman, one Philip Ricaut, almost causing him the loss of an eye. You have, moreover, been recently confined by this House of Lords for an attack on another of its members, my lord of Dorset.

'These are not matters which have concerned us on this present occasion, but they disallow consideration of any possible mitigating circumstances in this case. Today, my lord, you have been found guilty of the heinous offence of manslaughter. What have you to say for yourself why judgment should not be passed upon you to die according to the law?'

So the earl's criminal record was too scandalous for even his peers to overlook! Against all expectation, justice had been done; or so it seemed for a moment. But there was another surprise to come.

The prisoner stood flushed with anger at the majority's verdict and the Lord High Steward's words. He had lost his temper and thumped the bar with his fist so violently that the wood splintered. 'My life does not lie in your lordships' hands,' he shouted. 'I claim the privilege of the statute governing this case.'

He was invoking the protection of an almost forgotten medieval law, and the mob's rejoicing turned at first into puzzlement and then dismay as realization dawned that the whole of the day's elaborate ceremonial and judicial proceedings had been no more than a charade.

'You must have your privilege, my lord,' responded the Lord High Steward with a gesture of displeasure. 'It is your right and cannot be denied you. By Act of Parliament from bygone times a peer convicted of a felony must be set free without penalty. But I would have your lordship take notice that no man can have benefit of that statute but once. The axe hangs over you still and will assuredly fall unless you repent and mend your ways.'

The trial was over. 'Depart in God's and the king's name,' bellowed the Sergeant at Arms, and they all departed; amongst them an unnoticed figure who had been seated in a gallery screened from view.

The throne may have been vacant, for it was not considered fitting that the king should preside in person over the legal processes conducted in his name; but it was not in the nature of Charles, by the grace of God King of England, Scotland, France and Ireland, Defender of the Faith, et cetera, et cetera, to deny himself a treat. His Britannic Majesty had enjoyed himself immensely, a cynical smile playing continually on the royal lips while he watched the drama enacted below. It was better by far than a performance at Drury Lane.

The king was well prepared for the denouement, but he was also aware that this homicidal peer of his realm had not escaped wholly unscathed. The verdict entailed the forfeiture of all his lands, tenements, goods and chattels.

That could not be allowed. Unless he was arraigned for high treason, a nobleman's estates were sacrosanct, and the king therefore intended to restore the earl's to him by warrant the very next day. The law had run its course; justice had been seen to be done; and, he reminded himself, the reigning favourite among his mistresses (who was the earl's sister-in-law) would now be awaiting her lord and master in his closet in the palace at Whitehall.

— 1 —

THE NAVY OFFICE

Samuel Atkins was a fair-skinned, bright-eyed, sturdily-built young gentleman, aged twenty-two: handsome in features and venturesome by nature. In common with his contemporaries, he was intent on enjoying life and rising in the world. But, against the fashion of the day, he held truth and honesty in high regard.

This reverence for truthfulness had been instilled into him in childhood by his father, an uncompromising Puritan, who had enlisted in Cromwell's army in the late war between Parliament and king and risen to command a regiment. When the army was disbanded, Colonel Atkins had settled in Shoreditch and become a London merchant, supplying naval and military stations overseas with coal and other commodities. He sent his son to St Paul's school and intended him for Cambridge and the Inns of Court, but a sweating sickness carried him off before his time and his business foundered. Sam's education was thus cut short, and for the past six years he had earned his living as a clerk in the government's service with slender prospects of promotion.

Thwarted in his ambition to practise the law, obsessed by its waywardness and malpractices, he dreamed of some twist of fortune whereby he might one day exchange his clerk's pen for a judge's wig and introduce the laws of England to justice.

It was his habit to escape at every opportunity from his office in Whitehall and hurry down the street to gaze in wonder at the goings-on in Westminster Hall. The trial of the Earl of Pembroke that morning was an occasion he would never forget. After a struggle to gain admission, he had been squeezed in a corner until he could scarcely breathe. Only by climbing up and balancing precariously on a ledge could he free himself from the crush and gain a view above the forest of heads.

Not guessing at the trump card up the earl's sleeve, Sam had quickly become convinced that, however much arrogance and scorn he displayed towards them, his peers would find some excuse to acquit him. For if every earl who killed a commoner were put to death, surely there would soon be no earls; and if no earls, what of kings? Yet when the lords retired to consider their verdict and one hour passed and then another, he could not bring himself to leave.

That he would not have been missed at the office was a vain expectation. His heart was pounding with foreboding as he scurried through swirling drizzle, turned into Cannon Row, took the stairs of Derby House two at a time and threw open the door of the small back room which was his place of work.

Tom Walbank, his fellow clerk, looked up eagerly. 'So it is you at last,' he said. 'What news? Is that murderous brute of an earl to lose his head?'

'Guilty but acquitted,' Sam told him breathlessly.

Tom whistled. 'Others may not be so lucky,' he remarked. 'Mr Secretary has been inquiring after you most particularly: and more than once.'

'What did Mr Hewer tell him?' Sam asked with a groan.

'That you had gone on an errand, he supposed. That satisfied him for a while, but then he burst in again and fell into a rage to find you still absent.'

Sam crossed the corridor and knocked at the head clerk's door. Will Hewer had known his father and became his first employer when he was forced to leave school. They had worked together in an office at the dockyards in Chatham, and when Will had been promoted to the Navy Office in Whitehall he had brought Sam with him. Since then he had become a person of consequence, but was rarely without a twinkle in his eye.

Will's marriage was childless and he looked upon Sam as his adopted son. Now he stared at him with all the severity he could summon. 'Save your breath for Mr Secretary, you miscreant,' he said, holding up a hand to prevent Sam from speaking. 'I have turned a blind eye to your absences because of the excellence of your work and my friendship with your father, but you were warned when last caught playing truant. I won you a reprieve then, but I fear you will find that Mr Secretary shows little mercy to a persistent offender. You are to go to him straightway.'

Sam left the room like a naughty schoolboy. No second thoughts were needed to tell him how he would be received at his uncle's house in the City when he arrived with his baggage to confess that he had been turned out of his place. The names of his dead parents would be invoked, and there would be much talk of the shame they would have felt. His aunt, who always behaved as though she were too refined to be a wine merchant's wife, would shake her head and sniff at this latest proof that she had married beneath her. A nephew ignominiously dismissed from the king's service!

'Remember,' Will called after him as though throwing a lifeline to a drowning sailor, 'remember that this is Mr Pepys's special day. Be penitent and offer him some excuse to celebrate with forgiveness. Take my advice and be not too open with him about where you have been.' But even as he spoke the words he knew that Sam would pay them no heed. The lad was too honest for his own good.

The Secretary to the Admiralty was squat and ugly, low-born and self-important. Lack of inches, breeding and good looks had fired his ambition; and ability, diligence and a wholehearted devotion to self-interest had carried this tailor's son to high office and a gratifying familiarity with the highest in the land. He stood close to the king's brother and heir, the Duke of York, who had served as Lord High Admiral of England for fourteen years before being driven from office for professing allegiance to Rome. The duke's dismissal had unsettled, but not unseated, Mr Pepys, who had narrowly survived accusations of covert popery.

He was a widower, and Derby House was both the Navy Office and his home. Sam and Tom Walbank, who alone among the clerks were privy to confidential information, boarded in the house; but, unlike Will Hewer, he never treated them as sons. He was their master and they were his servants.

He stood now beside his desk in his elegant drawing room. The window behind him overlooked a walled garden so sheltered that he grew oranges there. But Sam could tell at a glance that this was no time to speak of the wonder of growing oranges beside the Thames: Mr Secretary, as Tom had warned him, was in one of his black rages.

'Where, pray, Master Atkins, have you elected to spend this day of your employment in His Majesty's service?' he demanded.

The question offered Sam no choice. Others might keep their place and advance their prospects by playing tricks with words, or by outright deceit, but he was handicapped for life by his commitment to a strict observance of the truth. 'I have been to Westminster Hall, sir,' he confessed.

'In the company of every other idle good-for-nothing in London, I dare say! I do not doubt that the whole metropolis was eager to witness the spectacle of a delinquent peer, but some of us have business to conduct whatever the temptation to fly away to the raree-show of the day. You, Master Atkins, have wantonly neglected your duties, and not for the first time. Did I not caution you roundly six months ago? Did I not inform you then in unmistakable terms what your punishment would be in the event of a repetition? And do you not know me for a man of his word?'

The caution and repetition could not be disputed, but neglect of his duties was a charge which Sam could truthfully deny. 'I worked late yesterday and rose early today,' he protested. 'All the despatches to the captains of the fleet in the Medway were completed according to Mr Hewer's instructions before I left this morning.'

'Early and late! It is not for clerks to decide for themselves their hours of work. Whose candles did you use, pray? You know full well that those skinflints in Parliament and the Exchequer are starving the navy of funds, and the Lords of the Admiralty will tolerate no extravagance. The safety of the nation is at stake.'

Sam pictured whole fleets lying idle at anchor unable to put to sea because of his reckless over-expenditure on candles. 'I will pay for the wax out of my own pocket,' he promised.

Ill health made Mr Pepys irritable at the best of times. Now the self-righteousness of this wilfully disobedient clerk served only to stoke the flames of his fury, which was already at a pitch of frustration because he knew that he could ill afford to dispense with Sam's services.

'Do not suppose that you will be let off so lightly,' he shouted. 'You are paid to be at your desk in the mornings and afternoons without fail, unless released on official business, not gallivanting on your own. Let there be no misunderstanding about that. This morning I had a task of the utmost importance to assign to you. It required your immediate attention, but you were absent without leave. I returned later and you were still not to be found. Even the king's most urgent commands must await your pleasure, it seems.'

'But Tom –'

'Master Walbank's writing puts me in mind of a drunken spider. His words wander all over the page. Mr Hewer must have taken leave of his senses to employ one clerk with such an execrable hand and another who gads about town without so much as a by-your-leave.'

In truth, although the lines could be straighter at times, there was little to complain of in Tom's penmanship. If Sam's guilt was being made an occasion for such fault-finding in others, then plainly an abject apology was overdue. 'Sir,' he said, 'it grieves me more than I can say to have caused you so much annoyance; and on this of all days.' At the last moment he had remembered Will's hint.

'You are a rascal to take advantage of me,' Mr Pepys reproached him, but less angrily. 'You have the neatest hand in the office and know that I must rely on you for the fairest copies. But do not depend upon it to save you from dismissal in the future. No man is indispensable – not even myself,' he added without much conviction.

Sam picked up the cue instantly. 'But you are the saviour of the navy,' he declared fervently. It was fawning talk, but sincere. Had it not been for Samuel Pepys, the king's ships would scarcely have been fit to put to sea.

Few men could resist flattery and Mr Pepys was not among them. He acknowledged the tribute with a slight inclination of the head and then picked up some papers from his desk.

'If they are to be transcribed I will attend to them at once,' Sam offered. He could see that the pages were written in Mr Secretary's private short-hand which only Will Hewer and Tom and Sam himself had been taught to read.

'Of all the documents which have passed through my hands during my many years as a servant of the Crown,' declared the saviour of the navy at his most pompous, 'this is incomparably the most precious. I am reluctant to entrust it to the care of one who chooses not to heed my commands.'

Sam understood this to mean that his master was impatient to entrust it to him and the threat of dismissal had passed. His curiosity was awakened.

On the previous day Mr Secretary had returned from answering a royal summons to Newmarket, where the king was wont to attend to affairs of state in brief intervals between the more agreeable pastimes of hunting, hawking and horse-racing. Business with those summoned was normally transacted within the day, but this visit had lasted for three. Gossip in the office speculated on the reason, but it had not yet been divulged. Sam, it seemed, was to be the first to learn the secret.

'Is it an order to the fleet, sir?' he asked. 'Is there to be another war with the Dutch or the French?'

Catholic France under Louis XIV was striving to subdue the Protestant Low Countries, which were Protestant England's fiercest commercial rivals. The English navy was therefore sometimes ordered into action on the one side and sometimes on the other, depending on whether religion or trade was the uppermost consideration at the time.

'This is no naval matter.' Mr Pepys brushed the suggestion aside. 'It concerns the king himself, with whom I would have you know that I have been closeted for many hours. This is his – and my – gift to posterity. Here is something which records, for the enlightenment of the whole world, not only in this age but also in centuries to come, how God intervened to save His Majesty's life during the late great rebellion; so that he was spared to restore the monarchy and reign over us so gloriously today. What you now hold in your hand' – and he placed it there with a gesture of reverence – 'is an historic, a sacred, document.'

Sam excitedly ran his eye over the opening words and then suppressed a groan. The king's account of his adventures and escape after the final defeat of the royalists at Worcester had been a thrilling tale when first told, but it had grown stale with repetition. The court had long wearied of hearing of the same once hair-raising incidents every time His Majesty took to reminiscing; which was not infrequently. The story of a fugitive prince evading his would-be captors by lying hidden in an oak tree was as good as a romance, but it was nearly thirty years old and for nearly twenty had been drummed into the ears of the whole nation as a miracle – a manifestation of the divine protection enjoyed by the House of Stuart, God's representatives here on earth. Eighteen years after the Restoration many of his subjects were far from convinced that Charles II merited this special relationship with God.

'His Majesty dictated it to me himself. These are his very own words set down for the first time. To which,' Mr Pepys added modestly, 'I have contributed a touch or two of my own. I am bidden to return to Newmarket tomorrow with a fair copy. Since your day has been wasted until now, you must work through this evening. But for that and your disgrace, you would have been a welcome guest among the company at my feast, but that cannot now be permitted. Do not stint the candle-light tonight, but if your eyes grow sorely tired you must stop and be up at first light. No errors, blots or mis-spellings, mind. Every sheet has to be perfect or done again. Hurry now and set to work.'

Tom greeted the news of Sam's reprieve with a hurray.

'But I am banished from the feast,' Sam told him and showed him the reason.

'Be sure to copy it in your very best hand,' Tom teased. 'Then – who knows? – our Mr Pepys may be knighted and you will be appointed Clerk Extraordinary to the King.'

The two clerks were firm friends. They shared living quarters in the attic and ate in the kitchen with the servants, but once a year towards the end of March or beginning of April they were invited to join Mr Pepys and his friends in an anniversary celebration. This year, with the sound of music and merriment ringing in his ears, Sam was condemned instead to accompany the king on his six-week flight long ago. While Cromwell's men searched the country and put a price of £1000 on his head, Charles was smuggled heroically from hiding place to hiding place, lying wet to the skin in orchards in Shropshire, chilled to the marrow in barns in Staffordshire, and squeezed into airless priest-holes in Somerset.

But before Sam and the king reached the discomfort of the ditches of Wiltshire, the door opened and Mr Pepys entered to inspect the work. When he had read it through closely, he nodded approval and clapped Sam good-humouredly on the shoulder. 'Come,' he said. 'The rest can wait until the morning. We cannot allow you to starve.' Wine had eased the pain of his gout and mellowed the martinet.

Sam had never seen such a choice of foods as was laid out in the room below. There were dishes of lobster and carp, a platter of roast pigeons, a fricassee of chickens and rabbits, a leg of boiled mutton and an enormous side of lamb. There were four different kinds of tarts, a lamprey pie and a dish of anchovies. Most were already depleted and the guests' plates piled high, but on the plate in front of the place left vacant for Sam was nothing except a round black object the size of one of the balls the king and his gentlemen played with at the tennis court. While his host filled a glass of wine for him, he attempted to smother his dismay, until every one burst into laughter and he saw that it was one of Mr Pepys's pranks.

A harsh disciplinarian to his inferiors, Mr Secretary was the most genial of hosts in company of his own choosing. He valued friendship and loved parties, especially those he presided over himself. Mean about money, he never grudged it when entertaining. The wines had already been dispensed freely, as Sam could tell from the empty bottles and the state of the company. Will Hewer, who winked at him reassuringly, was red in the face. Tom's eyes were on Susan, the maid, whose low-cut dress revealed two milk-white treasures whenever she stooped to pass or collect a dish.

'Friends,' Mr Pepys called out, rapping the table for silence: 'Dear friends all, we are gathered to celebrate the twentieth anniversary of the removal of that object from my bladder.' He picked up the ball from Sam's plate, threw it gaily into the air, missed catching it and had to hunt for it on the floor. Then, to general applause, he found it and held it in front of that part of his body where it had grown.

'Two ounces of solidified uric acid of renal origin,' he announced with pride: 'a record, so I was informed by Thomas Hollier of St Thomas's hospital, the greatest lithotomist of this or any age, who, under God's guidance, delivered me from unbearable pain. Most have perished under the surgeon's knife when cut for the stone, but in that year Hollier cut thirty men and women and all survived. I bid you rise to your feet, good people, and drink to his memory.'

All stood, some unsteadily, and drained their glasses in honour of the surgeon who had saved the life of their host. Susan refilled them, and the next toast was to the memory of Mr Pepys's cousin, Mistress Jane Turner, in whose house he had been cut.

She too was dead, but her daughter Theophila was present to receive a handsome kiss of thanks by proxy.

The toasts continued until Sam's head was swimming and Tom experienced some difficulty in rising. Mr Pepys grew maudlin and announced in a slurred voice that this was a solemn occasion. He blessed the holy name of God for the salvation of his body and solicited their prayers for the salvation (in due course) of his soul.

Sam joined in the fervent Amens, longing to be abed; but instead he was ordered to make a general confession of his wickedness and regale the company with an account of the day's events in Westminster Hall. His audience was fuzzy-headed and sleepy when he began, but wide-eyed by the end.

It was Mr Pepys who broke the ensuing silence, praying aloud that none sitting round the table would ever find themselves in such a predicament as the earl.

'What a notion, sir!' exclaimed Theophila. 'You cannot suppose that we have a murderer in our company.'

'That was not in my thoughts, madam,' Mr Pepys assured her. 'But one need not be guilty of murder to be accused of it in these times. Our expert on the law will tell you that.'

But Sam could only respond with a yawn. Taking a candle and bowing himself out of the room, he climbed the stairs to bed, to refresh himself for the ditches of Wiltshire at first light.

— 2 —

THE KING'S CLOSET

Lord Pembroke's trial in April was succeeded by a summer of ill omens and public and private discontent. Divine displeasure was seen in three eclipses of the sun and two of the moon. Up and down the streets of London and in and out the alehouses ran rumours of rival conspiracies to overthrow the government: by Jesuits with a mission to reclaim a heretic nation for the Catholic Church and by Fifth Monarchy men preparing to rescue England from a dissolute monarchy and restore a Puritan republic whose only king was Christ.

At Westminster opposition parliamentarians were hovering on the brink of rebellion – at loggerheads with the king over his reluctance to disband an army which had no foreign enemy to fight. Inside Pembroke House in Leicester Fields such storms raged after the trial that Henriette de Kerouālle, Countess of Pembroke, was demanding a separation from her husband and a passage home to her native Brittany.

One evening in August, in the most private apartment inside the palace of Westminster, the countess's sister Louise, Duchess of Portsmouth, was to be discovered on a sofa in an unbecoming position. Her body was barely visible beneath that of the King of England, Scotland, France and Ireland. A petite beauty with the innocent face of a baby and the manners of a lady, la belle Louise (vulgarly, 'the French whore') was ministering to the king's needs, which were seemingly insatiable. As one envious courtier remarked in a verse expressive of the coarseness of the age:

'Nor are his high desires above his strength;
His sceptre and his —— are of a length.'

A door opened, and the soft breeze blowing from the river through an open window became a draught, playing upon the exposed nether portions of the royal flesh. William Chiffinch, Keeper of the Private Closet (vulgarly, His Majesty's Chief Pimp) stood in the doorway leading to the back stairs and coughed discreetly.

'The devil take you, Chiffinch,' exclaimed the king. 'Can your business not wait until I have done?'

Chiffinch closed the door behind him and waited obediently, his gaze respectfully averted.

'The men to whom you granted an audience are here by appointment, sire,' he announced gravely as soon as the king began to adjust his dress. 'It is already gone half-past eight and you commanded the dukes for nine o'clock.'

'Who are these night callers?' Louise demanded to be told.

She had intruded into the king's private sanctum unbidden. Although his temperament was easy-going, it could be unwise to presume too far, but tonight he had been alone and in a welcoming mood. Pettish at the interruption and loth to leave, she stood at the window setting her disarranged clothing to rights while Chiffinch tidied the room.

'One of them accosted me in the privy garden this morning with a cock-and-bull story. I granted him leave to return with a companion who will show me proof. Or so he avers.'

Even as he spoke, His Majesty became distracted. His French duchess was pouting so prettily that he was minded to mount her again. *A tergo,* he thought lecherously as she pulled her skirts demurely down over what he would wager was the shapeliest posterior in the whole of Europe. The King of France had sent him gold coin in plenty, but never a gift so precious as la belle Louise. It was his habit to visit her for an hour every morning after tennis and breakfast, while his other mistresses performed their duties in turn during the afternoons and nights.

Chiffinch had learned from long experience to interpret the look on his master's face, and he hurried out to fetch the visitors before venereal operations could be resumed.

'What is this man's tale? I shall not leave until you tell me.'

Louise was forever asking questions, for state secrets were a valuable commodity. She was well paid to reveal whatever she could draw out of Charles about his doings and intentions; and not only by the French ambassador. Mercenary by nature, she did not scruple to do business with the Earl of Shaftesbury, the enemy of both France and the king.

'It is of no consequence, I do assure you.'

His impatient shrug of the shoulders heightened her curiosity and cupidity. What could he be concealing? Was it likely that mysterious strangers would be summoned into the royal presence so privily and in the hours of darkness on an errand of no consequence? She was not to be put off, she told him, and stamped her foot as a sign that she would stand her ground and hear their story for herself.

'I forbid you to remain,' he answered with a frown: 'but since you are so insistent, you may be the first to learn that I am to be assassinated. Now be off with you!'

He spoke easily, with a half-smile, but the vigour with which he bundled her out of the room told her that he was less easy in his mind. Assassination! Whatever would become of her then, she wondered as she hastened back to her quarters to decide what use to make of the information and how much to charge for it.

The visitors ushered in by Chiffinch made an ill-assorted couple.

Christopher Kirkby was an impeccably dressed young gentleman from a respectable royalist family in Lancashire. He lived in Vauxhall, and Charles was acquainted with him as a fellow dabbler in science. They had conducted chemical experiments together in the royal laboratory. Besides chemistry, his passion in life was antipopery.

His companion was a snivelling, dishevelled and obsequious old clergyman who introduced himself as the Reverend Israel Tonge. His eyes were staring unfocused as though at some heavenly vision beyond the palace walls. In his arms was a sheaf of papers clutched tightly to his chest.

Kirkby made his bow and did not wait for permission to speak. 'Your Majesty will doubtless be aware that Dr Tonge is the rector of St Michael's, Wood Street. He bears incontrovertible evidence of the very grave intelligence which I conveyed to Your Majesty this morning.'

The king had not previously been aware of the Reverend Tonge's existence and was silently regretting that he was being forced to recognise it now, for the clergyman had plunged to his knees and abased himself so violently that he bruised his head against the silver buckles of his sovereign's shoes. His precious papers shot from his hands and spilled across the carpet.

The fellow's brains are as scattered as his evidence, thought the king, smothering a smile and wondering idly what mare's nest was about to be revealed.

Kirkby stood pale and tight-lipped, soberly behaved but no less earnest than the reverend doctor. 'I must beg Your Majesty to discontinue your walks in the park,' he said. 'Your life is in danger there.'

After the beds of his mistresses, St James's Park was the king's favourite exercise ground. He had planted it with walks of trees and flowers, laid out a lake and a canal and stocked it with deer and waterfowl which he liked feeding and his spaniels enjoyed chasing. It was his custom to saunter there every morning after his visit to Louise and to converse without ceremony with any gentleman who approached him.

'Assassins will be lurking in the bushes,' said Dr Tonge.

'What means will they employ to kill me?' The king was amused and spoke to humour him.

'There will be two men armed with screw-pistols.'

'Do you perchance have the traitors' names?'

'They are called Thomas Pickering and John Grove. They are papist desperadoes. One is a Benedictine; the other a Jesuit lay brother.'

The rector's ready replies jolted the king into taking his tale seriously for the first time. Whether this was a real plot or a clever invention, the man might not be quite as mad as he appeared.

'That is but the beginning,' Dr Tonge continued, his fanatic stare now full on the king's face. 'Should they fail, a third ruffian will be waiting. He has orders to plunge a knife into Your Majesty's heart. I have his name too. All their names are here.' He tapped his armful of papers, which he had retrieved from the floor. 'It is Conyers and he is a Jesuit – an agent of Satan like all his kind.'

'An agent of Satan will surely fail too,' said Charles, concealing his thoughts behind a confident smile.

'In that event there are plans for you to be poisoned.'

'By whom, pray?' The tone of the king's voice grew sharp; his smile vanished.

'The name is written here with the rest. I do assure Your Majesty that when you have studied the evidence which I have assembled you will be satisfied of the truth of my words. Meanwhile permit me to say no more on this occasion.'

'By whom?' insisted the king. 'Who is this poisoner? All my meals are tasted before I eat them; so how can it be done? Give me the name at once if you wish me even to cast an eye over your so-called evidence.'

Dr Tonge spoke hesitantly for the first time, foreseeing trouble. 'Who tastes Your Majesty's medicines?' he asked. 'Who would suspect a doctor at court? But I beg you, implore you, entreat you, beseech you, sire: Beware of Sir George Wakeman, the queen's physician!'

Mention of the queen's name made the king both angry and alarmed, convinced at last that there was indeed a plot, though of what kind he could not yet fathom. 'That is a lie,' he shouted, 'a base falsehood; and upon my word you shall pay for it, reverend sir.'

Dr Tonge cringed at the threat, but was not cowed. He spoke with a humility which the words tumbling from his lips belied.

'On Your Majesty's sacred life depend the safety of the realm and the protection of the Protestant faith. Your death will be the signal for a general uprising by the papists. There are ten thousand of them in London and they are once more plotting to set fire to the city. In the panic and disorder, when the conflagration takes hold, one hundred thousand innocent Protestant throats will be slit according to their fiendish plan. The King of France will order his troops across the Channel to march on London and impose subjection to Rome. He will appoint Catholic peers to command the English army and serve as allies of France. I have their names too; and a copy of the secret papal bull nominating Cardinal Howard to be Archbishop of Canterbury. All this will come to pass – as sure as God is in Heaven – if Your Majesty is deaf to the warning of the most loyal of all your subjects, who (though unworthy) has been sent to you by the good Lord Himself. At this hour of peril to England and the true religion I pray to Him, the All-seeing, the All-knowing, to tear from your eyes the bandages with which the Devil hath blinded you.'

He sank to his knees, sobbing and gabbling and clutching at the king's legs, foam oozing from the corners of his mouth.

'Take this crazed fellow away,' Charles commanded in a fury, 'and never dare bring him into my presence again.'

Christopher Kirkby handed the papers to the king and escorted the reverend doctor from the room. At the door he turned and bowed low. 'Dr Tonge is not a well man, Your Majesty,' he said in carefully measured tones of respect, 'but I warrant you he is no liar.'

When they had gone, Charles sat on the sofa, so recently the seat of pleasure, recovering his composure. Here in the privacy of his closet he was surrounded by his collection of timepieces and choice paintings – Holbein portraits, sensual Titians and a Raphael Madonna and Child. His holy of holies had been defiled. He summoned a Gentleman of the Bedchamber to dispose of the papers left in his hand.

The ravings of the deranged clergyman had alarmed him, but not for his life. After spending the first eleven years of his reign in exile and poverty, he feared nothing so much as losing his crown, from which all pleasures flowed. Now he foresaw a storm which it would require all his skills to ride; otherwise it would surely sweep him back across the Channel.

About the safety of his person he cared less. To maintain a regal state, he was expected to live much of his life like a goldfish in a bowl, even dining in public; but he enjoyed being a spectacle. In an age when kings were no longer hedged by their divinity, he allowed himself to be approachable to strangers and accosted by supplicants, because he liked talking to his subjects. In the palace it was frequently impossible for his guards to distinguish those who had genuine business from those who had none but idle curiosity or criminal intent. The Stone Gallery through which he must pass to reach his private apartments was thronged from morning to night with sight-seers and office-seekers, among whom assassins might lurk.

At least the entrance to his withdrawing room was closely guarded, but not all who had right of access could be trusted. Even in the royal bedchamber, where the most confidential affairs of state were conducted, he was forced to play host to some who would make him a slave to the mob and others who wished him to return to the pain and poverty of exile.

To his closet alone was admission by personal invitation; and here his eldest and best beloved son, James, Duke of Monmouth, was always welcome. This evening he was admitted as soon as Kirkby and Tonge had obliged him by removing themselves.

The king beckoned him to the sofa, pulled him down beside him and put an arm around his shoulder. The lad was nearly thirty now, but as handsome as ever and prouder and more finely arrayed than any peacock. Others had been scandalised that a bastard should display the royal arms without a bar sinister, but Charles did not have the heart to rebuke him. He would have had every right to them, had his mother not been a slut.

'I have called you here tonight to be reconciled with your uncle,' the king told him with a show of severity. 'You must promise me to treat him with proper deference, Jemmie.'

The young duke's reply was to jump to his feet with an oath and declare that, as God was his witness, he would rather be damned than stay to meet that boorish, insufferable ogre. But even before he finished speaking, the door had opened to admit James, Duke of York. The legitimate heir to the throne paused with a start on the threshold when he noticed the presence of his nephew. Then, collecting himself and behaving as though they were alone, he bowed deeply to the king and advanced to kiss his hand.

The brothers had little in common except habitual fornication. Charles was tall and swarthy with the lazy, graceful air of a man who did nothing for himself. James was fair and stoutly built; blunt and breezy in manner, as befitted one who had commanded a navy. In character he was (sexual morals apart) as obstinately principled as Charles was flexible; and his wits were as dull as the king's were sharp and shrewd.

'There are ugly rumours abroad,' he observed. 'Those knaves from the Commons are conspiring to incite the army to mutiny. The regiments commanded by their friends will massacre Your Majesty's loyal Catholic subjects unless you act to save them. Pray recall Parliament immediately and have this shameful Test Act repealed.'

The king sighed. The Test Act compelled all office-holders to receive the sacrament according to the rites of the Church of England and swear an oath abjuring the ridiculed popish doctrine of transubstantiation. It was this which had driven James and every other Catholic out of the armed forces: unjustly, as the king recognised. But it was fantasy to pretend that he possessed the powers to have even the most innocuous Act of a hostile Parliament repealed, let alone this particular one at a time of national hysteria about popery.

'Others rumours reach my ears, uncle,' said Monmouth.

James snorted, turned his back and continued to address the king: 'Plots are being devised against myself, even as we meet. And against the queen, too, for the crime of being a Catholic. Even your own person is in danger, since Your Majesty remains an obstacle to the ambitions of republicans. Rouse yourself, brother!'

Charles was dismayed by a blundering heir so overblown with the enthusiasm of a convert that his bigotry and constant calls to arms in the cause of his faith could cost them both the crown. He did not intend to be deprived of the sweets of sovereignty for the sake of James's soul. But the welfare of the queen was another matter.

'Catherine at least shall come to no harm,' he promised. 'I shall make it my business to see to that.'

Marriage had not been allowed to cramp his style, but guilt at being unfaithful to her several times a day made him fiercely protective of her. She had proved barren – the only woman on whom he was incapable of fathering a child. Yet he refused to countenance any suggestion of divorce; even though it might lead to a legitimate Protestant heir and avert the calamity of James as heir presumptive and future king.

His eye rested regretfully on Monmouth, who was not to be put down and now boldly joined issue with his uncle. 'His Royal Highness slanders true Protestants,' he declared. 'These men are patriots who seek to protect Your Majesty from the scheming of traitors and the agents of foreign powers.'

'Lies!' bellowed James, stung into taking notice of his nephew's presence at last. 'Your friends are the traitors. My lord of Shaftesbury and what he chooses to call his Country Party are nothing but rabble-rousers and mischief-makers.'

Before Monmouth could remonstrate, the king silenced him with a frown and gave his brother an approving nod. 'That slippery little earl is the wickedest dog in England,' he pronounced.

In open defiance of the Crown, Shaftesbury was set on persuading Parliament to exclude the papist duke from the succession in favour of Monmouth, whom his party were supporting as 'the Protestant Duke'. But, however great his affection for his Jemmie and however low his opinion of his brother's worldly wisdom, Charles stood firmly by the legitimacy of Stuart rule. He would not have the rightful heir disinherited, and on that point (if on no other) he professed himself adamant. When rumours were spread that he had secretly married Monmouth's mother, he issued a public denial.

His purpose behind tonight's meeting was to effect a reconciliation between the rival dukes by convincing Jemmie that there were limits to a father's indulgence and it would be rash to harbour ambitions above his station. A disclaimer by Monmouth seemed the only hope of halting Shaftesbury's campaign. To gain that, the promise of some public show of favour and friendship towards his nephew must somehow be extracted from a mulish and unforgiving James.

The prospect of success was never bright. It grew dimmer and dimmer as James expatiated on the iniquity of Monmouth's champion. 'You should have taken my advice and never let him out of the Tower, brother,' he concluded. 'Except on a cart to Tyburn.'

The previous year Shaftesbury had overreached himself in questioning the king's right to gag the Opposition by proroguing Parliament indefinitely. He had been imprisoned twelve months for his impudence before he could bring himself to buy his release by confessing to an error.

'Your Royal Highness would do well to remember that the country is behind the earl,' Monmouth warned. 'I refer to peers as well as people.'

'Peers who are convicted killers!' sneered his uncle. 'He is welcome to the Earl of Pembroke. They are birds of a feather.'

'Gentlemen!' the king intervened sharply and proceeded to deliver his prepared lecture on the perils of divisions among them. He begged them to bury their differences for all their sakes. 'Do you wish for another rebellion, another republic, another king's head on the block?' he demanded.

His words merely served to reduce Monmouth to a fit of the sulks and James to a state of barely suppressed rage that he should be blamed for his nephew's unwarranted pretensions and abetment of treason.

'Unless there is a settlement I shall be forced to send you both into exile,' Charles threatened. 'For your own safety,' he added to placate them when they both protested.

'My safety is of no account beside Your Majesty's,' replied James. 'My duty is to remain by your side and defend you against your enemies. Did I flee from the Dutch at Lowestoft when they sought to invade your realm?'

'I am ever grateful for your gallantry, James,' the king acknowledged, 'but it would not protect me from an assassin's pistol or dagger.' He told them the Reverend Tonge's story.

'There!' cried Monmouth triumphantly at the end. 'What further proof of Catholic treason does any man require?'

'Lies again! Lies, lies, lies!' exploded James. 'I wager Your Majesty a thousand guineas that this is a trick by Shaftesbury and his vermin to commit an atrocity and blame honest Catholics for it.'

'I will not take your wager,' replied the king, 'because the plot does not exist. It is the invention of an addle-pated cleric.'

'You are too cool, brother,' James rebuked him. 'Let me see the papers and judge for myself. If they libel your Catholic subjects, I shall demand a public inquiry by the Council. Lies must be nailed and the perpetrators punished.'

'We are agreed at last!' Monmouth exclaimed. 'I too wish for an inquiry; and when it is discovered that the papers tell the truth, the plotters must pay with their lives.'

'I have sent the papers to Danby unread,' the king told them. 'I employ ministers to read that kind of nonsense for me. The Lord Treasurer will decide what to do.' The Earl of Danby was his chief minister and, as the king well knew, heartily disliked by both the dukes.

Above their protests he called for peace and harmony and an end to the meeting. But James had not finished with his bastard nephew yet: 'If His Majesty should fall victim to Puritan assassins (which Heaven forfend!), do not delude yourself with the prospect of a crown. I may then be driven from the country, but there will be no King Monmouth, as your false friends feed your vanity by pretending. There will be a new Cromwell – Protector Shaftesbury!'

The two dukes left the room by separate doors. The encounter had not been a success, as the king was forced to confess to himself. But comfort was at hand. Chiffinch reappeared.

'My lady Castlemaine awaits Your Majesty's pleasure,' he announced.

— 3 —

THE KING'S HEAD

The Duke of Monmouth's assertion that the country was behind the Earl of Shaftesbury could scarcely be denied. Hatred and fear of popery had become a national obsession. Every act in the calendar of popish terrorism was daily remembered and rehearsed: the burning of Protestant martyrs at the stake during Mary Tudor's reign; the massacre of the Huguenots in France; the Vatican-inspired attempts to assassinate Queen Elizabeth; the Gunpowder Plot to blow up Parliament; the Great Irish Rebellion; the burning of London in the Great Fire.

In Germany war between the two faiths had lasted for thirty years and ended with the banishment of Protestantism to the northern outposts of Europe. Yet even that victory had not sated the bloodlust of Rome. Across the Channel Louis XIV proclaimed his determination to bring England back into the Catholic fold by force, and the pope had forbidden English Catholics to take the oath of allegiance to their king, so that, if France should invade, the loyalty of a quarter of a million of His Majesty's subjects would be in doubt.

So this was not a time for tolerance or half measures. In a staunch defence of liberty and the Church of England as established by law, Shaftesbury's Green Ribbon Club employed pamphleteers to inform and arouse the nation, agents to lobby Members of Parliament, and spies to report on the machinations of enemies of the state. Those who withheld their support were denounced as covert papists. Xenophobia became epidemic, and foreigners walking the streets of London were liable to be set upon and knocked to the ground for being foreigners.

The headquarters of the club's 'No Popery' campaign was the

King's Head tavern at the corner of Fleet Street and Chancery Lane; and there, one morning some four weeks after the meetings in the king's closet, sat the earl himself drinking and conspiring in a private room upstairs.

Before ennoblement he had been known as Anthony Ashley Cooper. As a young man in the civil war he had deserted the royalist ranks to join the enemy, declared himself a Puritan and become a member of Cromwell's republican Council of State. At the Restoration he had turned his coat again. Being among those who invited Charles home, he was rewarded with office as one of the king's ministers and enjoyed it for thirteen years. His downfall from the summit of power after a year as Lord Chancellor was contrived by the Duke of York in revenge for the Test Act. From that day he had moved into Opposition, formed his Country Party and Green Ribbon Club, reverted to republicanism and sought his own revenge at the head of a radical, anti-clerical, violently anti-Catholic faction.

Physically, my lord of Shaftesbury was very short, very frail and very ugly. His face was often contorted with pain from an operation which had left him with a limp and a suppurating wound in his stomach. His drinking companion at the King's Head was, by contrast, a veritable giant in the rudest of health. It was the infamous Earl of Pembroke.

Few cared to be seen in Pembroke's company since his trial, but he was a leading member of the club and a wholehearted supporter of the Opposition in the House of Lords, and Shaftesbury was not above finding a use for him despite his reputation. Today they had serious and secret business to discuss. Although alone, their heads were close together and their voices lowered as a precaution against eavesdroppers at the door. Their conversation took the best part of two hours and three flagons of the landlord's best Bordeaux; after which they adjourned to a house of pleasure in Covent Garden.

Downstairs, meanwhile, two other conspirators were sitting with their heads together in a dark, secluded booth in the public bar.

'Have patience,' Christopher Kirkby urged. 'He will come as he promised. You may depend upon it.'

But the Reverend Israel Tonge was restless and would not be soothed. 'The Jesuits have run him to earth and he is a dead man,' he muttered. 'I warrant you we shall not see him again this side of Paradise – where he may not have long to wait for us, for you and I are like to be their next victims.'

He darted a sudden glance over each shoulder, for nowhere was a man safe from those unholy disciples of error and their hired cut-throats. Not even in the King's Head.

The Jesuits were Dr Tonge's particular obsession. He blamed them for the martyrdom of the king's father; for the loss of his own fellowship at an Oxford college; for the burning down of his former church in the Great Fire; and for his failure to secure the deanery for which he had applied and which all true Christians knew that he deserved. In doing the devil's work they had condemned a servant of God, a scholar and a gentleman, to poverty and obscurity; and now, perhaps, to death.

He and Kirkby had been summoned before the Earl of Danby as soon as he had read the incriminating papers. The Lord Treasurer had asked in whose hand the forty-three articles setting out the details of the plot and the names of its perpetrators were written. In acknowledging that the hand was his own, Dr Tonge had explained that he had copied them at the insistence of his informant, who wished to conceal his identity because he lived in fear of his life.

Could he nevertheless vouch for the truth of what he had written, the Lord Treasurer had demanded. On his admission that he could not, they had been dismissed with orders to produce their informant so that he might testify in person. In the meantime it was to be understood that no proceedings could be initiated or arrests made on the strength of unsubstantiated allegations. Further and better particulars were required.

They left Whitehall suspicious of his reluctance to prosecute those they had unmasked as traitors, and the task of tracking down their informant had not proved easy. Claiming that the Jesuits were hot on his trail, he had taken to moving mysteriously round the city, lodging here and there, night by night, under different assumed names.

During their vain pursuit Dr Tonge had grown uncomfortably aware that, so far from being rewarded with a deanery for exceptional services to the Crown, he was likely to spend time as His Majesty's guest in Newgate jail for having invented the whole story.

But the Lord looked after His own and the doctor's prayers had been answered at last. While conducting morning service the previous Sunday, he had looked up from his prayer-book, and there among the congregation stood the man for whom he had been searching: it was an unmistakable sign from Heaven. At the end of the service he had cornered him before he was able to disappear and borne him off to Kirkby's house, where they had not released him until they thought they could feel certain of being able to find him again.

The rendezvous at the King's Head had been arranged for eleven o'clock. It was now a quarter before twelve, and Tonge was twitching with despair. His eyes were closed and his lips were moving, but Kirkby could not tell whether in silent prayer or uncontrollably. Was he about to be seized by one of his fits or would the good Lord come to his aid again? Kirkby was preparing for the worst when the clergyman's eyes suddenly flew open and were flooded with joy.

'Praise be to God for this and every one of his blessings,' Dr Tonge intoned, while twitching more violently than ever with a relief which Kirkby shared to the full.

The apparition before them was a strange sight for which to praise the Lord. Dr Tonge's dishevelled appearance was unprepossessing enough, but by comparison with this it was order and beauty themselves.

The latecomer crossed the floor of the inn unhurriedly, with a rolling, bandy-legged gait which might have been mistaken for nautical or equestrian if it had not been accompanied by a strong odour of spirits. He was stout and ill-shapen. His head seemed joined to his body without benefit of neck. His forehead and chin both hung so low that his mouth appeared to be set in the middle of his face, which was as round as a clock's. His eyes were deep-set and matched his gait, rolling aggressively from side to side, on the alert for a surprise attack from any quarter. As he walked, he snuffled through a squashed, snub nose, apparently sniffing out his enemies. On his head was perched a fair, woolly periwig which looked as though it had been taken from the wardrobe of a theatre.

'I have come,' he announced, taking a seat beside them. 'I am a man of my word like your good self, Mr Kirkby.'

Kirkby took the hint and handed him the promised sum of

money which had bribed him into keeping the appointment. It was received, not with thanks, but with a grunt and the comment that these were hard times for honest men.

'Have I not provided proofs enough to convince the whole world?' the honest man continued as he pocketed the coins. 'If the Earl of Danby says that more is needed, then it is as clear as font water that the Earl of Danby is in the pay of Rome.' He spoke in a loud, bold voice for all to hear.

'Pray moderate your tone, Dr Oates,' Kirkby begged him in an agitated whisper. 'The head of His Majesty's government may have no friends in this hostelry, but spies are everywhere.'

'If the Earl of Danby is not satisfied with what we have given him,' said Dr Oates, not moderating his tone, 'then, by God, he shall have more, and in plenty. Have I not with my very own ears overheard Jesuit fathers speak of honeycombing England with fireballs? Do not imagine, good sirs, that they will confine their arson to London this time. They mean to burn Bristol as well – ay, and York and Norwich too. They will make conflagrations, I warrant you, such as no human being has seen since the sack of Troy.'

He paused for breath and refreshment, and Kirkby ordered him a dram of gin, which he downed at a gulp.

'Let no one doubt that I have sufficient proofs of papist knavery to hang every Catholic in England,' he continued with a thundering belch. 'If the Lord Treasurer chooses to pay no heed, then I will go with you, as I promised, and swear to them before the Secretary of State.'

In Kirkby's house Oates had agreed at Tonge's insistence – and for a consideration – to come out of hiding and swear an affidavit before Sir Joseph Williamson, to circumvent the inaction of Danby and the king. He would then put an end to living as a penniless fugitive by demanding protection and maintenance until the guilty parties were brought to justice. After that he would expect a generous pension from a grateful nation.

Dr Tonge coughed nervously. 'Sir Joseph will not see us,' he said. 'I was turned away from his door yesterday.'

'Another papist in disguise!' hissed Oates. 'The pope has a secret agent in every high place in this poxy administration. We must not flinch from exposing them. It is God's will and our bounden duty to flush them out, every one of them. And it shall be done. Never fear, Master Kirkby.'

His roving eye had caught Kirkby quivering, but not with fear at the threat from papists in high places; rather at the face of a fanaticism which exceeded his own and seemed to spring, not from conviction and principle, but from shameless self-interest.

Kirkby knew Lord Danby and Sir Joseph for devout Protestants and was beginning to regret his association with these two soiled men of the cloth: for Dr Oates too was in holy orders, though without a benefice. He dared not reveal to them what he had heard from a friend: that the Secretary of State had refused Dr Tonge an interview because he judged him insane. Instead he calmed Oates with another dram, which also vanished at a single swallow.

Dr Tonge treated them both to one of his wild stares. 'Rest assured that neither of us will permit the truth to be suppressed,' he promised Oates. 'We go instead to Mr Justice Godfrey. Our appointment is for midday, so we are late and must make haste.'

He led the way into Fleet Street and along the Strand until they left the bustle of the main thoroughfare for Hartshorn Lane, which took them winding down towards the river.

Sir Edmund Berry Godfrey was no Whitehall courtier. He was a City merchant, who also served as the chief metropolitan magistrate. In that capacity he was policeman, prosecutor and judge in one, and his name was a byword for fearlessness. During the Great Plague he had been the only Justice of the Peace to remain in the city, and once, when his officers refused to enter a pest-house in pursuit of a grave-robber, he had gone inside and dragged the man out himself. His knighthood and a silver flagon from the king had been the reward for his courage during that time.

His house stood at the end of the lane, and as they approached it Oates slowed his pace, reluctant to make his face known to such a zealous guardian of law and order.

Tonge tugged at his sleeve to urge him on. 'Godfrey is respected by every decent citizen,' he said; 'none more so. If you swear before him to the truth of what you have revealed, even the king and his brother and all the rogues in government will not be able to ignore you. Lord Shaftesbury and his men will see to that.'

'Do the swearing yourself then,' Oates replied truculently. He pulled his arm free and turned drunkenly on his heel.

'That I cannot do, as well you know,' Tonge cried and pleaded. 'No one but yourself has been a witness to the conspiracy. You have sworn to swear and been well paid for it. Would you be forsworn and return Master Kirkby his money?'

'And would you have the Jesuits unpunished and at liberty?' Kirkby demanded furiously.

At mention of the Jesuits Oates spat on the ground. 'Never!' he roared. 'But if this knighted thief-taker is in the king's pocket we shall be wasting our breath.'

They argued vehemently, arms flying, until Oates was persuaded by Kirkby's account of an occasion when Godfrey had displayed such stubborn opposition to the king that he had been imprisoned for it. The idea of a magistrate in prison restored him to good humour. He turned back and made ready to enter the house with a semblance of dignity and sobriety.

Mr Justice Godfrey was tall and forbidding. His visitors were unpunctual, and he received them in his office sternly, staring at Oates with unconcealed distaste. 'Dr Tonge has told me of your business, gentlemen,' he said. 'I have to tell you that, upon reflection, I have decided to have nothing to do with it. I am a businessman, not a lawyer. This matter is beyond me. In my public service I deal with common criminals, not affairs of state.'

'But we have come to you most especially, Sir Edmund, knowing you to be a man who, above all other men, will never shirk your duty, however unwelcome it may be.' Tonge bowed and scraped and cringed ingratiatingly. 'It is recognised throughout the entire kingdom that you are one of the few men of virtue in this sinful world.'

The magistrate was impervious to flattery. 'I have not been well of late,' he said, 'and the responsibility is heavier than my health can bear. You must forgive me. In performing my duties I have made many enemies, and my involvement in this affair would be too dangerous. The very fact of taking your statement could make me an accessory to acts of treason.'

'The safety of the realm is at stake,' pleaded Tonge. 'The lives of all of us are at risk. We will none of us lie safe in our beds until the plotters are arrested. Like ourselves, sir, and all other mortal creatures, you must put your trust in God. Will you pray with us for faith and guidance?'

Sir Edmund shook his head impatiently. 'I thank you, but have no need of your intercession. Now, if you will excuse me, my clerk and I must busy ourselves on other matters.'

Kirkby and the two doctors looked at each other in dismay. The colour drained from Tonge's face and reappeared in Oates's. Anticipating an outburst which would have them all evicted, Kirkby came swiftly to the rescue.

'We have brought two copies of the document in question. They are identical.' He laid them on the desk. 'The Reverend Titus Oates will swear to the truth of what they contain. The Reverend Israel Tonge and I will sign as witnesses to his signature. If you would be so kind as to relent and oblige us so far, I beg that you will sign as witness to his oath, and your clerk as witness to your own signature. I am advised that the law and your duty as a Justice of the Peace require nothing more. We do not ask you to read the document against your will, nor to be made aware of the details of its contents. We will take both copies with us when we leave, so that you will remain in complete ignorance of the nature of the plot and the names of the traitors.'

'But I have to be cognisant of the character of the felonies which are disclosed in the documents,' the magistrate objected.

'The firing of towns, sir,' said Oates, adding under his breath: 'amongst a multitude of other villainies.'

'The king himself has already been apprised of it,' Tonge interposed. 'Mr Kirkby will bear me out when I give you my solemn word as a man of God that he and I have informed His Majesty of it personally and handed him a copy of the very documents before you. Assuredly there can therefore be no question of your concealing acts of treason.'

Silence fell while the magistrate sat frowning in thought. 'That is a point on which lawyers may differ,' he said at last, 'but you have my agreement – my reluctant agreement – to the arrangement which Master Kirkby has proposed.'

The signatures were affixed and he bade them good day, saying that they had overcome his better judgment on that occasion and praying them to be considerate enough not to trouble him again. Kirkby and Tonge bowed their consent, well satisfied, but Oates, now that he had nothing to lose by it, assumed a menacing scowl.

'That I cannot promise and, as a true Protestant, you, sir, should not demand,' he replied. 'What we have with us here today is but the beginning. His Majesty and the Lord Treasurer have requested further particulars and, with the Lord's blessing on our enterprise, they shall have them. If we come to you again in Christ's name, you must not fail us or Him. The Devil take you otherwise.'

— 4 —

THE DEPOSITION

It was early one Saturday morning three weeks later when the two men of God returned to Mr Justice Godfrey's house. Dr Tonge was agitated, Dr Oates swaggered, and Christopher Kirkby was reported to have set out for the north in haste. The storm was about to break.

Apologising for the hour, Dr Tonge explained excitedly that they had been summoned to a meeting of the Council at ten o'clock – a meeting especially convened to hear their evidence. They were to be interrogated about a new and fuller deposition which had been delivered to the Lord Treasurer the previous day. It contained further revelations – information obtained at risk of life and limb by the intrepid Dr Oates, shortly to be hailed as defender of the faith and saviour of the nation (so Dr Tonge predicted).

The magistrate received them with reluctance and foreboding. Since their previous visit he had been making inquiries about this alleged paragon, and what he learned had plunged him into one of those black moods of dejection to which he was prone. This defender of the faith and saviour of the nation was also, it had transpired, a sodomite, an apostate and the king of liars.

Oates, it seemed, had been brought up as an Anabaptist, the son of the war-time chaplain to the famous Colonel Pride's regiment of Independents. He had been educated at Westminster School, Merchant Taylors' School and Caius College, Cambridge, all three of which honourable institutions had expelled him for homosexual practices. But these youthful indiscretions had proved no bar to his taking holy orders in the Church of England, where his career had ended in disgrace after the loss of a living in

Kent for stealing his neighbours' hens and pigs, followed by dismissal from a naval chaplaincy for buggery.

To his further astonishment and disgust, Mr Justice Godfrey had discovered that after his rejection by the Church of England this former Anabaptist had offered himself as a convert to Rome. The Provincial of the Jesuit order in England had listened sympathetically to the account of his maltreatment by heretics and despatched him as a novice to a seminary in Spain.

There he had lasted only six months. Sent instead to a Jesuit college in France, he had been disappointed to find that the order was not so leniently disposed towards unnatural vice as he had supposed. Summarily ejected from both college and Church, he had returned to London a fanatical Anglican reborn, vowing vengeance on the Jesuits and all who had slighted him.

Godfrey's informant was the rector of St Martin's in the Fields, where he worshipped. Casting charity aside, that worthy Christian had given it as his considered opinion that the man Oates was a consummate cheat, a vicious and perjured blasphemer, and an impudent, bawdy, foul-mouthed wretch whose pretence of patriotism was but bile and malice disguised.

Now, laid in front of him by this creature, the magistrate saw a thick set of folio pages headed *The True and Exact Narrative of the Horrid Plot and Conspiracy of the Popish Party against the life of His Sacred Majesty, the Government, and the Protestant Religion*.

'We have brought two copies of the document which was handed to Lord Danby yesterday,' said Dr Tonge. 'His lordship informed us that the Council would demand sworn copies, and my friend will now swear and sign in your presence. The deposition which he last swore before you contained forty-three articles. Thanks to Dr Oates's fearless investigations and wondrous memory, there are now an additional thirty-eight.'

'On this occasion, since the matter has become so weighty, you must permit me to read it for myself,' the magistrate insisted.

'Impossible! There is no time. The Council cannot be kept waiting.' Tonge flung his hands wildly in the air.

'Then you shall give me the gist of it and leave a copy for me to read at leisure after you are gone. There is more to it now than the firing of towns, is there not?'

The doctors moved to a corner of the room, where they conferred in whispers.

'I am adamant,' Godfrey warned them. 'Those are my conditions. If they are not acceptable, I shall have no more to do with the matter and you must take yourselves off to another magistrate. Already you have breached good manners by troubling me again despite my clearly expressed desire.'

'There is no time, Sir Edmund,' Tonge repeated impatiently. Tears sprang to his eyes, and he fell to his knees in supplication.

'Stand on your feet, man,' Oates ordered him roughly and swung round to address Godfrey for the first time. 'A magistrate who would obstruct the course of justice!' he sneered. 'A Protestant who would prevent the arrest of papists guilty of high treason! Had I the choice, I would wipe the dust of your house from my feet this very minute and report you to the Council for investigation. But I shall not allow you the satisfaction of frustrating my mission from Above, which is to thrust the secrets of knaves into the open before it is too late, so that the whole kingdom shall know of their villainy and be on its guard. So I will oblige you, sir. But should you betray my disclosures prematurely, do not expect your office and reputation to protect you from the punishment due to traitors.'

'Withdraw that threat or leave my house.'

Both men were flushed with anger, fists clenched. In height the magistrate had the advantage, but Oates was as strong as a bull and the younger man. Sir Edmund's clerk and Dr Tonge, rising abruptly from his knees, made haste to intervene.

'Calm yourselves, gentlemen,' Tonge implored them. 'It ill behoves two loyal servants of the Crown to fall out when country and faith are in peril. Proceed, I beg you, Dr Oates, but pray be temperate – and brief.'

Still scowling, Oates dropped his fists and threw himself into a chair. 'Last year I feigned conversion to Rome,' he said. 'Since then I have lived among the Jesuits in order to spy upon them and uncover their secrets. The person they call Pope Innocent has appointed them to the supreme power in this realm. King Charles, whom they call the Black Bastard, has been condemned as a heretic and is to be put to death. Father La Chaise, the French king's confessor, has lodged £10,000 in London to reward the assassins. The Jesuits' Spanish order will contribute another £10,000 to foment an uprising, and the Prior of the Benedictines at the Savoy has promised £6,000 to assist the enterprise.'

'Favour me next with the names of the recipients of these moneys,' Godfrey demanded.

'You have them in your hand. They are written in my narrative.'

'I desire them from your own lips before you leave.' That way it would be easier to tell truth from falsehood, the magistrate reckoned. He was accustomed to oral evidence.

'The queen's physician, Sir George Wakeman, was offered £10,000 to poison the king's posset cup, but the rogue bargained for £15,000, which he has now been promised. £8,000 has already been paid on account. In case Sir George is found wanting, four Irish ruffians have been hired to stab the king and two other men to shoot him with silver bullets while in the park. The names of the four I do not know. The two are Pickering and Grove – "Honest William" Grove. They should have made the attempt two weeks ago, but Grove fell sick and the flint in Pickering's pistol had worked loose and jammed. Had they succeeded, they would have received £1500 apiece.'

He spoke confidently and without hesitation, and Godfrey, who had marked him down as a liar, was amazed at the wealth of detail, which seemed beyond his powers of invention.

'If all else fails,' continued Oates, 'there is a Jesuit by the name of Conyers who has sworn to stick the heretic pig, as he dubs His Majesty. His weapon is a butcher's knife which he purchased for ten shillings and has consecrated. He is a fanatic who will undertake the deed without payment.'

'How have you come by all this knowledge?' demanded the magistrate. 'How have you, if innocent, acquired such a familiarity with acts of treason which traitors would surely have kept from strangers?'

'The plot was hatched at a Jesuit Consult, held on April the twenty-fourth at the White Horse tavern in the Strand. I was present and heard what was said. Since then I have seen the fathers' correspondence with their masters abroad. I have acted as a messenger for them and won their confidence.'

'So what information have you gained about their plans after the king is dead?'

'They mean to burn every town in the kingdom, just as they burned London twelve years ago, when the Jesuits alone spent £700 on fireballs. It may be doubted whether they will succeed again, but, I tell you, they are practised incendiarists. You will not be aware of it – no man suspected it – but the recent fire in Southwark was their handiwork.'

He paused and Tonge said urgently that they must be gone. But Godfrey bade him proceed and Oates obliged, not unwilling to keep the Council waiting and blame the magistrate for it.

'When the towns are ablaze, there will be a general insurrection and massacre of Protestants. In London three thousand Catholic cut-throats will be set to work on the citizens as they lie in their beds at night. The Duke of York will be offered the crown on conditions agreed with Rome. If he refuses them, he too will be killed. The French will then invade. England will be subjected to French rule and all the population converted by force.'

When he was finished, Oates stared Sir Edmund in the eye, challenging his disbelief with a look which said as plainly as words: 'I see you doubt me. Beware then lest I denounce you too.'

The swearing and signing were quickly done. Dr Tonge bade the magistrate and his clerk a hasty good morrow and hustled his friend away before there could be any further quarrelling or interrogation.

When the door had closed behind them, Godfrey gingerly picked up the document which Oates had certified as known to him to be 'true in the whole and every particular'. He turned the pages slowly, glaring at each one as though it were a malefactor brought before him for sentencing.

'I have encountered many liars in the course of my duties, Henry,' he said to his clerk, 'but none more adroit than this Titus Oates who styles himself a doctor, though God alone knows of what university.'

'He will meet his just deserts, never fear, sir. The king and his council will not be deceived.' Henry Moor had served him in his business for many years. He recognised his master's mood and sought to dispel the gathering gloom.

'Men believe what they want to believe, and there are many poor dupes who will gladly be deceived by this fabricated claptrap. Master Oates's concoction is designed to appeal to the prejudices of the mob, and it appears so cunningly put together that it may well succeed.' As he spoke, the magistrate continued to turn the pages, and his words were interspersed with groans and gasps at what he read.

There were passages from seditious sermons to be preached by Jesuits to launch the plot. There were the names of the Catholic bishops to be appointed to English sees under a secret Papal Bull dated the previous year. There were full details of the planned assassination of the king. There was a copy of the orders for setting fire to London. It was to be done when the wind was in the right direction and the tide was low, so that ships at anchor could not leave the quays; and Oates had identified himself as the person who would ensure that that part of the plot went according to plan. For that purpose he had been instructed to move to Wapping.

But the section of the sworn statement which caused the magistrate most distress was the one containing the names of those whom this plausible, devious scoundrel and his simple-minded associate were condemning to the gruesome death ordained for traitors.

At the head of the list of alleged conspirators were one hundred and fifteen Jesuits, ninety-nine of whom were named. These were followed by the names of nine Benedictines, nine Dominicans, three Carmelites, two Franciscans, two archbishops, fourteen other secular priests and two lay brothers. Eminent laymen among the accused included Sir William Godolphin, the ambassador to Spain.

Also listed were the Catholic peers selected to hold office after the coup. Lord Arundell of Wardour was to be Lord Chancellor and Lord Powis Lord Treasurer. The army was to be placed under the command of Lord Bellasis (General), Lord Stafford (Paymaster), Lord Petre (Lieutenant-General) and Lord Baltimore (Cavalry Commander).

Godfrey threw the papers down in dismay and disgust. What, he wondered, had so many prominent and noble and unquestionably loyal gentlemen done to incur the displeasure of one, Titus Oates? Was it merely that they still adhered to the old faith which had served England for centuries until Henry VIII fell out with the pope over his divorce? Or were there more personal reasons for the selection? How many were the target of a grudge-bearer settling old scores?

As the pages fell on to his desk, a name well known to him caught his eye. It was that of Edward Coleman, the Duchess of York's secretary and formerly the duke's. The magistrate knew him for an ardent Catholic, but also as a law-abiding citizen and a congenial companion. They frequently dined together, not in each other's homes (that would have been indiscreet), but at the house of an acquaintance. In the interests of friendship and justice, must he not take the risk of warning him?

Sir Edmund's own faith was firmly Protestant. Because the mood of Londoners expected it of him and because it was good for his business, he had even become a member of the Green Ribbon Club; although abhorring bigotry. He remained, nonetheless, strongly opposed to persecuting men for their beliefs. That he continued to live on good terms with Catholics had become the subject of some unfavourable gossip, and it was for that reason that he was suspicious of Tonge's and Oates's motive in choosing him as the instrument to help them authenticate their antipapist tale.

He smelt a trap. Was his friend Coleman the bait?

After some moments of reflection, weighing the odds and the rights and wrongs, he tucked the papers into his pocket and donned the broad-brimmed hat with a gold band by which all London recognised him.

Made apprehensive by his manner and sudden pallor, his clerk began to remonstrate with him and begged him not to leave the house. Politely, he brushed the protests aside, picked up the gold-handled cane which served as his sole precaution against the vengeance of the underworld, and stepped out into a dank riverside mist.

'No, no, Henry,' he said over his shoulder. 'Do not attempt to dissuade me.'

He strode up the lane, despondent but determined. He was mindful of Oates's threat and knew better than to take it lightly. But he had returned the ruffian no pledge of silence and was obeying the dictates of his conscience as a man of honour. For who would not hazard his own life to save an innocent friend from the suffering of being hung on the gallows and cut down while still alive to see himself castrated and feel the entrails drawn from his body?

— 5 —

THE DISAPPEARANCE

It was Tuesday, October the fifteenth. Two and a half weeks after taking Oates's second deposition Mr Justice Godfrey had disappeared and all London was in a hurly-burly. All London, that is, save at the magistrate's own house, which was shrouded in the silence of death.

Approaching down the lane slowly, groaning at every step, Sam was not more than half a dozen stone's throws from the bustle of the court at Whitehall. As on every weekday, an idle throng was jostling with the shopkeepers and litigants around Westminster Hall. Downstream, beyond the palaces which lined the Strand, sprawled the rough and raucous City itself, going noisily about its business. It was eerie that none of this clamour reached so far as to disturb the stillness in Hartshorn Lane.

When he paused outside the front door, his view across the water stretched from the archbishop's palace at Lambeth to the stews of Southwark. At his feet the Thames ran sluggish in the haze of an autumn morning: as sluggish as his own stomach and as grey as his face. The oaths of the boatmen and the cries of the gulls circling their wherries were drowned by a pounding in his head.

The brick building was shuttered like a fortress. Knocking brought no one to the door, but he dared not return to Derby House without an answer. His fists pummelled loudly enough to rouse the dead and split his head, until at last a chink appeared and through it he spied the face of Elizabeth the maid, pale with fright. She looked so pretty and so much in need of comfort and protection that his heart turned over twice: once with love and once out of fear.

'Go away,' she bade him with an anxious frown. 'The Justice is not at home.' She made to close the door again even as she spoke.

'The whole world knows that,' he replied, quickly advancing a foot across the threshold. 'But what news do you have of him, Elizabeth? My master has sent me to inquire most particularly, and we will both incur his anger if I return with nothing more than your refusal to speak with me.'

He might as well have saved his breath, for she was too distraught to pay heed. He was even denied the consolation of one of those shy kisses she had granted him on previous visits.

Vexed at his persistence, she was still struggling to shut him out when a figure whom he had glimpsed in the darkness within came forward. It was Judith Pamphlin, who kept house for the magistrate. Sir Edmund was a bachelor, and Mistress Pamphlin had been entrusted with sole charge of the management of his domestic affairs for as long as anyone could remember. She was the most businesslike of women, and Sam had never before seen her ruffled or in any way discomposed. Now she appeared wild-eyed.

'Forgive us, Master Atkins,' she stammered, 'but our master's brothers have this very morning come from the City and issued the strictest instructions that until he returns home the door is not to be opened to any visitor, whoever he may be.'

'Then prithee tell me, at least, what they believe may have befallen him,' he begged.

'They have suspicions but no knowledge and would not confide in me. What is the world coming to,' she continued with a sob, 'if the best-known, the most respected gentleman in London can vanish without a trace? We are much afeared.'

'Afeared of what, Mistress Pamphlin? Afeared of whom?'

'That we shall be carried off to Newgate. Or murdered here, asleep in our own beds; who can say by whom? There are wicked men in high places and low. Not even innocent womenfolk are safe in these lawless times. We are threatened from all sides, above and below, and without our master we are helpless.'

Sam was attempting to calm her when he was interrupted by a voice from behind. The magistrate's clerk had come quietly round the corner of the house from the rear and bade Sam follow him to his office. 'Those who call on business are welcome still,' he said. 'Otherwise we shall all starve.'

Magistrates were unpaid, but Sir Edmund earned a comfortable livelihood as a wood-monger and coal merchant, supplying departments of state and members of the court with timber and firewood and seacoal from the north. His wares were stacked in a yard between the house and a wharf on the river bank.

Like the housekeeper, Henry Moor, the clerk, had grown old in the Justice's service and was shaken and dazed by the sudden misfortune.

'Believe me, Master Atkins, none of us knows what has become of him – or of what will become of us. But we fear the worst. A man in Sir Edmund's position makes many enemies. We have been told to say nothing of his affairs or movements until he is found, but I would be ashamed if one of Mr Pepys's young gentlemen were to think himself unwelcome in Hartshorn Lane, whether or not he comes with an order from the Navy Office. It grieves me, too, to see you unwell, and Sir Edmund would not forgive me for sending you away in such a poorly condition.'

They were now in the office, overlooking the stackyard, and Sam was thankful to be seated. He made the mistake of shaking his head to signify that he had no order to deliver, and the pain made him wince.

'I drank too freely yesterday,' he confessed. 'In the course of my duties I was obliged to escort two gentlewomen on a visit to one of His Majesty's ships at Greenwich. The captain received our party with such liberality that we lingered overlong, and before the night was out I was, I fear, rendered quite unconscious.'

'So you spent the night aboard, tossing with the tide?'

Sam began to shake his head again, but remembered and saved himself in time. 'This morning I slept late and awoke in a strange bed without any recollection of how I came to be there. Mr Pepys was out of town in attendance on the king at Newmarket and has returned in an ill temper with me and the rest of the world. He reports that the news of your master's disappearance quite spoiled the pleasures of the racecourse. No one at court doubts that the papists have murdered him to prevent the discovery of some seditious act.'

Although they could not be overheard, Sam lowered his voice as he added: 'According to Mr Pepys, the hunt will soon be in full cry for the duke's blood.'

It was five years since the Duke of York's conversion to Rome had deprived him of office under the Test Act; yet, so far from subsiding, the hullabaloo over his apostasy was growing louder every day, orchestrated by Shaftesbury and his supporters.

Henry Moor nodded agreement. 'But first to be spilt will be the blood of those who have served him,' he said. 'I would not be in your master's shoes for all the coal in Northumberland.'

As Secretary to the Navy, Samuel Pepys had been at the duke's right hand during the whole length of his service as Lord High Admiral. If the Opposition in Parliament and the Protestant fanatics of the Green Ribbon Club now had a new opportunity to pursue their feud against the duke, those who had stood loyally by him would be judged guilty by association and their downfall was likely to be contrived as a stepping-stone to his.

Sam thrust such thoughts to the back of his mind. 'Mr Secretary is a true and faithful Protestant,' he declared. 'As I myself am, praise be to God.'

'Praise be to God,' responded the Justice's clerk, 'and if there be any danger to your master – or to yourself as a member of his household, may God avert it! But you must be on your guard. Did you know that before you entered his employment there were rumours that Mr Pepys's wife had died a convert, like the duke? Have you heard that a crucifix was reported to have been seen in his house? Why, he has even been accused of having jested that the Church of England sprang out of King Henry the Eighth's codpiece.'

These calumnies were new to Sam, and he sank his head into his hands with another groan.

'Falsehoods invented by his enemies, I do not doubt,' Henry continued soothingly. 'But perhaps I am not mistaken in believing that they explain his present anxiety. The duke is too high and mighty to be toppled at a single blow. Lesser men are more easily pulled down, and evidence fabricated against them can be used to incriminate him. It is as well that Mr Pepys is on terms of such familiarity with the king. You may take comfort from that.'

But Sam was not soothed or comforted. With a popish conspiracy against the king's life already under investigation, the malice or greed for reward of any rogue or malcontent would be sufficient to despatch a man on a cart to Tyburn, be he an important office-holder or a humble clerk.

'You are a young man, Master Atkins. If you wish to live to my age, take my advice before it is too late: avoid politics and abstain from wine. But first let us talk in confidence about the one and cure your sickness with one of Mistress Pamphlin's nostrums, which contains the other.'

A lonely old man who had no one but his missing master to converse with on matters of business and state, Henry Moor was in a mood for gossip. He rose and called across a courtyard to the kitchen for posset cups.

Elizabeth's blushes when she brought them cheered Sam's spirits, and the curdled milk, well laced with wine and spices, worked wonders with his aching head and stomach. After she had refilled the dishes and departed with a timid curtsy, the medicine which he had prescribed for his guest loosened the elder clerk's tongue still further.

'To oblige a good customer and gentleman of consequence such as Mr Pepys – as Sir Edmund would certainly command me if he were present – I will reveal to you all that I know, which is little, and all that I suspect, which is much. But my words must needs be kept close between the two of us and your master. Should you be interrogated, you must say that we have spent the hour arranging for the delivery of a supply of timber to the dockyards and that you were delayed here beyond expectation because of illness.'

He paused for Sam's assent and then opened the ledger on his desk, where the days of the month and the business conducted on them were set out in neat columns on facing pages headed 'October, AD 1678'.

'Let us see then. On what day did Mr Pepys leave town?'

'He was summoned last Friday and we believed that he would not return until today, Tuesday, but the news about Sir Edmund interrupted his business with the king and brought him back to Whitehall yesterday.'

'So that he found you absent – on duty in Greenwich, as you say – and unfit for your normal duties this morning?'

Henry spoke to establish the facts, not to administer a rebuke, but Sam hung his head.

According to Tom, Mr Secretary had arrived home from Newmarket shivering and sneezing. Since his operation he had suffered acute pain in his bowels and bladder whenever he took cold; and whenever he was in pain and provoked, his ill-temper and the roughness of his tongue exceeded all bounds.

A night's rest had not sweetened his temper. Sam had been summoned the very minute he appeared, to be reminded of his absence from the office on the day of the Earl of Pembroke's trial and of the warning given to him on that occasion. He was ordered to leave the Navy Office within the hour and never to cross the threshold again: if he dared to show his face there on any pretext whatever, he would be thrown out into the street. Only when Mr Pepys had become hoarse with shouting did Will Hewer's repeated assurances that his outing had been authorised win Sam a reprieve.

'He told me that my late return and insobriety were inexcusable, and that I was being sent on this errand only because I seemed to prefer life outside the office and was in need of fresh air to clear my head. To escape dismissal, I must perform it to his entire satisfaction.'

'Then I will help you, so far as it lies within my power. Sir Edmund left this house punctually at nine o'clock on Saturday morning. He went about his usual business, but did not return at night. We waited up for him and raised the alarm early on Sunday morning. From that moment no effort has been spared in searching for him, but no trace of him has been uncovered. There! That is the whole sad story in a nutshell.'

'But did he give no notice of his going away?'

'None, I do assure you; and in such matters he was always most considerate and particular.'

'Did he wear his customary dress?'

'Yes; although, as I now recollect, he at first put on his old coat and then changed it for a new one.'

'Is there anything missing from the house which he might have taken with him? And his behaviour – was it unusual?'

'He carried with him more money than was his wont, but nothing besides. The maid opened the door for him and watched him walk up the lane towards the Strand in his normal manner.'

'And there has been no sight of him since?'

'Indeed there has, but not since Saturday. In the morning he was observed walking in the meadows near Marylebone. If another report can be believed, he was noticed in Leicester Fields also. Then at noon he attended a parish meeting at St Martin in the Fields to settle some vestry business. During the afternoon he was recognised in the Strand near St Clement's church, and John Oakeley, a servant in the house across the lane, swears to having seen him near the watergate at Somerset House in the evening.'

'Might Oakeley have been mistaken?'

'He affirms that they took off their hats to each other. I can vouch for him as a man of truth, and there is no mistaking Sir Edmund.'

That at least was beyond doubt, thought Sam. The spectacle of the imposing figure of Mr Justice Godfrey striding the streets stern-faced was a familiar one to Londoners from Westminster to Wapping.

'Was he not accompanied?' he inquired. Gentlemen seldom walked the streets alone. Law and order had never been fully restored since a king was beheaded for the crime of committing high treason against himself. Always the haunt of common criminals, London had also remained, since then, a hotbed of Fifth Monarchy men and other dissenters intent on mischief.

'Never to take a servant with him is his settled practice,' Henry replied. 'Sir Edmund believes that servants are corrupted by the idleness and ill company they fall into when attending their masters abroad. Many evil-doers have a grudge against him, but he takes no care for his own safety. He is a brave man, Master Atkins. He and I are of an age – fifty-seven this year – and even as a young man I would never had had the courage to confront thieves and bravoes singlehanded, as he does. Even nowadays he will not hesitate to venture into back alleys unaccompanied by servants or constables. It is a wonder that he has not been set upon before.'

'So, Master Moor, shall I inform Mr Pepys that there is now no prospect of finding your master alive?'

'No; let us rather have faith and pray. It is too early to give up hope. Only this morning have his brothers gone to St Martin's to make a public announcement of his disappearance and invite anyone with knowledge of his whereabouts to come forward. They too are merchants, members of the Mercers' Company which owns this land, and they are troubled lest –'

'– lest he has been barbarously done to death?'

'That is not their belief.'

At first Henry would say no more, but when pressed his resistance quickly crumbled.

Sir Edmund, he confided, had been deeply distressed since taking a deposition from two rascally clergymen concerning a plot against the king's life and the safety of the realm. They had called twice, and since their second visit his behaviour had become very strange. He was a man whose conscience was always urging him to do his duty, but in this matter he appeared unable to decide in which direction it lay. He had muttered about a pack of lies and a trap being set for him; yet could not make up his mind whether it was right to break faith with the informers by revealing their wild denunciations to any who might suffer from them. Awareness of the penalty of capital punishment inflicted on those guilty of concealing knowledge of treasonable intent had deprived him of sleep.

'My master is as staunch a Protestant as yours,' Henry continued, 'but he has no zeal for persecution. He is lenient towards those who will not conform and reluctant to execute the laws against them. He will make no searches for houses where masses are held. So he is apprehensive of martyrdom, not from papists, with whom he lives on easy terms, but from fanatics within his own Church.'

Sam was shocked and incredulous. 'If the king himself would not have his Catholic subjects persecuted, who would dare harm Sir Edmund for following his example? His Majesty would surely protect him.'

'The king will not, and the reason lies here.' Henry tapped the ledger in front of him. 'Dr Alexander Frasier, the king's physician, is a mean Scotchman who does not honour his debts. As a member of the court he has immunity from the proceedings of the civil law. But when he persisted in refusing to pay the thirty pounds owed to us for firewood, Sir Edmund decided to challenge this privilege enjoyed – and most scurrilously abused – by courtiers. With the support of some of the judges, he issued a writ against Dr Frasier. But His Majesty was so incensed at defiance of the royal prerogative that he had Sir Edmund imprisoned in the gatehouse at Whitehall. No; the king, who once honoured him, loves Sir Edmund no longer.'

Here is a man after my own heart, thought Sam. Whatever the consequences, he stands by his conscience and devotion to justice and has no respect for the injustices of the law. 'Pray God he be found safe, for England can ill afford his loss,' he said and desired Henry to tell him more.

Henry readily obliged, casting discretion aside.

The previous Friday, the day before his disappearance, a messenger whom none of the household recognised had delivered a letter for the magistrate and stated that he was under orders to wait for a reply. The clerk had never seen his master so agitated. 'Tell him there is no answer, for I know not what to make of it,' he had said, and then thrown the letter into the fire and poked it to ashes.

After that he had begun counting his money and burning his papers, which Elizabeth had to bring to him by the apron-full. In the evening he paid a visit to the house of a friend, Colonel Welden, where he was observed to be in low spirits and where he refused an invitation to dinner the next day, although he had no other engagement. A servant had reported overhearing him say to his host emphatically as he left: 'Why, I'll tell ye; in a short time you will hear of the death of somebody.'

'Of himself, did he mean?' Sam's head was now completely clear, and he was memorising Henry's account word for word to retail to Mr Pepys and retain his post.

'He did not say, but why else would a man settle his affairs and make no engagement for the morrow?'

'Do you suggest, Master Moor, that Sir Edmund was speaking of his own murder and yet taking no steps to save his life?'

For once the magistrate's clerk made no response, but his face spoke plainly enough and Sam drew in his breath as he read the meaning.

'So he was preparing to take his own life! Is that what concerns his brothers? Does that explain why they have delayed a public announcement until today?'

Henry nodded. 'If Sir Edmund has committed suicide – and pray note that I say no more than "if" and divulge no more than what is common knowledge – his estate, which is considerable, will be forfeit to the Crown.'

'But is he – was he – not too devout a man to commit a mortal sin?'

'I tell you, Master Atkins, that my master is by humour a melancholic and never more so afflicted than during this last year. The terrible crimes committed all around him in this wicked city, the example of debauchery set by the king and his courtiers, the triumph of corruption and injustice in public life – all this became more than a man of Sir Edmund's virtue could stomach. It depressed him beyond endurance and carried him to the border-line of sanity.'

'So he was driven to madness? Is that what you say?'

'That is certainly what he himself long feared. Last year, during the summer, he abruptly left the country for France without a word of explanation. I had the task of minding all his affairs for him while he spent four months in the south at Montpellier to recover his health. But he returned no less morose and discontented with the life about him.'

'And now he may finally have given up the struggle and killed himself while his mind was disturbed.'

'Sir Edmund was always moody – private and solitary and hard to fathom. He has never married, as you know, and not for the reason blabbed by the malicious. Here is the reason – it is a secret for your and your master's ears alone: there is mental disorder in the family. His grandfather and father both became deranged, and his father attempted suicide. His enemies may not have killed him themselves, but they have aggravated an inherited darkness of the spirit and quite unhinged him.'

Sam was wide-eyed at this revelation. He could only wonder aloud where, if the deed were done, the body might be found.

'The person who reported seeing him wandering near Marylebone declares that he asked for directions to Paddington woods. There can be only one explanation for his making such an inquiry, when the woods are one of his favourite walks and he knows the way to them as plainly as he knows the back of his own hand. It has to be madness. We must suppose that the question betrayed an intention and he returned there after concluding his last items of business on Saturday.'

'So the world may soon learn that his body has been discovered hanging from a tree in the woods?'

'Not if his brothers should lead the search and be the first to find evidence of suicide. Nor would it suit those who seek to blame all calamities and crimes on the papists. Already it is being bruited abroad and treated as common knowledge that they have murdered him, and there are some who will stop at nothing to prove it. All of us who were close to Sir Edmund are in danger of becoming caught in the toils of plots and counter-plots. Before the week is out, any one of us may find himself a prisoner in the Tower. You will do well to hurry home and warn your master. And, Master Atkins, as you value your life, heed my advice and tread warily yourself.'

Those were the words which rang in Sam's ears as he ran breathlessly back to Derby House.

— 6 —

THE DISCOVERY

The body was discovered two days later.

William Bromwell, a baker, and his friend, John Walters, a blacksmith and farrier, both resident near the church of St Giles in the Fields, were out in the country hunting for hedgehogs – a succulent delicacy when baked in breadcrumbs. They were exploring the bushes and brambles in a field at the foot of Primrose Hill some two or three miles from the City when Bromwell spied some objects scattered on the ground beside a hedge: a belt, a stick, a pair of gentleman's gloves and the scabbard of a sword. Further searching revealed what appeared to be the body of a man sprawled face downwards in the neighbouring ditch. At this the two men took fright and repaired hurriedly to the nearest hostelry.

The White House tavern was approached by the road which led to the village of Hampstead. By the standards of the City and Westminster it was a mean hovel, but during the summer months its gardens were a popular resort for Londoners wishing to exchange foul air for fresh. On a sharp autumn day with the wind blowing from the north it at least offered a snug fireside retreat, and Bromwell and his friend had intended to join the inn's company of travellers and loungers to make merry and flirt with the serving maid before returning home. Instead, they took their jugs of ale into a corner booth and argued in whispers over what best to do about their find.

The law was notoriously ungrateful to ordinary men and women who reported crimes. Honest citizens doing their duty in this way ran the risk of falling under suspicion. For it had become a well-established legal principle that the first person known to be on the scene of a crime was the most likely to have committed it. In the case of murder this often cost innocent men their liberty and sometimes their lives. On the other hand, as Walters urged, valuable articles had not been stolen, so that this might not be murder, and Bromwell agreed that it would be foolish to forgo the opportunity of a reward.

From frequent visits the two men were well acquainted with John Rawson, the landlord. In the end they decided that the safest course would be to tell him about the articles but allow him to find the body for himself. They called him over and after listening to their tale he readily agreed to go with them, pledging his word that if their treasure-trove was worth the price they should have a shilling to drink for their pains. He would, he promised, keep the objects safe until they were claimed. At this, since the innkeeper's reputation was not of the most savoury, nods and winks were exchanged and there was some muttering about another shilling or two if warranted.

When they reached the spot and Rawson was stooping to pick up the scabbard, two more objects attracted his attention: a hat and a periwig half hidden among the bushes. These led him on to the corpse in the ditch. It lay face downwards with an expensive camlet coat turned up to conceal the head. Seven or eight inches of the blade of the missing sword were protruding from the back of the body.

'Poor gentleman!' he exclaimed in astonishment. 'Or, rather, rich gentleman! It may be that there is something in his pockets of which he will have no further need.'

'No stealing,' Bromwell cautioned him. 'I tell you, Master Rawson, I will take no part in theft from a dead man.'

'Nor I, as I hope for salvation,' declared Walters, taking up a stance to defend the dead.

'You mistake me, friends,' Rawson protested, backing away from the blacksmith. 'I intended but to see whether there are papers which would identify him.'

'Then I will do the searching,' said Walters. Bending, he groped in one of the pockets of the coat, and when he withdrew his hand it was full of gold coins.

'Put them back,' Bromwell begged him, frightened at the sight of so much temptation and the look of greed on the innkeeper's face. 'Put them back, neighbour, I say, and let us take ourselves straightway to a magistrate.'

But first they gathered the loose articles from the ground and carried them back to the White House out of the reach of other prowlers. There they further refreshed themselves to banish unease, before setting out again across the fields.

The parish of St Giles lay outside the boundaries of the City, and its civic authority was the churchwarden. When they told their story to his servant at the door he sent word that no magistrate lived near enough at hand and that he himself was too ill to attend them. They were referred instead to Mr Brown, the constable.

Brown was accustomed to being roused at all hours by callers with ill tidings, but never before with news as momentous as this. He was not surprised to learn of the churchwarden's sudden illness. 'You bring trouble, brothers,' he told them. 'For unless I am much mistaken you had no cause to stir a yard to fetch a magistrate. A Justice of the Peace, Sir Edmund Berry Godfrey himself, was lying there at your feet.'

This was what the discoverers themselves had come to suspect and fear. If the corpse they had stumbled across was indeed that of the missing magistrate, their reward was likely to be, not riches, but misfortune. What had seemed at first a stroke of luck would make them the hapless pawns of lawyers and politicians, from whose clutches men of their station could not expect to escape unscathed. And, as fate would have it, Bromwell and Walters were Roman Catholics.

To share the responsibility, the constable assembled an escort of two watchmen and a dozen inquisitive householders. They walked out of town along the country paths in small groups: some silenced by the solemnity of the occasion, others chattering with excitement.

By the time they reached Primrose Hill darkness was falling, but when Mr Brown bent down and rolled the body over there was still light enough for those who had known Sir Edmund to recognise his face. In life its paleness had earned him the nickname of 'The Ghost'. In death surprise had replaced the habitual look of strain and his cheeks had become as red as they ought to have been in life. The posse stood in a ragged circle, staring open-mouthed, mute to a man. The dead eyes stared back at them even more sternly than when alive, and even the Puritans amongst them made haste to cross themselves.

No blood gushed out when the constable withdrew the sword, which had pierced the left breast near the heart. On his orders the watchmen's staves were used to improvise a stretcher, and the mortal remains of England's most famous magistrate were borne through the darkness, twice nearly tossed to the ground when the bearers stumbled over tussocks on the way to the inn. There the body was laid on a bare table in an upper room. The citizens of St Giles then conferred solemnly over ale in the bar below, while Mr Brown and his watchmen set off to inform the Middlesex coroner.

Reports of the discovery ran through the City and Westminster at the speed of a forest fire, fuelling the smouldering antipopery of the citizens into a blaze. Since Dr Oates's meeting with the Council his revelations had become public knowledge and those who had doubted the existence of his plot had to confess themselves mistaken. The death of Sir Edmund, who had deemed it a pack of lies, was now believed to have proved its truth. The magistrate became instantly revered as a Protestant martyr; and where, it was asked, would Rome's assassins strike next? Every Protestant went to rest for the night fearing for his life – and every Catholic too.

Mr Pepys was one of the few who kept his head and remained sceptical. He was alarmed, nonetheless, and took to his bed, complaining of all the various illnesses to which he became prone at times of stress: a headache, wind colic, shortness of breath and pains in the leg.

From his bedroom he sent for Sam and ordered him to attend the inquest. 'On this one occasion you may indulge in your favourite occupation with my blessing,' he said. 'I do not doubt that it will be a fine example of English justice at work. As you have learned from his clerk, the unfortunate man was driven out of his mind to suicide, but the jury will assuredly do what is expected of them and return a verdict of murder. Should they prove obstinate, the wretches will doubtless be sent to Newgate as suspected papists and detained there in chains until they see fit to change their minds.'

Sam shuddered at the thought of innocent jurymen suffering for the truth. 'Is this then your considered opinion, sir,' he asked respectfully: 'that after finishing his business in London Sir Edmund chose to walk out to a secluded place and thrust his sword through his own body?'

'Yes, Master Atkins, it is. But before you pass judgment on a dead man remember that he must have acted while the balance of his mind was disturbed.'

'Among the Romans,' Sam took the liberty of reminding him, 'falling on one's sword was an honourable death, not the act of a madman.'

'Unlike the early Romans, Sir Edmund was a Christian.' As he spoke, Mr Pepys released some wind.

Sam took this for a rebuke, but would not be put down.

'His brothers may desire him to have been murdered so that they can keep his fortune,' he said. 'My lords of Shaftesbury and Pembroke and their adherents may wish it so that the Duke of York is tarred with treason and will therefore be exiled and excluded. But their motives and self-interest, however unworthy and misguided, do not prove them wrong. I concede that Sir Edmund may have been heart-sick and become distraught, but there is no evidence of insanity, and if he was too pious a Christian to have taken his own life whilst sane, then he must have been murdered.'

This time Mr Pepys's response was a belch of disapproval at Sam's presumption. 'Enough of speculation! Go and listen to what is said at the inquest,' he commanded. 'Be attentive. I must have it word for word. Keep your ears wide open and your mouth shut. Dangerous talk will carry me off to the Tower and yourself to Newgate. Always remember: *volto sciolto e pensieri stretti*.'

An open countenance and close thoughts. With this admonition firmly in mind, Sam rose early the next morning and took the road to Chalcot fields. He was not alone. To judge from some of the feverish conversations which he overheard, he was caught up in the greatest event in London since the execution of the king's father, Charles the Martyr, which had occurred before he was born.

Near the White House the press thickened until he became one of a multitude laying siege to the inn and banging on the doors for admission. Elbowing a path towards a window, he could glimpse another mob inside struggling unavailingly to get up the narrow stairs which led to the room under the roof beams where the coroner was due to hold his court.

There was nothing for it but patience. The coroner arrived at the head of a procession of jurymen, witnesses, physicians and surgeons. Somehow they squeezed through the throng, and as the day went on reports of the proceedings were passed down the stairs and out to the expectant crowd, which grew larger by the hour, swollen by fresh masses crying out against the murderers of their hero and clamouring to be allowed to view the body.

Upstairs, it transpired, the struggle was between those whose evidence pointed to suicide and those who were convinced that the common report was true and what had been committed was murder. The coroner was reported to be confused and flustered. Early in the afternoon he appeared at a window to announce an adjournment to less cramped quarters, and orders were given for the body to be moved before darkness to the Rose and Crown at St Giles, where the inquest would be resumed on the morrow.

Searching for a source of information among the crowd as it dispersed, Sam caught sight of the magistrate's clerk. The old man looked downcast and bewildered by the turmoil, and he willingly accepted the offer of a drink to revive his spirits.

'Were you called upon to give evidence about Sir Edmund's state of mind?' Sam asked when at last they had their ale.

'I was summoned, but have not yet been called upon. When the time comes I shall be hard put to it to know what to say. If I reveal how Sir Edmund's father attempted to kill his own children and had to be restrained and shut away, Master William and Master Benjamin will not think twice about dismissing me.' The old man pulled a long face.

'But you have to tell the truth, Master Moor. The brothers will understand that.'

'Often the truth is best not told. The sooner you learn that, the better for yourself, Master Atkins.'

'So the verdict will be murder, whatever the truth? Pray tell me everything that was said above,' Sam begged.

'The coroner is suspicious of Bromwell and Walters. He asked why, when they came across the stick and gloves, they made no further investigation. Bromwell gave a lame reply, stammering that he had supposed them to belong to some person who had gone into the ditch to ease himself and then forgotten them.'

'Do you think these tradesmen honest men?'

'The contents of Sir Edmund's pockets prove them so. Nothing of value that he took with him on the day of his disappearance is missing. Not that that will save them, for I am told that they are papists.'

Sam asked how much money was found, and Henry Moor drew out a piece of paper on which he had made a careful record of the sums in order to help the family reclaim them.

'In one pocket were six guineas, four broad pieces of gold and a half-crown; in the other one guinea, two small pieces of gold and four pounds in silver. There were also two rings. A large diamond was mounted on one of them, and Sir Edmund's favourite gold ring was still on one of his fingers. If my master was murdered, it was not by a footpad for robbery. That at least cannot be disputed.'

'Every man wants money, even Jesuits,' Sam brooded, puzzled. 'Was nothing taken at all?'

'One item only, to my knowledge: the pocket book which he always carried with him to take notes of his examinations. That has not been found.'

'Might he not have destroyed it himself? Did you not tell me when I came to Hartshorn Lane on Tuesday that he had burned all his private papers?'

'But not the pocket book. I saw it in his hand the following morning. Its disappearance is certainly strange – as strange as his carrying so much money with him if his intention was to take his own life.'

While they pondered the implications of this new mystery, Sam ordered more ale. Mr Pepys would cavil at the expense no doubt, but Will Hewer could be relied upon to see him reimbursed. 'What did the surgeons have to say?' he asked when the old man had swallowed a draught and finished wiping his lips.

'Two of them examined the body in our presence. They reported finding two sword wounds: one an inch deep stopped by a rib; the other penetrating clear through the body half an inch below the left pap.'

'Then the wounds could have been self-inflicted, and Sir Edmund may have killed himself at a second attempt?'

'So one might have supposed. But the surgeons maintain that they can detect no trace of blood, and their testimony was corroborated by some of those who had seen where the body lay. They swore that not one drop of blood was to be seen on the ground around, nor any appearance of it in the ditch, which was dry. That Sir Edmund's clothes were not bloodstained, the jury and all of us could see for themselves.'

Sam pushed his tankard aside and leaned forward in amazement. 'How does anyone imagine that a man can be stabbed to death without bloodshed?' he demanded.

Henry Moor leaned forward in turn, with the air of a man about to communicate a wondrous fact. 'The surgeons testified that the wounds were not the cause of death,' he said, 'and one of them explained that no blood is spilt when a person who is stabbed has already been dead for some days.'

At first Sam did not believe his ears, and when he did he could hardly restrain himself from running straight back to Derby House with the news. For here was a plot indeed, and surely one that was the portent and prelude of even greater events.

'Wait,' said Henry, laying a hand on his arm. 'Will Mr Pepys not expect to learn what the surgeons allege to be the real cause of death?'

— 7 —

THE JURY'S VERDICT

Mr Pepys, lying in bed feeling sorry for himself, was startled out of his depression by what Sam told him: that a man run through with a sword was thought to have died of strangulation.

'Master Moor reported it for a certainty,' Sam assured him. 'The sword thrust is no more than a deception. The surgeons pointed to a contusion behind the left ear and the mark of a circle round the neck and the settlement of blood there. The violence used was so great that the neck was dislocated. They said that you could take hold of the chin and set it on either shoulder. The breast below was bruised black from throat to stomach, either beaten or stamped upon, and the whole body was swollen. Sir Edmund must have fought hard for his life.'

'The body might have been assaulted after death,' Mr Pepys protested, reluctant to abandon his belief that the magistrate had killed himself in a fit of madness. 'Rather than murder made to seem like suicide, it could as well be suicide made to look like murder.'

Sam shook his head. 'Master Moor has signed an affidavit affirming the rumour that Sir Edmund hanged himself and he cut him down to be utterly false.'

'Yet others may have performed that service to safeguard the interests of the heirs.' Mr Pepys was always stubborn and hard to convince against his inclination.

After a night spent weighing the evidence in his mind he decided that he must attend the resumed inquest in person, his ailments notwithstanding. Sam was not to be allowed another outing. His master would determine the truth and judge the ensuing perils for himself.

When he arrived at the Rose and Crown, proceedings had already started and a witness was informing the coroner that the field where the body had been found belonged to his mother. He swore that two days earlier one of her servants had gone with a butcher and two boys to search for a missing calf. They had hunted through every part of the ground and could testify that no body or articles of clothing were lying there at that time.

'Let the jury be clear about your statement and its relevance,' said the coroner. 'To the best of our knowledge Sir Edmund was last seen alive on Saturday a week ago. The body which has been identified as his was found on Thursday, the day before yesterday. Are you telling the court that on Tuesday the body was not in the place where it was discovered?'

The witness signified his assent, and evidence was then given that, although the ground was muddy, the soles of the corpse's shoes were as clean as if their owner had just come out of his chamber at home. Another sign that the body had been carried into the field was the track of cart wheels near by.

Five surgeons and two apothecaries were in attendance – some, it was whispered, by the king's command. No post-mortem had been held, but all were in agreement that the bruises on the body must have been inflicted before death.

The sensational subject of the inquiry and the large number of witnesses elevated and prolonged the proceedings. The inn's upper room was filled with ladies and gentlemen of quality, amongst whom the Protestant Duke of Monmouth and the Catholic Louise de Keroualle, Duchess of Portsmouth, and her sister were conspicuous. Their presence unsettled the coroner and jurymen, who grew increasingly nervous and apprehensive at the expectancy with which the outcome was awaited at court and in the City. Lest they should forget, the shouts of an impatient crowd rumbled outside like an approaching storm.

It was late in the evening when the verdict was delivered. The jury found that certain persons, to them unknown, did feloniously, wilfully and of their malice aforethought tie and fasten a piece of linen cloth about the neck of Sir Edmund Berry Godfrey; and that therewith they did feloniously, wilfully and of their malice aforethought suffocate and strangle the said Sir Edmund Berry Godfrey, of which suffocation and strangling he, the said Sir Edmund Berry Godfrey, did then and there instantly die.

While he listened to the foreman's words after a long day perched at the end of a bare wooden bench, Mr Pepys was shivering pitifully, and not only with fever. This finding, he foresaw, would unleash a persecution of the innocent such as had never been known in England before. He would be lucky not to be numbered amongst the victims, for his services to his country would, he knew, count for nothing.

'You appear unwell, sir. May we see you home?'

He looked up to see himself addressed by Sir Edmund's clerk, who had been sitting behind him with two women whom he presumed to be other members of the magistrate's household. One was elderly and wrinkled as a walnut; the other as fresh as sunrise. Gratefully he seized the young one's arm and allowed himself to be assisted downstairs into the street.

He asked her name and she told him shyly that it was Elizabeth. Whispering that it was a beautiful name but not as beautiful as herself, he took advantage of the darkness and the autumn chill to put his arm around her waist and hug her to him for warmth as they walked together.

She offered no encouragement, but was too timid or polite to pull away from him. He felt all his bodily pains and half his forty-five years falling away at her touch, and he thought how wasted a girl like this was in Godfrey's house. If his experience was to trusted (and it was extensive), she still had the innocence and bloom of virginity about her.

'Pray, sir, remember me to Master Atkins, your clerk,' she said when the three of them took their leave of him.

So the wind blew in that direction! 'I will most certainly oblige you,' he promised and lowered his voice to add: 'Should you be in need of new employment, you may apply to me. I would not wish you to suffer from the misfortune of your master.'

In his parlour Will Hewer awaited him, eager for news, and the two men conferred over a late supper of botargo and cheese washed down with draughts of Mr Pepys's favourite medicine, which was the best claret the navy could procure for him.

Mr Secretary was as hard a taskmaster as the dead magistrate had been, but a close friendship between him and his head clerk had ripened over the years. He had come to realise that Will was the one person in the whole wicked world of public and private deceit whom he could trust implicitly. Had they not, together, overcome the obstacles of a nincompoop Board of Admiralty and a skinflint House of Commons to acquire the necessary funds and build and rebuild a navy strong enough to withstand the Dutch and avert the threat of a French invasion?

What a contrast with poor Henry Moor! While that downtrodden clerk lived in fear of rebuke and trembled to take a single step on his own, a resourceful and imperturbable Will Hewer quietly took charge of steering their political masters in the right direction whenever Mr Pepys was laid prostrate by his head, feet, chest or bladder.

'Why, do you suppose, did the surgeons refrain from opening the body and conducting a thorough post-mortem?' Will inquired, coming quickly to the point.

'It was reported that they began an examination but were deterred because the putrefaction proved so nauseous. But I dare say the truth of the matter is that they were ordered to desist lest an internal examination upset the verdict required of the jury. Or it may be that by his death Sir Edmund has become a Protestant saint, whose remains it would be sacrilege to mutilate. They have already been borne across the fields to town at the head of a rabble with hats doffed, like a papist procession with an idol of the Blessed Virgin. Now the body is to lie in state while the faithful file past to pay their respects and vow vengeance on Rome. I tell you, Will, the whole nation has gone mad.'

Mr Pepys concluded this pronouncement with a series of belches: in appreciation of the wine, disgust at the verdict, and scorn of the demagogues and the mob they manipulated. Will sighed in sympathy and predicted much turbulence and danger.

'The safety of the realm is threatened,' Mr Pepys agreed: 'but by whom? That is the question. I have it on the highest authority that all Catholics are to be ordered to take a new oath of allegiance to the Crown and will be treated as traitors if their religion forbids them to comply. Why then should not trouble-makers of a different hue be compelled to swear their loyalty too – first among them my lord of Shaftesbury, the fount of all sedition?'

'The safety of ourselves is of more immediate concern,' Will replied. 'The earl will not have forgiven you for defying him and defending the Duke of York's good name in Parliament. He attempted then to tie the label of papist round your neck. I wager you he will not be slow to seize a second opportunity to lay you low. The king will not desert his brother until his own throne begins to shake, but he may not deem it necessary or prudent to extend his protection to the duke's men.'

'Then we must make as sure as sure can be that even the most diligent of searches will not uncover anything in this building which could be twisted by the Crown's lawyers to incriminate any member of the household.'

'I can answer for the official files,' said Will, 'but take care not to overlook your own private papers. If they betray even the smallest indiscretion, you would be wise to destroy them. And, whilst speaking of indiscretions, pray do not take it amiss if I draw your attention to evidence of another kind which has recently proved fatal to innocent men unjustly accused of felonies. I refer to the false witness of a servant with a grudge.'

'Revenge for dismissal? I cannot believe it of Sam Atkins. He is honest to a fault, and you must know that I will always stay my hand while he enjoys your confidence.'

Will looked embarrassed. 'It was the maid I had in mind,' he confessed.

'Would you suspect Susan of such wickedness? How can you imagine the girl would be so disloyal!' Mr Pepys was seized by guilt and alarm.

'If inducements are offered to her, the temptation may be strong. I would advise paying the hussy well and promising her more if she keeps her pretty mouth well closed.'

The pregnancies of his maid servants were not infrequent occurrences in Mr Pepys's household. Although often himself responsible for their condition, he seldom treated them with generosity. Indeed it was not unknown for him to turn them out of the house without notice, branded as sluts, if they grew fractious. Susan was the latest to attract her master's attentions and become big-bellied.

'She shall leave on the terms you suggest,' he promised in a fluster. 'Pray arrange for her to be taken to her aunt's in Poultry and left there with sufficient coin in her hand and on offer to satisfy them both. The sooner she goes, the better; for I have this very day encountered by chance a most suitable replacement.'

Will knew well enough what a whoremonger like Mr Pepys meant by 'most suitable', but, having made and won his point, he chose to say no more on a delicate subject. 'As well as those who pay off old scores out of malice,' he went on, 'we must be prepared to defend ourselves against professional informers who swear to falsehoods for a reward.'

'If you mean Oates, he is already discredited. When he made his appearance before the Council, the king caught him out telling two bare-faced lies. I had an account of it from Mr Secretary Coventry himself. The rogue claimed to have been at the Jesuit College in Paris, which, as it happened, the king had visited during his exile. When asked where it stood, he placed it as much out of the way as if he had located Gresham College in Westminster instead of the City. His Majesty then bade him describe Don Juan, whom Oates claimed to have met, and he replied that he was tall and black-haired, doubtless thinking that a safe description of a Spaniard. But the king informed the Council afterwards that Don Juan is short and has red hair.'

'Take no comfort from that, sir,' Will warned. 'A few moments of discomfiture will not deter a monster as thick-skinned as Oates. He utters falsehoods unblushingly whilst on oath, and he is devilish clever. His lies are dashed and brewed with subtle infusions of the truth. Of all the liars ever born, he is the most adroit. He knows that men believe what they want to believe and is cunning in fashioning inventions to stoke the fears of anti-papists. No man is safe from him and his kind. Your enemies will not have forgotten that Mrs Pepys died a Catholic, and if they choose to turn him in this direction neither the truth, nor the law, nor the king will shield us.'

Will spoke passionately to jolt his master out of the mood of false confidence which was creeping over him with every fresh glass of wine. It was, though, a losing struggle.

'The bogus Dr Oates and his friends are too busy with the Jesuits to concern themselves with us,' Mr Pepys insisted. 'And here again has he not been proved a liar? When the Council forced him to produce the incriminating letters which he claimed to hold, they were seen to be palpable forgeries. Of course he argued in his usual brazen manner that the handwriting was purposely disguised, but no one who studied them believed him and he was exposed to ridicule.'

'Yet – except for Whitehead, the Provincial, who took refuge in the Spanish embassy one step ahead of the mob – did he not succeed in having every Jesuit who could be unearthed in

London hunted down and arrested by armed bands? Can you deny that, however guiltless, they will be fortunate to escape the hangman's noose and knife at Tyburn?'

Mr Pepys could not deny it and sought to turn the argument. 'It is all the fault of that secretary of the duchess,' he complained petulantly. 'Oates made a lucky strike there. Coleman's incriminating letters are genuine and prove the existence of a plot. No matter that it is a foolish and harmless one. It bestows credibility on every wild accusation. Were it not for Coleman's recklessness and negligence, Oates would now be languishing behind bars for perjury and we would all be spared anxiety.'

'Not since last Thursday,' Will respectfully corrected him. 'It is Mr Justice Godfrey's death which has made Oates's fantasies real and swayed the sceptics. His murder is what Oates and those who have been putting the words into his mouth will have most desired. It will seal the fate of the Jesuits and of lay Catholics as incautious as Coleman. I am therefore led to wonder who really killed him. *Cui bono*?'

They pushed aside the remains of the food, opened another bottle and pondered in silence on Godfrey's death and his connection with Edward Coleman, the secretary to Mary of Modena, the Catholic princess who had become wife to Mr Pepys's former patron.

Coleman's character and career were well known to them both. He was the ambitious son of a Church of England clergyman. After quarrelling with his father he had defected to Rome. Instruction by Jesuits had made him the most fanatical of converts. He was welcomed into the household of another convert, the Duke of York, where his zeal and impetuosity as the duke's secretary exceeded even the duke's own, and James became publicly embarrassed by activities of which he privately approved. Coleman was therefore dismissed, but quietly re-employed in the duchess's service.

All London had now learned that he had been conducting secret negotiations with the King of France's confessor and the secretary to Cardinal Howard, the leading English Catholic at the Vatican. His purpose was to gain support for James as heir to the throne and restore England to the arms of Rome through a change of government and religion.

'Until Godfrey's death,' mused Will, 'he might have escaped prosecution by pleading that his plan precluded the use of force.'

'Are secret correspondence with foreign enemies of the government and furtive consultations with their ambassadors not treachery enough?' demanded Mr Pepys indignantly. 'I would remind you that in the case of high treason the intention, not the act, constitutes the offence. Master Coleman richly deserves to be hanged.'

On this Will took issue. 'I am told that he makes the most agreeable company if the subject of religion can be avoided; and he is indisputably a man of talent and principle. Would you deny that, but for the Test Act, he is likely to have served the state loyally and with distinction? It is the law which has made him a traitor.'

'That may be,' Mr Pepys conceded, 'but as matters stand his folly has put other lives at risk as well as his own. Did he and Godfrey meet?'

Will nodded. 'My neighbour, Colonel Welden, is familiar with him and was also acquainted with Sir Edmund. They used to meet at his house. He has confided in me that Godfrey was convinced of Coleman's innocence and hurried to York House to warn him of the accusations made against him in Oates's deposition. That gave him time to burn his papers and go to Whitehall to demonstrate his innocence by offering to give evidence to the Council voluntarily before he was summoned.'

This was news to Mr Pepys. A warning of the charges against him accounted for Coleman's co-operation and his coolness as a witness, as a result of which he had at first been committed to the care of an officer and placed under house arrest instead of being consigned to prison with the Jesuits.

'According to Colonel Welden,' Will continued, 'his real defence, which could not be openly stated, is that he has acted throughout with the connivance of the duke and, at times, with that of the king himself. He has convinced himself that they will rescue him should he be condemned.'

Mr Pepys grunted. 'A man may be too confident for his own good,' he said. 'It may make him careless when destroying evidence which could be used against him. Is that the lesson which you have been trying to teach me, Will?'

A search of Coleman's chambers had revealed the damaging

letters, which he had overlooked or persuaded himself would not be found. They were hidden in a recess behind a chimney and were in cipher, like the diary and confidential notes which Mr Pepys kept. The key to the cipher had been left with them.

It was those letters, so guiltily encoded and secreted, which provided incontestable evidence that Coleman had been soliciting money from Paris and Rome. It transpired that his plan was to bribe both the king, so that he would dissolve his militantly Protestant Parliament, and the Members of Parliament themselves, so that they would legislate in the Catholic interest. As Mr Pepys alleged, the discovery had saved Oates from Newgate, where Coleman now lay instead, awaiting trial.

'Yes,' said Will, 'Coleman is an example to us all. He has brought himself to the gallows, unless the king grants him a pardon; which I doubt. No jury will dare acquit him. But how much light will his trial shed on the identity of Godfrey's murderers, do you suppose?'

'There were no murderers,' said Mr Pepys stubbornly. 'I remain of the opinion that his melancholic humour became aggravated by his involvement in Oates's deposition, and that he thereupon systematically put his earthly affairs in order and took his own life in such a manner as not to deprive his heirs of their inheritance. He was an unhappy sufferer from congenital mania. That is the truth which his clerk disclosed to Sam. But, as you acknowledge, juries must look to their own safety and find what is convenient rather than what is true.'

'Is putting one's affairs in order so meticulously the action of a deranged person? Would a madman pay such heed to the interests of his heirs?' Will demanded. 'Surely we deceive ourselves if we do not recognise that Godfrey is the victim of the same conspirators who will use Coleman's disgrace to have the king's brother and rightful heir barred from the succession.'

'Then the fate of Godfrey and Coleman will serve their ends and we shall not be troubled.'

'But suppose their ends are not served, and more is required? They are one route to the duke. You, sir, are another.'

— 8 —

THE FUNERAL

Never before had the life of the nation been so affected by the death of a man who occupied no higher position than that of metropolitan magistrate. The whole country was thrown into pandemonium. In London panic seized the entire population of one hundred thousand men, women and children. Fear ran from street to street like the Great Fire and from house to house like the plague.

The trained bands were called out to stand guard by day and patrol by night. Posts and chains were erected to block entrances to roads, and cannon were mounted at the approaches to Whitehall. No one could tell when and where the unknown enemy would strike, so every man and every building was equipped with arms for defence. An enterprising cutler who made daggers and inscribed them with the words, 'Remember the murder of Edmund Berry Godfrey', on one side of the blade and 'Remember religion' on the other, sold three thousand in a single day.

Most who ventured abroad made the pilgrimage to Hartshorn Lane, where they stood in patient silence in a long queue which stretched up to and along the Strand. The magistrate's body had been embalmed and, fully dressed, laid out on his dining-room table for all to view. Every day for more than a week the citizens of London came in their hundreds to pay their last respects to the man who had kept law and order for them and died for their Church and their religion. First taking care to wipe their boots and shoes, they entered by the front door, shuffled along the corridor and around the corpse, and left by the courtyard at the back after pausing only to mutter a brief prayer for the good man's soul.

Every day from dawn to dusk Henry Moor or Judith Pamphlin stood guard over their old master's body like faithful mastiffs. When Sam called on the first day, it was the housekeeper who was on duty, and after offering his prayer over the dead man's body he asked permission to speak with Elizabeth.

It was granted reluctantly. 'If you have come to entice her away, then you should know that Mr Michael and Mr Benjamin intend to take over the lease and carry on the business. One of them will come to live here, and Elizabeth need have no fears for her employment while I remain.'

'But for how long will that be, Mistress Pamphlin?' Sam inquired. 'For are they not both married men?'

'What promises I have had from them is my concern,' she answered sharply. 'But the girl is a hard worker and will keep her place deservedly, with or without me. She will be better looked after here than under your master, if what I hear is to be believed. Or have you come on a different errand, Master Atkins? Would you converse with her on your own account?'

Sam blushed at her directness. 'I cannot yet afford a wife,' he replied. 'But if I could, that might indeed be my errand.'

Elizabeth was busily engaged in the kitchen and embarrassed that he should discover her dirty and unkempt. She looked miserable, her pretty eyes ringed with dark circles. He wanted to take her in his arms and comfort her, but dared not lest she rebuff him. A snatched kiss before leaving would, he reckoned, be the most he could expect.

'I have a message for you from my master, Mr Pepys,' he told her. 'His maid servant has returned to her family and he is in want of another. He spoke to you about it after the inquest, and I am now sent to inquire on his behalf whether you will enter his service at Derby House. He engages himself to pay you the same wages as you are receiving here.'

She continued washing dishes, evidently at a loss how to reply and waiting for guidance from him. Her shyness, where most of her kind were so forward, was one of the arrows in her quiver which had pierced his heart when he first met her.

'Would I be welcome?' she asked at last, her eyes still meekly averted.

'How can you doubt it?' he answered gallantly. 'But I have to tell you, Elizabeth –' He stopped short, unable to summon the right words of warning.

She looked up and studied his face, puzzled and hurt by his hesitation when she had expected eagerness.

How was he to explain that the overwhelming joy which he felt at the prospect of their living under the same roof was crushed by the thought of his master's lechery and the inevitable consequence? He recoiled from the coarseness of telling her boldly and outright that he feared for the loss of her maidenhead, a treasure which he cherished above all else in the world.

'Mr Pepys –' he stammered tongue-tied, 'Mr Pepys is a great personage, a man of the highest reputation, but he is – is not the best of masters in every respect.'

'Mr Pepys fiddlesticks! If you are so lukewarm, I shall not come.'

He had wounded her and she flared with anger. Even as it scorched him – even as she tossed her head at him and bade him be off – his distress was outweighed by admiration for the strength of her spirit. Pride shone through her flushed and dishevelled appearance and gave it a beauty which took his breath away.

'You misunderstand me, Elizabeth,' he pleaded when he found his voice. Now was the moment to declare his undying love for her, to beg her to pledge herself to him and surrender her virtue to no other man until they could be married. 'Sweetheart,' he began, but it was too late. Mistress Pamphlin, who must have been listening at the door, entered the room in a fury.

'Pray cease tormenting the poor wench, Master Atkins,' she cried. 'Do not tempt her into sin. Elizabeth prefers to stay in a household where she is protected from the vice of men.'

Sam opened his mouth to rebut the charge, but his protest was swept aside.

'Even when Mrs Pepys was alive, her husband's maid servants were not safe from debauchery. I have heard of it from Master Moor and challenge you to deny it, Master Atkins. Elizabeth is an orphan, as you know. When Sir Edmund rescued her from the streets and took her into this house out of kindness, he consigned her to my care, and I owe it to his memory to act as her guardian now that he is dead. If she is so giddy and light-headed, she may choose of her own free will to run away with you. But if not, you may be sure that I shall never allow her to enter the house of libertines like your master and yourself. No; we will listen to you no more. Enough of your deceit! You lie if you profess that your infatuation with her is pure. Have you not a moment ago told me plainly that you cannot marry her?'

To be called a liar and humiliated in front of his beloved was more than Sam could bear. He left with hanging head, protesting vehemently that his intentions were honourable. His last sight was of Elizabeth in tears, with the housekeeper's arms round her shoulders where his own should have been.

He struggled through the multitude thronging the lane and was turning towards Charing Cross when a notice posted on a wall caught his eye. 'By the King,' it was headed: 'A Proclamation for the Discovery of the Murtherers of Sir Edmund Berry Godfrey.'

Others were clustered round it, painstakingly spelling out the printed words, which Sam read by peering over their shoulders: 'His Majesty is graciously pleased hereby to promise, to any person or persons who shall make such a Discovery whereby the said Murtherers, or any of them, shall be apprehended, the sum of five hundred pounds, which shall be immediately paid down.'

The proclamation was dated the previous day, the twentieth of October. That was the day immediately following the conclusion of the adjourned inquest, and a Sunday to boot. Sam marvelled at the haste of a customarily slow-moving government and the size of the reward offered by a notoriously niggardly Treasury.

The guilty men would be lucky to escape with their lives, he thought; and so would anyone else accused by informers so handsomely tempted. The alehouses and stews of London were full of scoundrels who would lie through their teeth and see their own grandmothers hanged for a fortune of five hundred pounds. Every Catholic who had quarrelled with a neighbour would be in peril from the unscrupulous and avaricious.

On his way to Derby House to let Mr Pepys know that he would have to look elsewhere for a good-looking girl to make his bed and tickle his fancy, Sam daydreamed of throwing scruples to the winds, excelling Oates in invention and claiming the reward for himself. He could then afford to buy a house of his own, marry Elizabeth, become a lawyer and bask in the respect which wealth commanded. He sighed at the thought that his conscience would never permit it and that he would live in terror of the punishment awaiting him on the Day of Judgement.

The proclamation signalled the start of another feverish week. Even as Sam had been reading it and the citizens were preparing to sell their lives dearly in the coming campaign of fire and slaughter, Parliament was reassembling.

It was the sixteenth session of a Commons elected more than seventeen years before. The dominant faction were full-blooded pope-haters. Over the years which had passed since the Restoration, members had grown disenchanted with the Stuarts, whose return they had once greeted with so much joy. Not only had the heir to the throne gone over to the enemy, but even the loyalty of the king himself to his own Church was suspect. He had too many French relatives for Parliament's liking, and altogether too close a relationship with Louis XIV, Europe's Catholic tyrant.

The discovery of Coleman's secret correspondence had now laid bare the source of His Majesty's extra-parliamentary funds, and members were speculating with alarm what promises he might be making to Louis in return. It was widely suspected that he would concede almost anything to gain financial independence from a Parliament which he would have dissolved long since had it not been apparent from the mood of the country that elections would bring in another even less amenable to his wishes.

Meanwhile, with some clandestine *pourboires* from Louis (and the gift of the callipygous Louise de Kerouaille), Charles contrived to jog along agreeably enough, albeit on a tight rein. For it was in the interests of both Parliament and the French king to ensure that he was never sufficiently in funds to recruit the standing army which would make him the master of his realm in fact as well as name.

When his 'faithful' Commons passed unpalatable legislation, the king had to rely on his influence with the Lords to see that it never reached the statute book. When both Houses became unmanageable he would resort, not to dissolution, but to prorogation, not permitting them to meet again until it was convenient to him or he was compelled by poverty or disorder. The ministers who governed the country (in so far as it was governed at all) were appointed and dismissed by him without reference to the people's elected busybodies or their troublesome and often refractory lordships.

On October the twenty-first 1678 Lords and Commons were recalled because the Popish Plot threatened both king and Parliament. It was an occasion when they could stand together and if, as Charles supposed, there was really no plot at all, the suffering of a few guiltless persons would be a small price to pay for what might be gained from a period of reconciliation and the opportunity to be rid of mischief-makers, like Oates and Coleman, on either side of the Great Divide.

His Majesty was also hopeful that the pestilential little Earl of Shaftesbury would over-reach himself again, and he even visualised this as the right moment to win some popularity and strengthen his increasingly shaky hold on crown and sceptre by bowing to the Commons' frequently expressed wishes and exiling his dear and loyal but incorrigibly stupid and pig-headed brother.

Exhibiting the tactical skill which had served to keep him on his throne thus far, Charles opened the new session with a characteristically judicious announcement: 'I have been informed of a design against my person by the Jesuits, of which I shall forbear an opinion, lest I may seem to say too much or too little. But I will leave the matter to the law.'

It was generally known that close examination of a mountain of papers seized from the Jesuits had yielded not a word of treason nor the whiff of a plot. The Commons were nonetheless unanimous in the belief that Mr Justice Godfrey's death proved the existence of a damnable and hellish conspiracy by the pope's army of fanatical recusants, who would not scruple to kill the king, subvert the government and root out the Protestant religion.

When Charles retired from the chamber to console himself with the titillating vulgarity of Mistress Gwyn, currently Louise's most favoured rival, members expressed themselves dissatisfied with the Council's handling of the affair. The Earl of Danby, the chief minister, was roundly accused of a criminal lack of diligence, and the Commons thereupon proceeded to appoint their own committee to inquire into Oates's allegations and the magistrate's murder.

The Lords followed suit the next day, so that three separate inquiries were at work simultaneously, each interrogating the ever fluent Oates in turn and all burrowing for nuggets of truth among his various charges, some plausible and others contradictory and barely believable.

The Council had cooled towards him since he had been confronted with the most prominent of his accused, Edward Coleman and Sir George Wakeman, and failed to recognise them despite having boasted that he knew them well. After several meetings Henry Coventry, the presiding Secretary of State, had seen through his blustering farrago of fact and fiction and dubbed him an unmitigated liar, but Oates's first performance before the Lords' committee was so well judged to exploit the hysteria which he had helped to create that orders were given for the immediate despatch of five Catholic peers to the Tower and the arrest of some Benedictines living in harmless poverty in a tumbledown house in the Strand.

On the Thursday of the same week a second proclamation was issued: 'Whereas His Majesty has received information that some persons who can discover the manner and circumstances of the murder of Sir Edmund Berry Godfrey are withheld from so doing out of a fear that their persons may be in danger from the revenge which the murderers or their friends may take upon them, His Majesty is pleased hereby to signify, and on the word of a king to promise, that if any person shall speedily make such discovery to one of His Majesty's Principal Secretaries of State he shall not only receive the five hundred pounds and pardon (promised by His Majesty's late Proclamation) but His Majesty shall take such effectual courses for the security of such discoverer as he shall in reason propose.

'Given at Our Court at Whitehall this twenty-fourth day of October in the Thirtieth Year of Our Reign.

'By His Majesty's Command, Henry Coventry.'

Sir Edmund's body was buried a week later, and Mr Pepys and Will Hewer were among the mourners: partly out of curiosity but mostly because they were frightened men who judged it expedient to make a public demonstration of loyalty.

They joined a cortège of more than a thousand distinguished persons of quality who mustered near the city wall at Bridewell to escort the coffin to St Martin's in the Fields, where the magistrate had served as a vestryman. The solemn procession crossed the

Fleet and paraded along the Strand. It was headed by no fewer than seventy-two Protestant divines, and a vast rabble brought up the rear. Prominent among the pall-bearers were the ill-assorted earls of Shaftesbury and Pembroke: one much too short and the other much too tall to dignify the company.

A strict silence was observed during the march, and there were no demonstrations except when the little, limping earl raised an angry roar by brandishing his stick in the direction of the now empty Benedictine house. This set the mood for the funeral service inside the church, where a fiery sermon was preached on a text taken from the second book of Samuel: 'Died Abner as a fool dieth?'

It was a time for taking inspiration from the Old Testament, not from the New with its injunction to Christians to turn the other cheek. The congregation were reminded that Abner had been stabbed to death under the fifth rib, and that the biblical king and his people had responded by rending their clothes, girding themselves with sackcloth, weeping for him and then taking their revenge in the name of the Lord.

'The Lord shall reward the doer of evil according to his wickedness,' quoted the preacher. Godfrey's death, like Abner's, must not be in vain: it must be avenged, he urged. His peroration was a thundering denunciation of Rome and all Romish practices. The threat from that city of Satan was real, he declared – as the congregation were able to judge for themselves from the presence of two other, burly clergymen, chosen for their size, who stood in the pulpit throughout the sermon to guard the preacher against attack by a papist assassin.

'We live in strange times indeed,' remarked Mr Pepys to Will as they left the church. 'I have never before seen two such thumping divines, nor witnessed three parsons in one pulpit.'

He spoke lightly, but his stomach felt as heavy as stone. A few days earlier the government had instructed the Admiralty to close all ports and mount a watch day and night to prevent suspects from escaping abroad. Within the Navy Office it had seemed as plain as could be that any guilty person intent on fleeing the country would have taken flight before the discovery of the body. But it was Mr Secretary's responsibility to arrange for orders to be transmitted and obeyed, and he had at once alerted all port commanders.

A thorough search of every vessel about to leave port was instituted, but at Gravesend there had been a disturbing lapse of duty. This presented the parliamentary critics of the Admiralty with an opportunity to cast doubt on the anti-Catholic zeal of a service which was rumoured not yet to have rid itself of Catholic officers, as Parliament demanded.

A man of suspicious appearance and behaviour had arrived in Gravesend two days after the magistrate's body was found. When challenged, he had disappeared, only to return later and board a vessel outward bound for Lisbon by bribing one of the searchers. A sailor who had observed the transaction reported it too late for the sailing order to be countermanded.

A warship sent in pursuit overhauled the vessel in the Downs, but it was then discovered that the fugitive had disembarked at Margate. A sweep of the Channel by naval boarding parties, hurriedly despatched from Portsmouth and Plymouth to stop and search every ship sighted, failed to locate him. It was later discovered that he had ridden by night from Margate to Folkestone, where a fishing boat had taken him to Dieppe.

When it became apparent that the mysterious runaway would never be traced or identified, Oates had announced that the man who had slipped through the navy's net was Father Simons, a notorious Jesuit, in disguise. According to Oates, he was among the most dangerous of the plotters and the leading instigator of Mr Justice Godfrey's murder.

Could it, Oates demanded, be mere negligence which had allowed this diabolic agent of the Roman AntiChrist to escape his just deserts and live to plot and plot again? Or could it be that there were traitors in high places who were fearful of being implicated in what Father Simons might have revealed under interrogation?

Mr Pepys's political instincts and experience were acute and seasoned. They told him that these words from the arch-informer's mouth had been put there by my lord of Shaftesbury, the inveterate adversary of the heir to the throne and all associated with him, not least the navy and Mr Pepys himself. He did not doubt that 'high places' included the office of Secretary to the Navy, and that 'Father Simons' did not exist outside Oates's imagination. Urgent steps were being taken to discover the true identity of the fugitive, in the hope of unmasking him as a Green Ribbon man or an associate of Oates.

Good fortune had blessed Mr Pepys with the most watertight of alibis for Godfrey's murder: during the weekend of the magistrate's disappearance he had been on official duty in attendance on the king at Newmarket. On that score he was safe from the perjuries of false informers tempted by the royal reward and, no doubt too, by inducements secretly offered by Shaftesbury's lackeys. Where then would the first blow fall? And how quickly? He put the questions to Will Hewer.

'Where we least expect it, and very soon.'

Will's prediction was correct on both counts. The answer was to come the very next day. While the Secretary to the Navy and his head clerk were walking home from the funeral of the Protestant martyr, in Whitehall the finishing touches were being put to a plan for the arrest of a member of his household, charged with the martyr's murder.

— 9 —

THE ARREST

Sam was at work the next afternoon when Tom Walbank's head appeared around the door.

'A Mr Smith has called with a message that he has business with you, Sam. He would not stay, but asked me to tell you that he will be waiting in Lawrenceson's Rhenish wine house.'

Sam puzzled over the name. He could think of no Smith who might have business with him; but an excuse to leave the office was welcome, even on a cold grey day. November had come overnight, and winter with it. He put on his hat and a heavy coat and ran down the stairs.

'If Mr Hewer notices my absence, tell him I shall be returning in a few minutes,' he called over his shoulder to Tom, little suspecting how wide of the mark that might be.

At the wine house a hard-faced stranger introduced himself as Mr Smith. 'I am a king's messenger,' he said. 'My errand is to desire you to go with me to Mr Secretary Coventry.'

'I shall go with you most willingly,' Sam replied, 'but upon what occasion?' He was taken aback.

'Mr Secretary does not inform me of the nature of his business,' answered the messenger. 'But since you are a gentleman, sir, and mean to cause me no trouble, I will show you this in confidence. My instructions are not to speak of it nor put it into execution unless refused; so if you are asked, you will say you never saw it.'

He put a finger to his nose, winked slyly and emptied his glass. Then, after peering around to make sure that they were not observed, he pulled out of his pocket a warrant for Sam's arrest.

Sam needed a drink, but they left at once. During the short walk through the streets to the Secretary of State's office he attempted to clear his mind and prepare for interrogation. What information did he possess of such importance that a man was sent to apprehend him? Was he himself really under suspicion and, if so, of what misdemeanour could he possibly stand accused? He was innocent of any crime and, so far as his memory served him, no man had reason to bear him a grudge.

The journey was hurried, but the wait on arrival a long one. Mr Secretary, it seemed, was engaged on more pressing affairs of state. After sitting for more than two hours, wondering what Mr Hewer and Mr Pepys were thinking of his disappearance, Sam was told that a message had been received from the newly appointed Committee of the Lords requiring his presence for an examination into the murder of Mr Justice Godfrey. A letter was prepared to accompany him and Sergeant Farraday (alias Mr Smith) to the Marquess of Winchester's house in Lincoln's Inn Fields, where the committee was in session.

The sergeant kept his silence for the length of the Strand, but as they turned into the fields he at last responded to his charge's pleas to be told at least the names of the members of the committee whom he was to meet. Sam knew the marquess to be a Catholic turned Protestant and an implacable enemy of the Duke of York. He was hoping to be reassured that some of the others might be well disposed towards the Admiralty and his master, but he was due for disappointment.

The most senior was the Duke of Buckingham, who had resigned his office as a minister of the Crown after insulting the king to his face. Now a leading member of the Green Ribbon Club, he was a close ally of the other lords mentioned by the sergeant: Essex, Halifax – and Shaftesbury himself. At these names Sam's stomach churned over in dismay. When that of the Bishop of London, the most fanatical of all the bishops, was added, only the sergeant's strong grip on his arm prevented him from running away. He feared that no justice or mercy could be expected from men like these.

This time there was no waiting. He was ushered into the marquess's great chamber for immediate questioning by Shaftesbury, the huntsman of the Opposition pack. There were no preliminary courtesies, and he felt the hairs on the back of his neck rising when he found himself treated as though a guilty man already convicted of some heinous offence. He prayed to God to give him strength and courage.

'Mr Samuel Atkins,' the earl addressed him sternly, 'do you know one Mr or Captain Charles Atkins?' He spoke with a slight lisp, like the hiss of an adder.

'Yes, my lord.' Sam bowed his head dutifully and answered with all the appearance of respect which he could muster.

'Are you related?'

'No, my lord; although for the sake of our names we have called each other cousin.'

'Do you know or believe that he has any reason to be prejudiced against you?'

'No, my lord; nor have I ever given him any such occasion.'

'Did you ever tell him that there was a want of friendship between Mr Samuel Pepys and Sir Edmund Berry Godfrey?'

So that was where the little lord was leading! Sam felt his bowels loosening as he began to realise what the charge against him might be. This was becoming the worst nightmare of his life, but he determined not to be overawed and to tell nothing but the truth, cost what it may. 'No, my lord,' he replied firmly. 'I never mentioned Sir Edmund's name to Captain Atkins in my whole life.'

With a piercing glare of disbelief Shaftesbury passed the interrogation to the Earl of Essex, whom Sam had once heard reported as saying that talk of popery made him imagine his own children frying in Smithfield.

Essex's first question was whether Sam was acquainted with a man called Child, and when Sam replied that he had no remembrance of anyone by that name, a rough seafaring person was brought into the room.

'Now pray you, do you not know this man?' the earl demanded.

'No, my lord; I never saw him before in all my life.'

'No!' Essex rounded on the newcomer. 'What say you, Child?'

'I never saw him before in all my life.' To the earl's confusion the man repeated Sam's very words.

He was dismissed in disgrace and replaced by Charles Atkins, who had been better rehearsed in what was required of him and affirmed without hesitation that Sam had told him of a difference between Mr Pepys and the murdered magistrate.

'My lord,' Sam protested to Shaftesbury, who had resumed the questioning, 'I cannot guess at what has led Captain Atkins to say this. I can assure you that I said not one word of it.'

'Did you not ask Captain Atkins whether this Child was a man of courage and secrecy and bid him send Child to Derby House to inquire for your master?'

Sam made a vehement denial. He now understood the precise nature of the accusation. It was that Mr Pepys had hired an assassin to murder the magistrate, and he, Sam, had acted as an accomplice and intermediary. His quaking spirits revived a little, for it was hard to believe that such an improbable fabrication could be sustained, even under what passed for the law in England.

Captain Atkins stood beside him, a shifty, skimpy youth not many years older than Sam himself. He was trembling, but stuck to his guns: 'This discourse, as you know, Mr Atkins, took place between us in the window recess in the Lords room at Derby House.'

Such perfidy and mendacity roused Sam to anger. 'Captain Atkins,' he said, 'God, your conscience and I know that there is not a word of truth in what you say. On the last occasion when I saw you in the Lords room at Derby House you pulled me to the window and begged me for the loan of a crown; to which, as you will doubtless recollect, I assented.'

'Come, come, Mr Atkins,' Shaftesbury swiftly intervened, seeing his witness shamefaced. 'This will not do, you know. Captain Atkins has sworn this positively against you, to whom he bears no prejudice or malice, as you have yourself acknowledged. Rather, he has confessed to several obligations towards you. To tell you truly also, I do not believe he has wit enough to invent such a lie.'

That, thought Sam indignantly, is the first piece of truth I have heard from any of these noble schemers and their perjured parasite. He suspected that the person who had invented this tale was the secretary to the committee, who was writing notes at the far end of the room but otherwise seeming to play no part in the proceedings. Sam had recognised him as Sir Philip Howard, a magistrate with a reputation for corruption, and was aware that Charles Atkins was his nephew. There sat just the man who would concoct false evidence to ingratiate himself with his superiors and contrive to enrich a member of his own family at the same time.

Sam made yet another denial and, despite the fear he felt, ventured to call their lordships' witness a rascal. When he made the accusation, neither the captain nor Sir Philip would meet his eye.

'Indeed!' said Shaftesbury. 'We believe Captain Atkins to be someone who has loved wine and women and been a debauched man, but on what grounds, pray, would you have us think him a rascal?'

'Why, my lord, I would offer you this,' Sam answered boldly. 'Charles Atkins was a naval officer who basely surrendered one of His Majesty's ships to Barbary corsairs. He no longer has any right to the rank of captain, by which title he continues to be known only because his family have protected him from the disgrace which he has fully deserved. By all of us in the Navy Office he is pitied and despised as an officer dismissed the service for cowardice in the face of the enemy. I trust that your lordships will not think me presumptuous in dubbing a man without honour a rascal.'

Shaftesbury's face turned white with rage, and he ordered the witness to leave the room. 'Mr Atkins,' he then demanded in a menacing voice, 'what is your religion?'

'I am a Protestant, my lord; and my family ever so.'

'Have you taken the sacrament recently?'

'No, my lord,' Sam was forced to confess, 'but it is my intention to receive it next Sunday.'

'Then you must have us believe that it is your intention to forgive Captain Atkins; else your conscience will not be clear. Now tell us, pray, how long you have lived with Mr Pepys.'

'Four years last August, my lord.'

'And where were you housed before you came to him?'

'I lodged with Commissioner Middleton. He was a friend of my father, who was a Puritan – like yourself, my lord – and a commander in the parliamentary army.'

'I did not ask about your father, whose faith and loyalty to Parliament I do not question. Nor do I dispute that Mr Middleton's household was Protestant. But now that you are brought into government business and move in different circles, it is thought that you may have become other than what you once were. We find that those employed in the business of His Majesty's navy are strangely prone to fall under the influence of popery.'

'I never yet had temptation from within or without to alter my religion,' replied Sam, 'and I trust to God I never shall.'

This momentarily silenced the assembled peers, and the others looked towards the Duke of Buckingham, who rose and crossed the room to stare into Sam's face and wheedle him into compliance.

'I swear to it that you are an ingenious young man, Mr Atkins,' he declared in a flattering voice. 'You have shown us a ready tongue. For your own sake I would gladly have you use it now to reveal to us without further ado what you know of this matter.'

This opened a new phase in the examination, when the bullying was set aside and each of the lords in turn begged him to speak without fear. They repeated the duke's high opinion of him and expressed their great sorrow at his obstinacy, which would, they warned, create prejudice against him, whereas a confession would do him no injury but bring him advantage. Captain Atkins, who was recalled, promised faithfully to make Sam's fortune by sharing the reward with him.

'Mr Atkins, dear cousin,' he pleaded, 'do pray recall for their lordships how you told me that Sir Edmund Berry Godfrey had greatly vilified your master and if he lived would be the ruin of him. Why else would I have made an assignment to meet Child in an upper room at the Three Tobacco-Pipes in Holborn to tell him in secret that Mr Pepys would speak with him? Why else, when I next met him, did Child endeavour to engage me to join him in an act of murder, as I have plainly and in duty bound informed this committee?'

But, frightened though he was, Sam's life-long devotion to the truth remained unshaken by threats and blandishments alike. While expressing his deep regret at having to disoblige their lordships, he reiterated his utter inability to say one word avowing a conversation with his namesake which had never occurred. He was thereupon ordered to withdraw.

When his presence was required again, Shaftesbury addressed him with a crooked smile and an affectation of pity for a sinner who would not confess.

'Truly we are, every lord of this committee, most unhappy to be forced to be thus blunt with you, Mr Atkins, but there being such a positive oath sworn against you, we cannot answer to Parliament for doing less than committing you to Newgate.'

'As your lordships please. If you send me to be hanged, I can say no more or otherwise.' Sam spoke with a bravado which his knocking knees belied. Newgate! It was almost a death sentence.

'Fine words!' sneered Shaftesbury. The mask of pity slipped and he banged the table sharply with his cane. 'For the last time let me advise you to declare what you know of this abominable crime or you will rue the ill fortune which will assuredly attend you. You must know the laws of this nation to be such as will bring you under severe punishment for concealment.'

'My lord,' said Sam, 'I know very well the laws of this nation on that point and on others. But I know as well the laws of God, which are such as would draw a worse punishment on my head if I were to tell a lie or invent aught to the prejudice of another man.' His throat was dry, and he almost choked over the brave words.

'Call Captain Richardson,' ordered Sir Philip Howard at a nod from Shaftesbury.

An attendant led in the keeper of the jail, who had already been summoned to wait outside with Child in his custody. The secretary then read him the warrant: 'You are hereby to receive the body of Mr Samuel Atkins for suspicion of felony in concealing the murder of Sir Edmund Berry Godfrey and to keep him safely until he shall be delivered from your custody by due process of law.'

Outside it was raining so hard that it seemed as though all the angels in Heaven were weeping for Sam. Miserably he hid his head, both for protection and lest an acquaintance should notice him in the keeper's charge. Together with the dejected seaman Child and another warder, they threaded a path through the stews of Whetstone Park, which bordered the road to the City. Skirting Lincoln's Inn, where the lawyers plied their trade, they were soon at the prison, which stood beside the City gate of which it had once formed the upper part.

Sam gazed in anguish at the frowning stone walls, parts of which were still blackened with the marks of the Great Fire. Inside, the corridors were dark and narrow and pungent with the smell of urine and ordure and rotting humanity. Newgate served not only the City but the whole county of Middlesex as well. Only the frequency of death within relieved its perpetual and notorious overcrowding.

'Where shall we put him, Captain?' the turnkey inquired, sizing Sam up for what he was worth. 'If their lordships have sent him, I suppose the gentleman will be with us for a long stay.'

'Master Atkins is to have quarters to himself in my own house,' ordered the keeper.

Sam thanked him profusely. The prospect of spending his days and nights in the company of robbers and cut-throats had been terrifying him. Now his overriding concern was to let Mr Pepys know where he could be found. 'May I be permitted the use of pen and paper to send a message to my master?' he asked.

'You have nothing to thank me for,' replied Captain Richardson, shaking his head. 'Your accommodation with me is at their lordships' bidding. They have instructed me to keep you a close prisoner in solitary confinement. You will talk to no one, write to no one, be visited by no one until you have ceased to defy them and come to your senses. Those are my orders.'

Sam groaned, and the captain extended a comforting hand. 'You can be released tomorrow,' he said. 'You have only to tell them what they are waiting to hear.'

'Never!' Sam vowed under his breath as the turnkey led him away.

— 10 —

EVIDENCE OF MURDER

'No,' said the king, releasing himself with a sigh from the encirclement of Louise's soft pink flesh. 'I will grant you anything but that.' Swinging his legs over the side of the bed and looking back over his shoulder, he studied her naked body with the eye of a practised lecher.

'You are unkind to me, Charles,' she pouted, arching her rosy buttocks and waggling them at him reprovingly.

He was lost for a reply. If the grumbles of Lord Treasurer Danby were to be believed, she had had £50,000 in cash from him over the last two years alone, as well jewellery and other gifts. And all those calculated indiscretions which he so thoughtfully planted in her mercenary little ear during their pillow talk would have earned her a handsome retainer from the French ambassador.

'It is such a very small favour,' she pleaded.

'Yet it is one which touches my honour. I acceded to your request to find a husband of rank for your sister. She was reputed to be the plainest girl in all Brittany and now enjoys the good fortune of being the plainest countess in all England. For Henriette to desert the earl would show base ingratitude on her part, and on mine if I were to assist her. She must stay and make the best of him.'

'There is no best in my lord of Pembroke. Whenever she displeases him the brute puts his hands round her neck and lifts her in the air and shakes her. One day he will strangle her. Do you imagine you have made my sister content by marrying her to a convicted murderer?' Louise laid a hand on the king's thigh and gave him her most appealing and reproachful look.

'The Mighty Giant was not a felon when she became his wife,' he reminded her. 'Maybe it is the marriage which has turned him to drunkenness and savagery. But if you wish it and she is willing to forgo the pension I pay her at your insistence – £600 a year, is it not? – I will meet you this far: she may leave as soon as her husband consents. It would surprise me if he were not glad to see the back of her, but I incline to think she will first have to oblige him with an heir.'

His tone had softened as her hand crept up his thigh. He was relenting fast, but not fast enough for someone as determined as Louise. 'Pig!' she cried.

Charles was unsure whether this referred to himself or the earl's bedtime behaviour. 'Be patient, my sweet,' he coaxed. 'All ports are closed to prevent the plotters from fleeing. If I were to issue a warrant authorising your sister to cross the Channel, Parliament would demand my head for aiding the escape of a papist.'

'Plotters!' she scoffed. 'I will tell you who the real plotters are. They are sitting pretty in your Parliament. It is their victims who are fleeing. At least you must promise me that you will let Henriette go when the queen and I are sent packing; or I promise you I will arrange her escape myself.'

Charles was even-tempered to a fault, but mention of the queen by his mistresses always made him angry, as she well knew. 'Her Majesty will not be leaving,' he answered sharply.

His treatment of his wife was one of the few subjects on which his conscience pricked him. It had been a most unfortunate match, he reflected. A pretty Infanta had been on offer, and the Spaniards had nearly gone to war when they were outbid and he chose a Portuguese princess instead. But what else could they have expected of an impoverished monarch? Her dowry had been half a million pounds in gold coin, with Tangier and Bombay thrown in, and – a great prize for London merchants – free trade with Brazil and the East Indies.

The cost had proved too high, all the same. When she arrived, Catherine had turned out to be a plain girl with protruding teeth which her mother and his ministers had refrained from mentioning in advance. As a pious Roman Catholic, she was unpopular and booed in the streets. Her court had become a safe haven for

Jesuits and other popish undesirables. Her piety in bed quite unmanned him.

'The poor creature has nothing to do in Somerset House all day except play basset with her maids – and nothing to do all night except sleep,' persisted Louise maliciously. 'It would be a blessing for you both if she left and never came back. Then you could remarry and get a little Protestant heir of your own at last.'

As she taunted him, Louise was still flaunting herself invitingly, but talk of the queen had extinguished his lust. Before he could restrain himself he had slapped the lovely posterior hard. She tumbled out of bed with a shriek and ran from the room, calling loudly for her maid.

Politics were a wearisome distraction from dalliance, he meditated while he dressed. How could even the most generously endowed of the Lord's Anointed keep a mistress happy when his rascally Commons were threatening her and his queen with banishment, his chief minister with impeachment, and his brother and heir with exclusion from the succession? Ah well, he consoled himself, if mademoiselle chooses to sulk I still have Nellie, who never troubles me except with laughter at the wrong moment, and my lady Castlemaine, who is so prim and proper on her feet and lascivious on her back.

Leaving Louise's chamber, he crossed the privy garden preoccupied, acknowledging no bows or salutes. Beneath his breath he was cursing his meddlesome Commons and vowing to stand by all those around him whom they had the impudence to attack: brother and wife, mistresses and ministers. Upstairs in his closet he found his brother awaiting him impatiently.

'There is no time to be lost.' James was in one of his wild moods and waved a sheaf of papers in the king's face as soon as he entered the room. 'Your Majesty must act, and act today, or the traitor Shaftesbury and his lewd dogs will drive me into exile and tumble you right off the throne.'

Charles smiled faintly. 'What would you have me do, brother?'

'Free the Jesuit and Benedictine fathers, order the immediate release of that unfortunate clerk from the Navy Office and announce that if Coleman is put on trial and convicted you will exercise the royal prerogative and grant him a pardon. All are as innocent as unborn babes. They are suffering for my sake. They must be protected as a matter of honour, and not for that reason alone. Their trials will be seen by our enemies as a prelude to yours and mine. The little earl and his henchmen are still republicans at heart, whatever they profess. They are of the same mind as those atheists and regicides who brought our father to the scaffold. You are his successor as God's elect in this realm and you must stop them before they break out into open rebellion again. Silence them. Show them your mettle by proroguing Parliament and putting Shaftesbury back in the Tower. That is how you must act – decisively.'

First Louise and now James. He had asked for advice and received commands. However easy-going in his regal state, the king did not take kindly to being told what he must do, but he concealed his irritation and appraised his brother's proposals coolly.

'Have you considered that your remedies may provoke what they set out to cure?' he asked. 'The new session of Parliament has barely begun. To send Lords and Commons scurrying back to the country like whipped children would invite an insurrection. Shaftesbury is riding so high with the mob that arresting him may be what the knave would welcome. We would have another martyr on our hands.'

James was about to burst out in protest, but Charles signed that he would not be interrupted.

'We will do what can be done for the fathers, but it is Coleman as much as Oates who has put their lives at risk. His behaviour has been criminally indiscreet. I wonder at you for giving employment to such a bungling fanatic. As for Mr Atkins of the Navy Office, you know that I have no powers to order out of custody a man awaiting trial. He is of no consequence, and a pardon would not be appropriate for a person of his low standing. If Shaftesbury's hounds are baying for blood and must be appeased, Mr Atkins's will do as well as any man's and much better than yours or mine.'

'It is my duty to protect those who serve me,' insisted the duke, still blustering with indignation. 'And Your Majesty's to protect your innocent subjects.'

The king refused to be put out of countenance. 'You may do as you please,' he responded courteously, 'but allow me to offer you advice on the highest duty of a monarch in times such as these. After my death you may find it useful. A monarch's first obligation to his subjects is to survive. He cannot defend them from the grave. Would you have me end on the scaffold for the sake of a rash secretary and a mere clerk?'

'It will not come to that,' James assured him. 'Shielding those in your service is your strongest line of defence: it would be folly to stand aside and allow it to crumble. Coleman has committed no crime, and there is no corroborative evidence of young Atkins's guilt. His sole accuser is an officer who has disgraced his command and would have been shot for cowardice in the face of the enemy had I still enjoyed the privilege of being Your Majesty's High Admiral.'

'Then we can be confident that the lad will be acquitted,' said the king with a sardonic smile. 'But it is of another captain of ill repute that I wish to speak to you. He styles himself Captain William Bedloe, although it seems that his captaincy is no more genuine than Oates's doctorate. He has emerged from the Marshalsea prison to confirm Oates's lies and clear his own debts by claiming the reward. Yesterday he was examined before myself and the Council, and I fear that he has been well coached to furnish the promoters of this imagined conspiracy with what they now need to proceed with the trials of those arrested. To obtain a conviction for murder, no more than one witness is required, but for charges of high treason the law demands at least two, as you will know. For treason, even the sworn testimony of Titus Oates, the hero of our nation, is deemed insufficient.'

'I have had inquiries made about this Bedloe and can tell Your Majesty what kind of man he is, so that you may judge what degree of credence to place upon his word.' The duke tapped the papers in his hand.

'He has already obliged us by telling me himself. "Your Majesty," he said before all the Council, "I have been a great rogue." He confessed to having led a vicious life and cheated many persons. Yet he is handsome and has a frank air about him, and I must own that if he were to take a seat in the House of Lords as though of right I for one would be deceived.'

'He is a fiddler's son from Chepstow and was Lord Bellasis's stable boy!' exclaimed the duke. 'I have it all here. The man is a swindler, a horse-thief, even a highway robber. He has practised as a confidence trickster all over Europe. Your Majesty speaks the truth about his passing for a peer of the realm. In Flanders he called himself Lord Newport. In France he went under the name of Lord Cornwallis. In Spain he was known as Lord Gerard. He lived on credit as an English milord, and his debts were never paid. The Spaniards imprisoned him, and he was sentenced to death in Normandy.'

Although his brother spoke in a tone of outrage, Charles's expression at this catalogue of infamy was one approaching admiration. 'I remember that you and I were once compelled to live in much the same manner,' he remarked. 'It requires great ingenuity.'

'We deceived no one, and all our debts were paid.'

'That is true,' the king conceded. 'Thankfully, the French king and others came to our assistance. In Captain Bedloe's case, when his credit expired, he turned to the Jesuits. They accepted his bona fides because Lord Bellasis is a Catholic and they believed him to be one too. He claims that for the last four years he has acted as a messenger for them and gained secret information by opening the letters entrusted to his safekeeping. That is how (so he says) he learned of their plot to depose me and replace the government with one nominated by the pope. Whether or not you are to have my crown, he did not divulge. His story bears a remarkable similarity to that of Oates, but he swears in the name of Our Lord that they are not acquainted with each other.'

'With this he takes the name of Our Lord in vain,' declared the duke, crossing himself. 'The two are birds of a feather. I am told that they met in Valladolid and probably here in London as well. They speak like Ananias. The Jesuit fathers are not stupid. It is absurd to suppose that they would employ such fellows to carry their confidential correspondence. I tell you that every word which comes out of the mouths of this pair of ne'er-do-wells has been put there by that limping pygmy.'

'Yet my lord of Shaftesbury is not stupid either. He may be behind those who are behind Oates and Bedloe, but he will take good care to keep his distance from perjury.'

After delivering this judgment the king signalled for silence and proceeded to pace his closet in thought until his reverie was interrupted by a mess which one of his lapdogs had deposited on the Turkey carpet presented to him by the Sublime Porte. He noticed it just in time and stepped round it with a muttered curse, which James took for a sign that he might speak again.

'Are Your Majesty's thoughts the same as mine?' he inquired. 'Must we presume that the earl murders from a safe distance too? What, pray, did Bedloe allege about Godfrey's death?'

The king was examining his shoes and did not respond at once. When he did, he ignored the first two questions. Keeping one's thoughts to oneself was a cardinal rule of kingship, and one that James had yet to learn.

'Bedloe told the Council that early last month he was approached by two Jesuits, named Le Fevre and Walsh. They offered him £4000 to join them and several others in killing a man who was an obstacle to their design. When he asked who was their master, they replied that they were employed by Lord Bellasis.'

James snorted. 'The only truth to be learned from that deceit is that young William Bedloe did not give satisfaction in his lordship's stables. I warrant the scoundrel is taking revenge for punishment or dismissal.'

'Bedloe agreed their terms,' continued the king, 'but when they met again to inform him of the rendezvous for the next day and all that was to be done then, his nerve failed him and he did not keep it. That was on Friday, the eleventh of October, the day before Godfrey's disappearance. On the Sunday Le Fevre accosted him in Fleet Street, apparently by accident, and told him that the murder had been committed, as they had planned, the previous day.'

The duke cast his eyes to the ceiling, where two stucco cherubs were fondling each other. 'Is that to be believed?' he demanded.

'Not only that,' the king replied coolly. 'Furthermore we are expected to believe that, so far from feeling resentment at Bedloe's failure to keep his word, the Jesuit offered him half the original reward for his help in disposing of the body. Bedloe accepted, and on the evening of the following day he was taken through a side gate into a dark courtyard in the queen's palace and led into a small room where he was shown a corpse lying on the floor.'

At this, James finally lost control of his temper. He sprang to his feet with an oath. 'Godfrey murdered inside Somerset House? The queen incriminated! This is treason indeed!'

Charles waved to him to calm himself and be seated.

'He and his associates will, of course, deny suggesting that the queen had any knowledge or involvement in the affair; while leading the country to suspect otherwise. The scene of the crime has not been set in Her Majesty's apartments. Their master mind has been clever enough to choose a location near the servants' and tradesmen's entrance to the palace. That is a position from which they can advance or retire as the plot is developed.'

'I smell more than Shaftesbury in all this cunning,' said the duke. 'Buckingham, Essex, Halifax, Pembroke – yes, and your beloved son Monmouth too – all these rebel whiggamores must be rounded up before they trick us back into exile. Leave this sham captain to me and I will get their names for you. If he has confessed to moving the body, he has confessed himself an accomplice after the fact and will squeal to save his neck.'

'For the second time I beg you to be seated.'

The king was at last showing signs of anxiety, but less for the safety of his wife and realm than for his precious collection of timepieces, threatened by the duke's rampages round the room. Only when his order had been obeyed did he resume his narrative.

'When Bedloe first saw the body, he promised to return the next evening after dark to join the others in carrying it off in a coach to Primrose Hill. But when, on closer inspection, he recognised the magistrate's face he became frightened and broke his word once more.'

'So his account clears him of the charge either of committing the murder or of being an accomplice to it?' James made a gesture of disappointment.

'That would seem to be part of its purpose,' the king acknowledged.

'And does that complete his evidence?'

'By no means! Le Fevre, so he told us, revealed to him every detail of the murder; first, of course, taking the precaution of binding him to secrecy. It may appear strange to you and me that the Jesuit should place such trust in the word of a man who made a habit of breaking it, but, as we have seen already, this whole story rests on the premise of Jesuit imbecility.'

'And public gullibility,' added the duke.

'According to Bedloe the murder was committed thus. The two Jesuits and a gentleman in the service of Lord Bellasis encountered Sir Edmund in the Strand on the Saturday afternoon. They inveigled him into Somerset House on the pretext of possessing information about where the plotters were meeting and how they might be seized. Once inside, they set upon him and dragged him into an unlit store-room. There, at pistol point, they demanded that he send to his house for the depositions which he had taken from Oates and, in the meantime, tell them all he knew. When he refused, they murdered him.'

'Were they not aware that the depositions had long since been passed to the Secretary of State's office in Whitehall?' asked the duke in surprise.

'It appears not,' answered the king, 'but you must suspend disbelief if you are to hear me out. This is Bedloe's tale, not mine. Upon Godfrey's repeated refusal to oblige them or to answer any of their questions, the plotters decided to kill him because he had seen their faces and declared that he would never yield to threats to hold his tongue. They knew his reputation for bringing men of violence to justice, so they stifled him with a pillow, and then, to make sure of their work, strangled him with a cravat. On the Monday night the body was taken out into the fields and left there with a sword thrust through the breast to suggest suicide.'

'What a monstrous tale, whether true or false!' James exclaimed in disgust. 'But either way there is nothing to be done for Sir Edmund except pray for his soul. Now we must bestir ourselves and look to the salvation of the monarchy and to safeguarding the lives of all true believers in this realm, afflicted as it is with the devil's curse of heresy.'

The king was lounging at ease and displayed no sense of urgency. 'Yes,' he murmured. 'True believers must certainly be accorded the privilege of our protection, whoever they may be.'

'Those standing in the greatest peril are the Jesuit fathers. Some are already imprisoned; others are in hiding and hunted. All face a traitor's death.'

'If they are as innocent as you would have me believe, we will do our best for them,' the king promised soothingly. 'But I forbid hasty action. Cunning must be met with cunning. And do, I pray you, bear in mind this point in logic: the fact that the informers against a man are liars does not, of necessity, infer his innocence.'

'Do we live in a realm where an accused must prove his innocence and not the prosecution his guilt? I tell you, brother, I know these Jesuits for honest men of God.'

'Then we must have faith that God will look after his own,' responded the king, not troubling to disguise his cynicism. 'My especial concern is for yourself and the queen. Bedloe was considerate enough to absolve Her Majesty from playing any part in the plot, but he claims to have read letters from her pledging herself to contribute money to bring in the Catholic religion.'

'What harm in that?' demanded James.

'Little enough,' granted the king, 'but he also mentioned some letters of your own which he said he had seen in the study of Cardinal Barbarini in Rome. Without making an outright accusation, he hinted that they were incriminating and that you were guilty of some measure of engagement in the plot. Not, however, in so far as it would involve my death; for which I thank you.'

'Pray forgive me, but Your Majesty's jest is ill-timed,' said James indignantly. 'If this be not another of Bedloe's lies, I can say only that I know not what poor Coleman may have written in my name. He had no authority from me, I do assure you. All the world knows of my longing for this country to return to her old faith. God knows I have never concealed it. But it should be as widely known that I would never stoop to treason, even to realise my fondest wish. England and Rome must be reunited by legitimate means – and that could be brought about tomorrow if only you would cease dissembling and declare yourself.'

Weary of his brother's insistent demands that he sacrifice the reality of earthly joys for the promise of heavenly ones hereafter, the king found his attention drawn elsewhere and seized on a diversion. 'What news, Chiffinch?' he asked.

The man's movements were so discreet that no visitor could be sure how long the confidential Keeper of the Closet had been standing in the darkness beside the door behind him, or how much he might have overheard.

'A messenger from Mr Secretary Coventry has brought this for Your Majesty.' Chiffinch bowed, handed the message to the king, bowed again and disappeared as silently as he had come.

'Bedloe is being examined before the Lords' Committee today,' the king explained, 'and I desired Sir William to send me word if the rogue chose to treat their lordships to any fresh revelations. Ah, yes,' he went on as he read the paper, 'it is as I suspected. There is one important item of information which he says he forgot to tell the Council yesterday, but which, it appears, came to him suddenly during the night.'

James greeted the news with another of his snorts. 'I wager it came to him from someone else's lips and not out of his own head unprompted.'

'He has remembered that one of the murderers around Godfrey's body told him his name was Samuel Atkins and that he was one of Mr Pepys's clerks. I fear there may be no saving poor Atkins now,' said the king.

— 11 —

IMPRISONMENT

'Well, Mr Atkins, we hope you have considered of this business and are now ready to shed some light upon it for us.' The speaker gave an encouraging smile.

Sam recognised him as Viscount Halifax, a gentler interrogator than Shaftesbury, but no less slippery. No one could tell quite where Halifax stood or for how long he would stand there. What every man knew was that it was never safe to trust him.

As a prisoner with no company but his own, Sam had ruminated for nearly a week on his previous examination. After six uninterrupted days and nights he had desired Captain Richardson to acquaint the Lords' Committee of his request to be brought before them at their next meeting. That very same afternoon he had been taken here to the Lord Privy Seal's chamber, where they were sitting.

'Indeed, my lord,' he answered Halifax respectfully, 'I have well considered of it.'

Their looks were expectant but doomed to disappointment, for imprisonment had not broken his spirit. The cold, the discomfort, above all the humiliation of his confinement had hardened his resolution. 'Having searched my heart, my conscience and my memory,' he continued, 'I am now prepared to show your lordships that nothing is to be expected from me and there is no reason why my liberty should be denied me.'

Their lordships conferred in whispers among themselves before Halifax spoke again: 'If, as we understand from your words and demeanour, there is aught you would say against Captain Atkins or his deposition, then you must stay till we send for him.'

Sam bowed to show his gratitude. 'My lord,' he said, 'I trust I shall refute him in several circumstances which I have better considered, and thereby convince you of my innocence and clear my good name.'

This proved too much for the Earl of Shaftesbury, who was seated beside Halifax and at once took up the questioning. 'Why, Mr Atkins,' he threatened, 'you had better beware lest you provoke your accuser. The captain has declared to us that he has much more against you. He would have us believe that he has other circumstances to relate by which you will appear the most wicked man living.'

'If your lordships please,' Sam replied, 'I desire that he be sent for.' Although he spoke boldly, his courage was ebbing.

After more whispering they ordered him out of the room to wait in a downstairs passage, where he was guarded by his custodian from Newgate. Half an hour passed, and then Captain Atkins appeared. He scurried past and up the stairs like a scared rabbit, but Sam gave chase and caught him by the sleeve.

'What has induced you to bring this mischief upon me?' he demanded. 'Do you design to ruin a man who has been your benefactor?'

'No, no.' The captain was craven and recoiled shamefaced. He made to pull himself away, but Sam would not let him go.

'Do I look like one who has done, or is party to, any murder? Do you believe in your conscience that I could ever be guilty of such a crime?'

'No, faith,' stuttered the captain. 'I will swear for you on that. Against you I will swear naught except the words which passed between us.'

Again he attempted to free himself and again Sam tightened his grip, crying: 'God and you and I know it was not so.'

The cowardly officer was cringing with fear as Sam's hands on his coat and cravat sought to shake the truth out of him. 'What are these new lies you are about to tell the Committee so that I shall be hanged at Tyburn?'

While he struggled, the captain kept repeating that he had nothing more to swear against Sam and that, in sooth and before God, he verily believed that Sam knew nothing of the murder.

'Note that down; take notice of what he has said,' Sam panted to his warder, who had joined the affray and at last succeeded in pinioning Sam's arms behind his back to release the witness.

Soon they were called before the Committee, and there the argument was conducted in a more seemly fashion. Captain Atkins swore once more to the truth of his former statement, but he had no new charges to bring, despite Shaftesbury's prompting. Sam maintained his denial and added that, before their confrontation at the Committee's previous meeting, he had not set eyes on the captain since the middle of August. That was a few days before Bartholomew Fair, as he remembered, and long before the discovery of any plot or Sir Edmund's murder.

'Captain Atkins swears one thing and you swear it is not true,' said Halifax. 'If you are innocent, then it is he who must be the greatest villain in the world. Pray, look one another in the face.'

They turned to confront each other. 'Come, Captain Atkins,' Halifax urged him, 'confess truly: have you belied Mr Atkins or no? Perchance you have been mistaken. Consider the injury you do this young man if what you avow be not the truth.'

The captain persisted in his story: his uncle's eye was on him, and so was Shaftesbury's. But under Sam's steady gaze his own wavered and he grew deathly pale. 'There!' cried Sam in triumph. 'Pray observe, my lords, how his look shifts and the colour of his countenance is altered.'

'I do not see it,' pronounced Shaftesbury, grim-faced.

'My lord,' Sam protested, 'I humbly submit that it is very apparent.' But the earl merely looked away and the others said nothing.

So this was their idea of justice! In despair he pressed hotly for his liberty and appealed to the Bishop of London, the only man of God amongst them. He told him of his Puritan family and religious upbringing and how he had never gone to mass, nor ever known or met a popish priest in all his life.

'Truly, I believe you are a Protestant,' said the bishop, 'but this oath is greatly against you and your accuser affirms it most positively.' He was as unyielding as Shaftesbury.

'But, my lord,' Sam pleaded, 'does it not seem strange to you that I should invent such a lie as to tell Captain Atkins of ill will between my master and Mr Justice Godfrey when the only time I saw them together they appeared as great friends as could be, expressing mutual kindness and respect? What is more, my lord,

I swear to you that Mr Pepys has never committed any secret of any kind to me, nor ever spoken to me of Sir Edmund. Your lordships would readily be persuaded of the truth of this if you but knew how tottering is my position with him. He has parted with me once and at this present time I do not at all stand high in his esteem.'

'It grieves me to hear it,' said the bishop sternly. 'Are you given to drink or debauchery?'

'To neither, I thank God. But Mr Pepys is an exacting master. For the least absence from duty he will withdraw his favour.'

Tempers frayed as the examination dragged on, until Sam came to understand that even if he won every argument it would not gain him his release. His pleas for bail, for visitors, for a lawyer, even for pen and paper were all peremptorily refused.

'Enough of these obstinate denials and impertinent demands!' Shaftesbury at last cut Sam's pleadings short and pointed towards the door. 'Another witness has been kept waiting this past hour. Let us now hear what Captain Bedloe has to say.'

The journey back to Newgate in chains and a closed carriage was almost too much for Sam to bear. Glimpses of others freely walking the streets brought the tears which he had fought to suppress during the long interrogation. He was now without hope and returned to lie in his cell, refusing all food and drink for two full days.

On the third morning he was dozing, fretting in his mind over his beloved Elizabeth and what might have become of her, when the door was flung open and the keeper entered with a visitor; although visits were still forbidden.

His joy quickly melted when he was confronted with the last person in the kingdom whom he would have wished to see: Captain Charles Atkins.

He scrambled hastily to his feet, pummelled the door with his fists and called to Captain Richardson, whose footsteps were retreating down the corridor. The keeper obligingly returned and consented to Sam's urgent appeal to be allowed to speak with him in private.

'For God's sake do not leave me alone with this man,' Sam begged when they stood in the passageway together. 'He has already sworn falsely against me and will, for aught I know, go back to the Lords and swear anything else that he lists.'

'Their lordships have directed that he must be alone with you.' The keeper spoke with sympathy but firmly. It was his wont to treat Sam with kindness, like a son in trouble, but he would never break the rules or disobey an order.

'Suffer it not, I pray you,' Sam pleaded. 'It will be useless to them. I vow I will not utter one single word to him except in the presence of a witness.'

The answer was a shrug, and Sam was pushed back into his cell with no more than a promise that it would not be long before the keeper returned.

No sooner had he gone than the visitor began to wring his hands and make tears start from his eyes. 'Oh, Mr Atkins,' he moaned, 'we are both undone.'

'How undone?' Curiosity prompted Sam to ask the question despite his vow of silence.

'The man who was summoned to the Lords after us on Wednesday has sworn against you. He affirms that you were present at Sir Edmund's murder. He has identified you positively.'

'Well, God bless him!' exclaimed Sam bitterly. 'For he is as positive a perjurer as yourself. Both of you will need to stretch the bounds of His mercy if you are not to burn together in hell-fire. Assuredly, Captain Atkins, you are undone in the next world. But inform me, pray, how this fellow fibster has undone us both in this.'

'He will filch my reward – our reward – if you do not confess. My uncle bade me come to you and tell you of it. Confess, Master Atkins, while there is still time. Then you will come to no harm and your fortune will be made. We will share what the king has promised. You have my word upon it. No hurt has ever been intended towards yourself. Why be so solicitous for a master who treats you harshly?'

From his sly grin Sam could see that the rogue believed his offer of freedom and wealth would be a temptation too great for any man to resist. He was quick to disabuse him: 'You might as well ask me to forgo my salvation,' he replied. 'I do assure you that a thousand deaths shall not extort a lie from me which would ruin Mr Pepys or any other innocent person.'

Sam's indignation proved infectious, for the captain now became angry. He asked whether Sam remembered telling him that his master kept a secret house in France, given to him by the French for services rendered. 'At Rouen, is it not?'

'Have you sworn to that too?' Sam was aghast at this new invention.

'Not yet, but I intend so to do. At the same time I shall swear to the occasion, which I now recollect, when you expressly desired me to impeach your master for this murder in order to divert suspicion from the Duke of York.'

'Heavens above!' Sam exclaimed. 'Thou art a prince among liars.'

'Come now, Master Atkins,' said the captain, 'you know you told me so, and I have my duty to do as a loyal Protestant and subject of the Crown.'

'Captain Atkins,' said Sam deliberately, 'I verily believe you to be the wickedest man alive. You will one day repent of this cursed mischief that you are doing me with your damned inventions and false oaths.'

Weak though he was, Sam raised his fist, but the captain cried out and the keeper answered the call and hurried him away. 'Consider what I have said before this afternoon when you will be called to the Lords again,' was the visitor's parting shot.

Captain Richardson insisted on his eating and drinking to gain strength for his third examination. His display of violence towards another witness caused him to be searched and put in leg irons before being carried to Westminster. There he was kept waiting an unconscionable time. When at last called into the Lord Privy Seal's chamber, he found a stranger with the Committee – a man wearing a black periwig and campaign coat who looked him over earnestly and saluted him gravely.

The Earl of Shaftesbury was once again presiding. 'Do you know this gentleman?' he asked Sam, and Sam replied that he had never seen him before in his life.

The stranger was then asked the same question and addressed Sam directly: 'I believe, sir, I have seen you somewhere, but cannot tell where. I don't indeed remember your face.'

'Come, come, Captain Bedloe,' Shaftesbury chided him. 'Look more closely. Is this not your man?'

'My lord, the person I saw at Somerset House was a young man and he told me that his name was Atkins and he was a clerk belonging to Derby House, but I cannot swear that this is the same person.'

The Committee was disappointed, and Bedloe abruptly dismissed. Shaftesbury then turned again to Sam: 'Where were you, Mr Atkins, on Monday, the fourteenth of October, between nine and ten o'clock at night?'

Sam was dizzy from two days' hunger. His mind went blank. 'I cannot well remember, my lord,' he stammered, 'but I suppose I was at home, for I am seldom out at that hour of night.'

'So you cannot remember!' The scowl with which Shaftesbury had greeted Bedloe's uncertainty was replaced by a wintry smile. 'Mr Atkins, if you are innocent, you are the most unfortunate wretch alive. Pray attend carefully to what I have to say, for I would be your friend. Confess all you know and make a discovery of this matter and your life shall be saved.'

Quietness fell on the room. The five lords and the bishop sat motionless behind the long table. At the secretary's desk Sir Philip Howard's hand and pen hung suspended in the air. Sam stood before them tight-lipped, with his leg irons chafing his flesh and one of Captain Richardson's men on silent guard at his back. He could tell that all their minds were occupied with the same thought: this was his last chance.

Freedom awaited him outside. Through the window behind their lordships of the inquisition he could glimpse the first frost of winter on the roof of the Parliament House. Was he never to feel fog in his throat or the sun on his face again?

After an instant of turmoil in the pit of his stomach, anger mastered his fear. Did he not stand before them in irons guiltless? Were they not fully aware of his innocence and yet feigned ignorance of it? They might lord it over him with their grand titles of Duke, Marquis, Earl, Viscount and Bishop, but beneath the finery they stood lower in his eyes than the meanest commoner, for they were nothing more than base perverters of justice. How he yearned at that moment for the return of the Commonwealth for which his father had fought; for the rule of the Lord Protector, who was hard and stern but God-fearing and just.

'My lords' – he chose to address them all – 'as I am innocent in every respect of what is said about me, I sincerely trust that you will neither advise nor desire me to wrong my conscience and stain my soul in an endeavour to postpone death, which at length must overtake us all. I pray God to give me the strength and grace rather to suffer an early passage to the next world than swear to a lie.'

His speech drew no touch of pity. The whole Committee was enraged. Their faces were moulded and set in cruelty. He consoled himself that he had been right not to throw himself on their mercy: their expressions told him that they had none.

'Since you are so gallant, Mr Atkins,' Shaftesbury sneered, 'I must tell you that you will either be knighted or hanged – knighted if the papists rise and cut all our throats; hanged if they are prevented. What Captain Atkins has told us that you said to him was damning enough. Now we have Captain Bedloe's oath which, though not positive, yet with other circumstances against you must prevail upon a jury to find you guilty.'

'My prayers shall be that the real murderers be detected,' said Sam. 'Then I am confident I shall be acquitted.'

'Why hear him further? Mr Atkins will confess nothing,' said the bishop. 'I dare say he expects a pardon.'

'I shall guard against that, I warrant you,' Shaftesbury promised and signalled for the prisoner to be removed.

'I require no pardon, my lords,' Sam called out as he was led away, 'for I have committed no crime.'

During the journey back to Newgate he shut his eyes against the world. When the wicket gate closed behind him, he felt his fate sealed. Kept in irons, he found himself no longer the keeper's guest. His new accommodation was a solitary, windowless cell below ground level in the darkest and dampest bowels of the prison.

Visitors were still denied him. But he soon discovered that some means of communication was open, even to prisoners held incommunicado. Like Captain Richardson himself, the warders and servants bore no malice towards those of their charges who gave them no trouble. Dick, the unseen scullion who brought him his food, became Sam's friendly informant on the promise of payment after his release or in his will.

From him Sam learned that one of his neighbours was Edward Coleman, the Duchess of York's secretary and Justice Godfrey's friend: the papist who had so carelessly failed to destroy all his indiscreet correspondence with fellow Catholics in Paris and Rome. But Coleman, although in even greater straits than Sam himself, was, according to Dick, by no means downcast or reconciled to his fate. He was constantly at prayer and in hourly expectation of God responding to his supplications with a pardon from the king.

One day, through the food hole in the door of Sam's cell which was their channel of communication, Dick reported excitedly on a procession which had wound through the city all the way from Moorgate to Temple Bar, headed by a bellman ringing his bell and crying: 'Remember Justice Godfrey!' A dead body had been carried on a horse behind him. It was dressed in the magistrate's clothes and supported by a rider impersonating one of his murderers taking his corpse from Somerset House to Primrose Hill.

Sam felt a noose round his neck as he stooped to catch every word of the hoarse whispering. If the frenzy of the mob was still being whipped up, anyone accused of the murder was doomed indeed. The procession, it seemed, had been mounted by Shaftesbury's Green Ribbon Club, and the body was followed by pageant scenes representing Jesuits and cardinals with daggers and poison. The final tableau had featured effigies of the pope and the Devil hand in hand.

The scullion's voice revelled in the description, while Sam listened in horror. The mob's enthusiasm had been fuelled with free wine dispensed at Temple Bar to drink to the pope's damnation while his effigy was burned on a bonfire. The toast of 'No Popery!' had been given by Shaftesbury himself from the balcony of the King's Head tavern, and the cheers which followed were accompanied by screams of agony from inside the belly of the pope, where imprisoned cats were being burned alive. By the time Dick had finished his gloating account, Sam felt almost glad to be locked away from such wickedness.

Dick became so engrossed in the fun of the pope-burning that he lingered too long and was caught and reprimanded. Thereafter his news came only in single snatched sentences.

As the days passed, Sam grew accustomed to the loneliness and discomfort. Enforced inactivity brought a strange contentment, and he sensed a bond of comradeship uniting all the inmates of the jail. Some were there for no more than a few days or weeks before taking the road to Tyburn. For others – prisoners with long sentences and jailers who could find no better employment – it became their home, where at least they did not starve.

Then one morning his breakfast of rancid bread and murky water was accompanied by a softly spoken: 'Say nothing'. Puzzled, Sam sprang to the food hole and echoed the words: 'Say nothing? What is your meaning?'

'Message from W.H.' That was all and Dick was gone.

Will Hewer! So he was not abandoned! A flood of relief surged through Sam, only to be followed by a return of unease. New expectations had replaced resignation and unsettled him.

Later that day he was taken to the keeper's house and presented to four members of the House of Commons who had come to examine him. To them he repeated what he had said to the Lords, and they repeated that his life was in desperate peril.

Did he know one Welch or one Prichard? Did he remember circumstances on Monday the fourteenth of October relating to a dark lantern? Was he at Somerset House on that day? How and where had he spent his time on Saturday, Sunday and Monday, the twelfth, thirteenth and fourteenth of October?

Sam's answers to the first three questions were 'no'. He then assured the solemn gentlemen that he was never at Somerset House, either on that day or at any time before or since in his whole life. Mindful of Will Hewer's warning, he informed them that in his present condition he could remember much less about his movements on those days than he would wish, but hoped to be able to oblige them upon consideration. It was the truth, but also, as he confessed to himself, an evasion.

The message and the visit broke his peace of mind. Back in his dungeon, he wept with frustration at having no means of setting out in writing all he remembered of those fatal days. The month which had passed since seemed a lifetime.

The fact that he had an alibi was now clear in his memory. But would revealing it bring about his release without trial, as it ought, or would prior knowledge of it enable the prosecution to suborn witnesses and discredit it in the eyes of a jury? He suspected the latter; and so, if he interpreted the message aright, did Will and Mr Pepys.

A week later it appeared that he was about to find out. Captain Richardson came to his cell early, bade him rise and dress himself and ordered his legs to be secured with a heavier pair of irons.

'You are to be tried this morning at the King's Bench bar,' he said. 'May God be with you.'

Sam protested that he had been given no notice and had no witnesses prepared for his defence.

'Go you must,' the keeper replied. For that was the way of the law.

— 12 —

TRIAL FOR TREASON

While Sam was lying incarcerated awaiting trial, the turmoil created by treason and murder had run on unabated.

The terms of the Test Act were stringently applied, and new anti-Catholic measures announced. Every holder of public office was ordered once again to receive the sacrament according to the rites of the Church of England and to take an oath against the obnoxious doctrine of transubstantiation. All popish recusants were required by proclamation to remove themselves at least ten miles from London.

In the matter of Mr Justice Godfrey's murder Sam was but an afterthought, incidental to the main thrust of Captain Bedloe's evidence, but he remained the sole suspect in custody. Despite the most assiduous of searches, the three Jesuits named by Bedloe as the murderers – Le Fevre, Walsh and Prichard – had vanished. Nor had 'Lord Bellasis's gentleman' been identified.

Bedloe himself was now discovered to have obtained his commission – not in the British army, but in that of the Prince of Orange – by fraudulent means. Yet king, Council, Lords and Commons continued to hang on his every word, even though his every word was not always the same from day to day. As examination succeeded examination, the details of his story varied and the discrepancies multiplied.

The reward offered him by the Jesuits fluctuated between £4000 and two guineas. Sometimes the murder occurred at two o'clock, sometimes at five. At one time the victim was stifled with one pillow, at another with two. The body was at first said to have been moved on the Monday, and then not until the Wednesday. According to one of the captain's sworn statements, it had been hidden in a room in Somerset House where the Duke of Albemarle's body had once lain in state; according to a later one, it had been secretly taken into the queen's chapel.

A story was thereupon circulated that Roman Catholic devils in the shape of the queen's ladies had performed a ritual dance of triumph round the corpse of the Protestant martyr. The proof of this was seen in the droppings of beeswax which had been detected on the deceased's clothing at the inquest and not previously accounted for. Tallow candles, made from animal fat, lit homes like the magistrate's; the more expensive beeswax candles were used only by the rich and in churches and chapels. This became such a telling point and roused such feeling against the queen that by the end of November it had emboldened first Oates and then Bedloe to name her openly as one of the guilty plotters.

The trial of Sir George Wakeman, her physician, was being postponed only until the prosecution could be sure of the verdict. The obstacle was the king, who recognised that, in all but name, the queen herself would be on trial: Sir George's conviction would precipitate her disgrace and exile. He was therefore adamant that he would not have the physician found guilty. The judges – *his* judges, he made plain – would have to choose between obliging him or Shaftesbury and could expect no mercy if they ventured to incur his displeasure.

Although, like Sir George, he was not the real target of his accusers, Sam enjoyed no such protection. The hounds of the Green Ribbon pack were baying for blood, and there was no reason closely affecting king or state why his life should not be sacrificed. Mr Pepys would still stand between Shaftesbury and the Duke of York.

The veering course by this new Oates who had arisen in the shape of William Bedloe, his constant weaving and dodging among the facts, were not attributable to a poor memory. Like Oates, he had mastered methods of deceit, and so grown wary of exactness. In a fog of uncertainty about detail one was less likely to be caught committing an indisputable falsehood. His hesitation over recognising Sam when confronted with him before the Lords was calculated caution.

But two facts he stood by unswervingly, to make good his claim to the king's reward. First, Mr Justice Godfrey had been murdered in Somerset House on the afternoon of Saturday the twelfth of October by, or at the instigation of, the three named Jesuits. Secondly, he, Bedloe, had seen the body there – and someone who said he was Sam beside it – on the following Monday evening between nine and ten o'clock.

The Jesuits were not available to deny their involvement and would not have been believed had they done so. It was commonly supposed that Catholics had a dispensation from the pope to lie on oath in the cause of their religion. But the precision with which the time of Sam's presence was alleged and the witness's doubt over his identification opened a narrow avenue of escape.

From strict confinement the task of preparing his defence was impossible, but Mr Pepys too was feeling the noose tighten round his neck and recognised that he must rescue Sam to save himself. A game was now being played outside Newgate of which Sam knew nothing. Mr Pepys's moves to establish his clerk's alibi were spied upon and reported, so that the government decided to postpone his trial until such time as the witnesses so painstakingly assembled for the defence could no longer stay in London without losing their employment elsewhere.

So, even as Sam was shuffling in irons towards the prison gate to face his accusers in Westminster Hall, the order was countermanded and he was returned to his cell, feeling like a puppet jerked hither and thither at someone else's whim. In his place, so as not to disappoint the mob, a respected Catholic goldsmith named William Staley was taken out and tried for the capital offence of 'malicious speaking' against the king.

The witnesses against Staley were a pair of disreputable topers at a cookhouse in Covent Garden, who swore to having overheard him call the king a rogue and a heretic. His denials were not believed, and the fact that he had at the time been talking to a foreign customer in French, a language which the topers did not understand, was not enough to save his life. To speak in French was in itself prima facie evidence of treason.

Dick's excited whispering informed Sam of the gruesome details of his execution three days later. Convicted of high treason, the goldsmith had suffered the traitor's death of being taken down from the gallows while still conscious, in order to be castrated and disembowelled alive. His body had then been hacked into four pieces and handed to his family and friends, who had created a scandal by celebrating four masses: one over each quarter.

Dick had obtained special leave to attend the execution and delivered this last tidbit with relish, leaving Sam to brood miserably on the fate of the fellow prisoner who had taken his place.

A few days later Edward Coleman was taken to Westminster for trial on the same charge of treason. The sounds of his departure from the neighbouring cell were all too audible in Sam's, but on this occasion no news was delivered by Dick and it was to be several weeks before he learned of Coleman's fate. Sprawled on the damp stone floor, he passed the time recalling the days when he attended trials as a curious spectator and reflecting on the irony that the next would be his own.

At Derby House, meanwhile, news of the day of Coleman's trial reached Mr Pepys in time for Will Hewer to be despatched to observe the proceedings and report on their relevance to those threatening Sam.

Inside Westminster Hall the gravity of the crimes of which the Duchess of York's secretary stood accused was impressed on the jury by the length of time it took the Clerk of the Court to read them.

The prisoner had, it was alleged, falsely, maliciously and traitorously proposed, compassed, imagined and intended to stir up and raise sedition and rebellion within the kingdom of England, and to procure and cause a miserable destruction among the subjects of the king and wholly to deprive, depose, deject and disinherit the said sovereign lord the king of his royal estate, title, power and rule of the kingdom of England, to alter the sincere and true religion of God in this kingdom by law established, to levy war against the said sovereign lord the king within his realm of England, and, with the aid, assistance and adherence of the French king, to alter the true religion in this kingdom of England to the superstition of the Church of Rome, and to subvert the government of the kingdom of England.

The voice of the clerk continued in a steady monotone for several minutes, while Will scribbled a summary for Mr Pepys.

To all of this Coleman listened with the superior air of a man who judged such an absurd farrago to be beneath his notice. In pleading not guilty, he drew the attention of the court to the violent prejudice against every man in England who confessed to being a Roman Catholic. As an undefended prisoner so heavily charged in such circumstances, he begged leave to be allowed the advice and assistance of counsel.

The team of prosecution lawyers, headed by the Attorney-General, Sir William Jones, and the Recorder of London, Sir George Jeffries, expressed amazement at the impertinence of this demand. Sir William Scroggs, Chief Justice of the court of the King's Bench, fortified by precedent and strong spirits, concurred and dismissed it out of hand.

Squeezed among the throng surrounding the well of the court, Will allowed himself a wry smile. The practice of the law decreed that the accused be brought to trial in ignorance of the charges against him until they were read out, and that he must then fend for himself as best he could against skilled advocates who had spent weeks preparing the prosecution's case.

Without a copy of the indictment or the services of a defence lawyer, Coleman was further handicapped by having no knowledge of what witnesses the prosecution intended to produce; nor, when they appeared, was he permitted to cross-examine them. To load the dice still more heavily, the court was also pleased to admit hearsay evidence against him.

The verdict was therefore not in doubt. It was taken for granted that the prisoner was condemned before the trial began. An acquittal would have been an affront to the Crown, and to the judges whose duty it was to conduct a successful prosecution in the king's name. Among the public, convinced by Shaftesbury's pamphleteers and rabble-rousers of the guilt of every Catholic accused, it would have provoked a riot.

That the witnesses for the prosecution were under suspicion as the two biggest liars in the kingdom was of no significance. To the mob they were heroes; to the Crown a necessary formality. The really damning evidence was Coleman's undestroyed correspondence, but without witnesses the case could not have been brought to court.

After solemnly acknowledging an admonishment from the bench to speak nothing but the truth, Oates testified how the accused had employed him to carry letters from himself and Jesuits in London to the French king's confessor and Jesuits in St Omer.

He said that he had not broken open the letters himself, but had been present when they were opened. He had then contrived to read their contents, which included Coleman's acknowledgment of the receipt of £10,000 for the propagation of popery in England. Oates testified that the Jesuits' plot to assassinate the king met with the approval of the prisoner, with whom he was well acquainted.

Coleman's expression, as he listened, conveyed his determination to expose perjury and the wickedness of those who stooped to it for gain. When given permission to address the court, he burst out impatiently: 'I would have it known that at my examination before the Council this fellow was brought in at my request. He told the king that he had never seen me before. Yet he would now have it believed quite otherwise.'

'My sight is bad by candle-light,' explained Oates readily. 'The Council was meeting in the evening, and Mr Coleman had taken the precaution of changing his periwig.'

But when pressed to answer why he had not thought to mention to the Council the serious charges which he was now bringing against the prisoner, he was for once lost for words. There was a long pause before he stammered that his memory must have failed him – from weariness after sleepless nights spent in the pursuit and arrest of the king's enemies, he added.

Bedloe was then summoned and testified that he too had acted as a messenger for Coleman in his treasonable intrigues to destroy the king, the government and the Protestant religion. He swore to having heard the accused say that he would adventure anything to bring in the popish religion. The very words used were, as he recalled them: 'If I had a hundred lives, I would spend every one of them in the cause of the Church of Rome; and if there be a hundred heretical kings to be deposed, I would see them all destroyed.'

When he went on to describe how he had seen the prisoner at a Jesuit consult in London in August, the prisoner stopped staring at the roof-beams in scornful disbelief and interrupted with a vehement denial.

'I spent that month in Warwickshire and can prove it,' he declared. 'This witness, like the last, is as trustworthy as Beelzebub, the prince of mischief himself. I swear to the court that I never uttered those words; nor have I ever so much as set eyes on this very gallant captain before today.'

When the testimonies were done, sixteen of the most damaging letters discovered in the accused's house were read at length. In Will's ears these did not ring of treason, but the Chief Justice pronounced differently. His summing-up informed the jury that unless they found the prisoner guilty they must find the two witnesses for the Crown perjured. This, he indicated, was not to be contemplated by loyal citizens, and a verdict of guilty was delivered accordingly without further ceremony.

On hearing the sentence, Coleman lost none of his defiance and self-possession. 'Pray hear the words of a dying man,' he said. 'It was never my intention to bring in the Catholic religion by rebellion or by bloodshed, but by toleration only. As God is my witness, I have kept a resolution not to utter a single untruth to save my life. Good people, I have nothing to confess but my innocence.'

'It was bravely spoken,' commented Will afterwards, when he made his report seated in the privacy of Mr Pepys's parlour. 'He was as valiant for the truth as our own Sam.'

'We must pray for the continuing strength of Sam's will-power and purpose,' said Mr Pepys gloomily, 'for if his spirit is broken we are all sunk, true Protestants and loyal subjects though we be. Coleman's courage will have been raised by the expectation of a pardon from the king, but our Master Atkins must know full well that, in spite of my every endeavour, a junior clerk can have no such prospect.'

'But has Coleman too any real hope, or does he not deceive himself?' mused Will. 'He never denied the plain truth that he formed a design to bring popery back to this country and to promote the interest of the French king against our own government. Nay, he boasted of it.'

'If promoting Louis' interests be treason, how many others are guilty of it?' demanded Mr Pepys in a flurry of indignation. 'The king's favourite mistress, the Duchess of Portsmouth, is without doubt Louis' agent. Danby, his chief minister, is assuredly on the French pay roll. The king himself must be in the French king's pocket: from what other quarter does he procure the funds which Parliament refuses him? As if that were not enough, I hear that my noble lord of Shaftesbury and his cronies, who are so rabid in their abuse of the French, secretly receive bribes from across the Channel to keep their opposition confined to words. If that be so, nothing stands against the French but the will of the people and myself and the navy.'

Having learned from experience not to interrupt Mr Secretary when he spoke of himself and the navy, Will responded with nothing more than a muttered *'O tempora! O mores!'*

'Such are the times we live in that a pardon for Coleman would bring down the government,' Mr Pepys continued, 'and perchance the monarchy as well. So the king himself fears. I was at St James's with the duke this morning. He confided in me that he has been pleading with his brother daily for the poor creature's life, but, as you have guessed, all to no avail. However, I am pleased to say that my importunity has achieved something for Sam.'

'He is to be released?' Still agile, Will leaped to his feet with a hurrah, but a shake of Mr Secretary's head dashed his joy.

'Alas,' sighed Mr Pepys, 'our young clerk is a prisoner by order of the Lords; so only the Lords can order his release. That cannot be expected while our old adversary rides so high. Even Danby is powerless – Shaftesbury is coming ever closer to having him impeached for not moving against the plotters with sufficient zeal. But His Majesty has consented to instruct Sir William Coventry to recommend to the Chief Justice that Sam be allowed pen and paper and a visit from a lawyer to help him prepare for his trial. Scroggs is a time-serving wretch and can be relied upon to comply with His Majesty's wishes.'

Will's congratulations were tempered by a suspicion that the lawyer would be a hack nominated by the court and therefore not to be trusted. 'Do you not foresee a danger that Sam's written statement will be taken from him and studied by the prosecution so that it can be countered and rebutted in court?'

He made the point diffidently, but offence was taken nonetheless. Mr Pepys was notoriously touchy and rebuked him sharply. 'How dare you question my foresight?' he demanded. 'I put forward the name of Mr Hayes and it has been accepted.'

Mr Hayes had undertaken work for the Navy Office on occasion and always with exemplary diligence. He was not, however, of a sanguine humour, and when on the following day he entered Sam's cell in Newgate in the company of Captain Richardson, it was with the cheerless look of a hangman come to size up his next victim. His opening words, too, were not designed to raise false hopes.

'Mr Atkins, I have been instructed to assist in the preparation of your defence and will act for you to the best of my ability. But it would be idle to conceal from you my considered opinion that you are a dead man. Now that Captain Bedloe has informed and sworn against you, and now that his evidence has been found to be truthful by the jury in the case of Mr Coleman, I see no likelihood of saving your life.'

'Yet you shall have my thanks for making the attempt.' The comfort brought to Sam by the presence of a visitor who had come as an ally outweighed the man's black looks and words. That he was already as good as dead was not news, and his spirits had no lower to sink. 'You have my word that I am unjustly accused and wholly innocent of the charge against me,' he continued earnestly; 'although that is not of the least concern to the law, as I am perfectly aware.'

The lawyer frowned at this sentiment. He was ill at ease in the presence of the keeper, who would not leave but stood as a silent witness to all that passed between them. Sam's eager questions about Mr Pepys and Will Hewer and progress in the discovery of those engaged in the plot went unanswered.

Instead Mr Hayes handed him pen, paper and ink and signed to the keeper to leave the candle. 'Write whatever you can remember about that Saturday, Sunday and Monday, the twelfth, thirteenth and fourteenth of October,' he instructed. 'I must have the names of all the friends and acquaintances whose company you kept during those days. Search your memory for the times to the nearest minute. Make haste about it, for your trial will be in a day or two.' He made to leave, but Sam put out an arm to detain him.

'Pray take a message for me.'

The lawyer put a warning finger to his lips and nodded his head in Captain Richardson's direction, but Sam paid no heed.

'It is for Mistress Elizabeth Curtis, formerly Sir Edmund Berry Godfrey's maid-servant,' he said. 'Pray find her and tell me when we next meet what has become of her.'

Mr Hayes was shocked and read him a stern lecture. 'Master Atkins,' he said, 'I must caution you against mentioning the name of any person not relevant to your defence, and most particularly against requests to carry messages. The keeper here is under orders to report any irregularity of that nature, and whoever is named by you may very well fall under suspicion as an associate in the crime with which you are charged. I would stress, furthermore, the especial danger incurred in the case of mention of a member of the murdered man's household.'

Sam was contrite but persistent. 'In every other instance I would bow to your advice, Master Hayes,' he replied, 'but this is a message which must be delivered before my death and I may not be granted another opportunity. I respect Captain Richardson enough to believe that he would never be party to ensnaring an innocent girl in the meshes of the law. What I beseech you to convey to her has no relation to murder or treason. It is that I love her and will go on loving her beyond the grave, and that I desire her with all my heart to be happy with another of her choice when I am gone, but to remember me always in her prayers.'

Sam cast an imploring glance at the lawyer and another at the keeper, then sank to his knees and covered his face with his hands to catch the tears which he could not hold back. When he rose and dried his eyes, he was alone.

— 13 —

THE ALIBI

Mr Pepys was sitting behind the desk in his office awaiting a visitor. His chief clerk was at his side. A fat dossier lay open in front of them. It contained depositions attesting to Sam's whereabouts on Monday, the fourteenth of October.

Mr Hayes's prediction that Sam would be tried in a day or two had proved wide of the mark. November was over and nearly half of December too, and the Navy Office's neatest amanuensis still lay imprisoned in limbo, suspended between indictment and trial. One legal term had ended without his case being called, and another was about to begin.

The reason for the delay was no riddle. As Will Hewer had foreseen, the statement which Sam wrote for Mr Hayes had been taken from him and copied before it was passed to the lawyer. The prosecution now possessed the names of his witnesses, and they had been summoned to appear that day before the Lords' Committee.

'So you are still of the opinion that Sir Edmund took his own life?' Will inquired.

'His own clerk believes so, as Sam reported to us,' Mr Pepys replied. 'That is strong evidence, for no man knew him better than Henry Moor; and nothing that a rascal like Bedloe swears to on oath will alter my opinion one whit. Godfrey hanged himself in Paddington woods. His body was discovered by men who decided to make use of it for their own mischievous purposes. That much is plain. The mystery lies in their identity. His brothers would have wanted to disguise the fact of *felo de se*. Catholic fanatics might have wanted to make an example of him. Our friends, the Protestant fanatics, would have praised the Lord and seized the opportunity to make his death appear the work of papists.'

Will was too old and trusted a colleague to play the flatterer. At the risk of another rebuke, he shook his head and ventured a contradiction. 'You forget the marks of assault and battery on the body.'

'The most significant marks were round the neck,' argued Mr Pepys. 'They are proof of strangulation. The surgeons are agreed that the sword thrusts were not the cause of death. They were wounds inflicted on a corpse to conceal the cause. The bruising of the chest and face will have occurred when the body was moved.'

'How then do you account for the internal haemorrhage?' Will asked. 'Could that have occurred after death? It is common ground that Sir Edmund was beaten, stabbed and strangled. The question is, in what order?'

Mr Pepys threw up his hands in perplexity, not (he was careful to indicate) surrender. 'Whatever the truth may be and wherever it may lurk,' he declared, 'it must not only be uncovered but susceptible of proof. Without unimpeachable evidence, all our suppositions and speculations will be of little use to Sam.'

They were interrupted by the arrival of their visitor. Bearded and tanned, he was unmistakably a man of the sea.

Mr Pepys received his respectful salute and responded with a warm handshake. 'You are very welcome, Captain Vittells. Deliver your intelligence and spare us no detail.'

The captain was master of His Majesty's yacht *Catherine*, to which Sam had paid a visit with two ladies on the day when Bedloe swore to having seen someone answering to his name standing beside Godfrey's corpse at Somerset House. His was the most important of the names disclosed in Sam's statement, and he and five of his men had been called for interrogation by their lordships.

'Pray excuse my lateness, Mr Secretary,' he apologised, 'but we were examined at length – and without overmuch courtesy. To hear some of the questions you might suppose that the lords of this land believe the navy to be under popish command. One even hinted that I might have led my crew up from Greenwich and taken a hand in the crime myself.' He took the chair which Will vacated for him and sat down heavily with a grunt of disgust.

'That would be my lord of Shaftesbury. He is as great a threat to ne navy as the French or Dutch. If he is seeking traitors, he need look no further than himself.' Mr Pepys's bitterness overcame his discretion.

'The little one? Ay, that would be him. The rest deferred to him, and he fired all their broadsides for them. He was at me as soon as I began to tell them how Mr Atkins had sent word that he would be bringing two gentlewomen to inspect the yacht on that day.'

'Did they demand the names of the ladies?' It was Will who put the question.

'Lord Shaftesbury asked for them particularly and I told him, as I had told you, Mr Hewer, that they called themselves Mistress Jane and Mistress Sarah. Those were the only names by which Mr Atkins introduced them. I assured their lordships that they were respectable ladies of quality, not women of the street, but unless I am mistaken my word was not believed.'

'Yet that is what you yourself believe, is it not, Captain Vittells?' Will pressed him.

'I presumed that the visit would have been authorised by you, Mr Hewer, to oblige some gentry; so their real names were no concern of mine. Mr Atkins is an honest young gentleman and, as I judged, not the lad for amorous jaunts on his own account while on the king's service.'

Will exchanged glances with Mr Pepys, who then addressed the captain: 'This is a matter of some delicacy, as you will have surmised. At that time I was with His Majesty at Newmarket and was not informed of the expedition until my return. But, in case you undergo a second interrogation, there has to be a clear understanding between us that it was properly sanctioned by Mr Hewer, who alone was made aware of the identity of the ladies. Mr Atkins was never told, and I trust that today's examination will not lead to any disobedience of Mr Hewer's orders to you and your men not to hazard guesses and bandy names, even among yourselves.'

'You have my word on it, sir,' the captain assured him. 'My men are not blabbers, and all of them have served long enough to respect the punishment for disobeying orders. Lord Shaftesbury was curious, but idly so. The drift of his questioning was to tar Mr Atkins with debauchery and find the Navy Office guilty of some malpractice.'

'As like as not, he will be content to let the matter rest there,' said Will. 'The discovery of two more witnesses in Sam's defence would not suit his case.'

Captain Vittells then resumed his report. He had informed the Committee that the visitors' party boarded at Greenwich at half-past four on that Monday afternoon; and that, at the ladies' request, he conducted them round the crew's quarters and other parts of the vessel before taking them to his own cabin for a glass of wine. He had not informed the Committee that, although they conversed in English, he thought the two gentlewomen foreigners; nor that they were extravagantly dressed for a river trip.

'I had heard that green stockings have become the height of fashion,' he said, 'but I never saw such articles of attire before these ladies seated themselves in my cabin and exposed their ankles.'

'I desire to hear no more of that,' said Mr Pepys curtly. 'I command you to hold your tongue about the ladies' appearance, whether you are talking to me or anyone else. Pray proceed with what you did tell their lordships.'

'I described how we drank until seven o'clock and the company grew so merry that the ladies accepted my invitation to stay for supper and bade Mr Atkins send their boat away.'

'What, pray, did the ladies do or say to you while Mr Atkins was absent?'

The question came shrewdly from Will, and Captain Vittells looked for and received Mr Pepys's consent before answering.

'One of them inquired how long it would take the *Catherine* to cross the Channel and whose permission I would need before sailing. She was on the point of making some proposition when Mr Atkins returned and no more was said. I have kept this to myself, you will understand, and would never have spoken of it but for Mr Hewer's asking.'

'Were you offered a bribe, Captain Vittells?' Will leaned forward accusingly, as though a bribe was hitherto unheard of in the Navy Office.

'No, Mr Hewer; I swear not. But I verily believe that to have been her intention.'

As always, Mr Pepys was quick to pounce on a dereliction of duty. 'Would you deny, then, that it was your responsibility to report the affair to your superiors?' he demanded. 'If the ladies were foreigners, they were like as not Catholics. They may have been among those plotting treason. Imagine, if you can, the consequences of fugitives from justice making their escape in one of His Majesty's ships. The Admiralty would not have survived the disgrace.'

The captain swallowed miserably. 'That was the very reason I dared not report it,' he muttered.

Mr Pepys glowered at him. 'Your story is nonsensical,' he stormed. 'How could your fine gentlefolk in green stockings have supposed that a vessel in His Majesty's navy might sail for France or the Low Countries without Admiralty orders? Did they take you to be so corrupt or foolish as to choose to end your career in ignominy and chains?'

'They told me that they intended to bribe you to issue the sailing orders.'

'Me?' Mr Pepys assumed an expression of astonishment.

'Yes; they were confident that, if the sum were large enough, you would readily hit upon a pretext.'

Mr Pepys's reserves of indignation were exhausted by this slander. The captain sat stony-faced, but Will allowed himself a furtive smile. 'That sufficiently explains your silence, Captain Vittells,' he said. 'Let us now return to your report to the Committee.'

'I told them that after supper there had been more drinking. The gentlemen toasted the ladies, and the ladies toasted the gentlemen, until we all became merry as can be. Mr Atkins kept repeating that he never drank more than one glass at a time, but the ladies would not consent to leave and plied him with more, so that he grew pretty fuddled. It had gone half-past ten when I gave them some parting gifts of wine and cheese and put them aboard the yacht's wherry homeward bound.'

'Pray proceed.' Mr Pepys looked up from his desk, where he had been comparing the spoken account with the captain's statement. He was on the alert for discrepancies and indiscreet additions, but Will, it seemed, had rehearsed his witness well.

'I repeated it all word for word, I do assure you,' said the captain, 'and when I had finished, the crew of the wherry took up the tale and told how the tide was flowing too strongly for them to shoot the bridge, so they landed the party at Billingsgate. They said they had to row for a full hour, and Mr Atkins was in such a state that he snored during the whole journey. At Billingsgate they threw him into a hackney coach and the ladies carried him off.'

'Were the men questioned?' asked Mr Pepys.

'No, sir. When every one had given his evidence, even Lord Shaftesbury was left wondering how Mr Atkins could have been at Somerset House between nine and ten o'clock that evening.'

'Bravo!' said Will, seeing that Mr Pepys was still simmering. 'They did well, and so did you, Captain Vittells. Pray reward them – but with spirits, not money. There must be no suggestion of bribery.'

'Let us pray that Mr Atkins will now be released, and I shall be free to take up my posting to Tangier.' The captain rose to take his leave.

'Your prayers will be in vain,' Mr Pepys told him. 'Mr Atkins will be held until he is tried, and what has occurred today will serve only to delay his trial. His innocence is so transparent that nothing but the non-appearance of his witnesses in court will ensure a verdict of guilty. For, as you know, witnesses must appear in person. You can be sure, therefore, that their lordships will procrastinate, and it may be some months before you enjoy the pleasures of a command on the Barbary coast.' He bowed the captain out.

Three days later came another trial which boded ill for Sam. Three Catholics – Pickering, Grove and Ireland – were brought to the bar of the Old Bailey, to be convicted and sentenced to death on the evidence of Oates and Bedloe.

Thomas Pickering was the Benedictine, and John Grove the Jesuit lay brother, named as the king's would-be assassins in Oates's original revelation of the great Popish Plot which had reeled and staggered in its credibility until brought back to life by Mr Justice Godfrey's death. William Ireland, the third accused, was an older man and a higher functionary. He was Procurator of the English province of the Society of Jesus.

It was Will Hewer once more who attended the trial, Mr Pepys judging it imprudent to be seen taking too close an interest. Will listened incredulously as Oates testified how a Jesuit consult held at the White Horse tavern in April, at which he claimed to have been present, had decided that the king must die; and how in

August Ireland had met Pickering and Grove at the same rendezvous and commissioned them to do the deed.

According to Oates, Grove was to be rewarded with £1500 and Pickering, who had no use for money, with thirty thousand masses for his soul. Armed with pistols and silver bullets, they had crept round the parks at St James's and Windsor, lurking in bushes and dogging the king's footsteps. Once they failed only because the flint of Pickering's pistol had worked loose; once because he had forgotten to put powder in the pan. As a penalty for his blundering, he had undergone a penance of thirty lashes.

When Bedloe took the stand, he blustered in his usual manner, but it soon became clear that he knew nothing of the affair. The accused denied the whole story, and evidence was produced that Oates had previously lied on oath. Testimony that Oates had been at the Jesuit college in St Omer throughout April, so could not have been in London, was offered but disallowed.

On Ireland's behalf, four witnesses swore to his having been away from London during the whole of August, and another forty-five were said to be at hand to testify if called. But Chief Justice Scroggs ruled that their evidence was nullified by that of Oates, Bedloe and another witness, who was hurriedly brought forward to swear to Ireland being seen in London at that time.

The conduct of the trial plunged Will into despair. 'On this form the Chief Justice will prefer Bedloe's word to that of six honest seamen, and Sam will be lost beyond retrieve,' he lamented when he made his report.

'What of the jury?' demanded Mr Pepys. 'Were they hoodwinked or cowed?'

'They were instructed by the Chief Justice to ignore the prisoners' denials because their religion allowed them a dispensation to lie. He railed against Catholics as people who eat their own God, so will feel no qualms about killing their king and making a saint out of the murderers. It was a fiery summing-up, and when the jurymen obliged him by bringing in a verdict of guilty, he commended them as good Christians; by which, he said, he meant good Protestants. At least we can take comfort that Sam is not a God-eating papist.'

Mr Pepys stared dejectedly out of the window and shivered as he felt the chill of winter run through his body and stab at his ailments from head to foot.

'Scroggs knows the king's mind,' he said, 'and although His Majsty has made no secret of his belief that this plot against his life is plain invention, the verdict will serve to discourage other attempts. Sam's case is altogether different, and His Majesty must be persuaded to intervene. He must be made to realise that, if the verdict goes against Sam, his own brother and heir will be the next victim – after myself.'

Will sought to cheer his master. 'The duke may not be in such danger as you suppose,' he said. 'Oates told the court that the assassins intended to dispose of him as well – for backwardness in promoting the Catholic religion. He would surely not have spoken those words except under instruction from Shaftesbury or one of his minions.'

'Pah!' exclaimed Mr Pepys, not to be comforted. 'Shiftsbury is more apt a name. He will practise pretence until he is ready to strike. The king and duke must not be deceived.'

'There is one thing more that we can do for Sam,' said Will hesitantly.

'No!' Mr Pepys cried, catching his meaning at once and swinging round in alarm. 'If we reveal the true identities of Mistresses Sarah and Jane, it will be at the risk of precipitating our own ruin earlier rather than later. I had supposed that you were commanded to exercise discretion about a wanton but harmless pleasure trip. I believed that betrayal of that trust might lead to Sam's trial being abandoned; that it would cause embarrassment and subject us to severe displeasure, but no more. Now, from what Captain Vittells has told us, I understand the ladies' real purpose.'

'A threat might suffice,' suggested Will.

Mr Pepys swept the idea away. 'I would not venture to threaten a king,' he replied. 'Not only that, but the truth would almost certainly emerge. You and I, my dear Will, would have to face the consequences of a scandal which could well dethrone His Majesty. No, my friend; there can be no escape for Sam by that route.'

— 14 —

A NEW WITNESS

It was Christmas Eve, frost was on the ground and his Council was to meet at midday, but the king would not forgo his morning saunter through St James's Park. The Duke of Monmouth had been commanded to accompany him and walked at his side with chin held high, more regally attired than the king himself. The usual posse of guards, courtiers and hangers-on kept their distance out of earshot.

Charles admired his bastard son's athletic build and prowess and the manner in which he bore himself like a prince. But he was not blind to his faults. Although close on thirty, the duke had not yet grown up. He had the face of an angel, but was vain and vicious, impetuous and impressionable. He thrived on public adulation, and with liberal doses of flattery Shaftesbury was leading him by the nose towards calamity.

'Jemmie,' said the king without preamble, 'I require you to use your influence with your Green Ribbon friends on behalf of Her Majesty.'

He discoursed on the events of the past week and the progress of what the duke angrily interrupted to dismiss as 'that damnable and hellish plot', but about which the king insisted 'some truth there was, but brewed with lies'.

The duke's was the popular view. During this season of good will prisons across the country were bulging with bewildered and despairing Catholics, many unaware of what they were accused.

Oates's pride in this achievement had emboldened him to denounce the queen herself as one of the conspirators. According to the latest broadside from the saviour of the nation, Sir George Wakeman, her physician, had written in a letter of her complicity in the plot – a fact which he regretted he had forgotten to mention earlier. Also, during a visit to her apartments in Somerset House, he had himself overheard her say that she would no longer tolerate the affronts she had suffered from her husband and would avenge his violations of their marriage bed.

'Let her find safety in exile,' advised the Protestant duke. 'Her Majesty is homesick for Braganza and Your Majesty cannot bear the sight of her.' Catherine's banishment, he reckoned, would suit him well. It would put a final stop to any prospect of a legitimate heir.

'All Catholic Europe would be affronted,' replied the king, moodily picking up a twig and throwing it for his toy dogs to chase. 'Portugal would never forgive the insult. Nor would our own merchants here in London: they would lose the trade with the Indies and Brazil. Besides, my honour is at stake.'

'She will stay at her peril,' warned the duke. 'But I promise to do my best for her,' he added grandly as though already seated on his father's throne.

The king put an affectionate arm round his waist. 'I am right glad to hear it,' he said. 'If this latest news is to be credited and there is confirmation that Godfrey was murdered inside Somerset House, Her Majesty will have need of both of us to preserve her.'

The latest news was that the traitor's fate suffered by William Staley, the goldsmith, had inspired a tenant fourteen months in arrears with his rent to level a similar accusation of treason against his landlord, Miles Prance, a Catholic silversmith. Prance's guilt was taken for granted because he had been acquainted with the assassins Grove and Pickering, and his customers included Jesuits and the queen.

This new revelation was hailed as Heaven-sent by the informers Oates and Bedloe and by the ardent Green Ribbon regulars at the King's Head tavern. Their God had manifested himself at last by delivering into their hands an accused papist without an alibi for the time of Godfrey's death. Frustrated by Sam's religion and obstinacy, Bedloe had seized the opportunity to revive his flagging claim to the £500 reward. He immediately identified Prance as one of the magistrate's murderers.

The silversmith had been arrested and examined in turn by the House of Commons Committee for the Plot and the House of Lords Committee for Examinations which had interrogated Sam.

At each interrogation Bedloe had pointed a bony finger at him and declaimed in a loud and menacing voice: 'This is one of the rogues that I saw with a dark lanthorn about the body of Sir Edmund Berry Godfrey at Somerset House.'

Prance was consigned to prison with the caution that it would be better to confess than be hanged. His denials of any involvement in murder or treason had fallen on deaf ears and closed minds. Their very fervour was held to be suspicious.

After two nights spent enduring the torment of confinement in a cell in Newgate known as Little Ease, he had promised a true and perfect discovery if granted a royal pardon. That morning, before setting out on his walk, the king had sent a messenger to give him that assurance, and on His Majesty's return to Whitehall the prisoner was to be brought before a specially convened meeting of the third investigative body: the Privy Council Committee for Examinations.

'Come,' the king urged when he and the duke reached the end of the lake. 'We must quicken our pace. This dawdling has chilled me to the marrow, and we shall be late for the meeting.'

Monmouth offered to demonstrate how fast he could run to the council chamber, but the king restrained him and they entered the chamber together ten minutes behind time.

The others were already assembled and rose at their entry. The king took his seat at the head of the table with his son on his left. The place of higher precedence on his right hand was already occupied by the Duke of York, who eyed them with undisguised suspicion. At a nod from the king, Secretary of State Coventry, seated at the foot of the table, ordered the prisoner to be produced.

Miles Prance was a sorry sight – a small, bespectacled craftsman in chains, shivering with cold and cowering in terror. Desperate to give satisfaction and be freed, he swore to the untruth of his former denials and unburdened himself of as full and plausible a confession as could be desired. A wealth of detail lent credibility to his deposition, so that the mystery of the magistrate's death seemed to be resolved at last – to some of his audience at least.

He began by telling them that during September he had heard whispers of an armed rebellion to be led by Lord Bellasis and two other Catholic peers. Then, towards the end of the month, he had been approached by an Irish priest called Gerald who was employed in the Venetian embassy and privy to the rebels' secret. This priest, whose good will had brought him the custom of the ambassador, begged him to repay the favour by helping in the killing of an unnamed man who was alleged to be a great enemy of the queen and the members of her court and to have treated some Irishmen harshly.

It was not (he said) until a further meeting a week later that he learned that the intended victim was Mr Justice Godfrey, against whom he himself also bore a grudge. At Middlesex County Sessions some three years earlier Prance's plea that he be excused parish duties had been dismissed by the magistrate with a brusque reminder that even those who served the Catholic queen were expected to shoulder their responsibilities as citizens of a Protestant community.

At that second meeting the priest had been accompanied by two other men, both of whom were known to Prance by sight. One was another Irishman, named Robert Green, a cushion-layer, carpenter and general handyman in the queen's chapel. He was elderly, but his companion, Lawrence Hill, a servant to one of the queen's chaplains, was a tall, stalwart youth. They told Prance that the murder was ordered by Lord Bellasis, who had offered a reward which they would share with him. They had demanded he join their enterprise. Had he not, when knowing of the plot, his own life would have been in danger.

Taking turns so as not to arouse suspicion, the four of them had kept watch on Godfrey for a whole week, trailing him wherever he went. On the day of the murder they dogged his footsteps from the moment he left home until nine o'clock at night, when he was walking past St Clement's church in the Strand on his way towards the Somerset House water-gate. To be sure of not losing him, Green had even called at his house as soon as he had left. He had spoken to the maid-servant on some pretext and tried, unsuccessfully, to discover where her master's business might be taking him and at what hour he was expected home. They were all determined to make an end of him that Saturday.

The Committee were all ears as the plot was unfolded. When Prance's voice faltered and he began staggering with fatigue, he was provided with a stool and a jug of water and told to rest awhile until the faintness had passed. Outside, the sky was overcast and the room had grown shadowy, illuminated only by the fire in the hearth.

The Secretary ordered candles to be lit, so that the gleam of the sconces flickered over the oak panelling and played on the prisoner's features, which were under close scrutiny for truth or falsehood. His narrative was approaching the murder itself, and the king forbade all questions till it was done.

As the magistrate neared the palace in the darkness (Prance resumed) he and Hill slipped ahead of him through the wicket gate leading to the stable yard. Hill at once re-emerged, crying out for help to separate some drunkards who, he said, were brawling within and would assuredly do each other mortal injury if the affray were not brought to a speedy conclusion.

Sir Edmund had responded to the appeal without hesitation, as they had known he would. He was closely followed down the steps into the yard by Gerald and Green, pretending that they too were answering the call. Waiting on a bench at the bottom were Henry Berry, one of the Somerset House porters, and another Irish priest, who answered to the name of Kelly. In accordance with a pre-arranged manoeuvre, Prance, at the sight of their victim, ran back past him to mount guard at the wicket, while Berry took his stand beside the opposite entrance to prevent any approach from within the palace.

The others thereupon set about their unsuspecting victim without warning. Hill and the two priests pinioned his arms so that he could not draw his sword. When he was held helpless, Green winded him with a blow to the chest and threw a twisted handkerchief round his neck, throttling him and jerking his head back until the neck broke. When Prance returned a few minutes later, the body lay slumped on the ground, inert but still warm. Thus he had not, he insisted, been a party to the actual murder, nor even a witness: he was told later what had occurred and had no reason to doubt it.

The corpse had then been carried down several dark passages, up and down steps, across the upper Court, through a doorway in the left-hand wall and finally, after many further twists and turns, into a house in the palace precincts belonging to the chaplain who was Lawrence Hill's master. There it was left, propped against a bed in an upstairs chamber little larger than a closet. To authenticate his story, Prance traced the journey in meticulous detail.

It was (he said) two nights and days before the murderers' fear of its discovery overcame their reluctance to run the risk of detection whilst moving the body again. On the Monday night they carried it back into the palace to a deserted room overlooking the garden. On Tuesday there was a near discovery by an inquisitive steward and it had to be hurriedly removed once more as soon as darkness fell. Again Prance took the attentive Council through a maze of corridors and back-stairs in the service quarters to the body's next resting place in a servant's empty room.

The murderers were now desperate to be rid of the evidence. At nine or ten o'clock the next evening Hill and Berry brought a sedan chair into the palace and stood it in an unlit entry while the body was fetched and propped up inside. Gerald and Prance then carried it out through the wicket gate, which Berry held open for them. They hurried across the Strand to Covent Garden and thence to the new church in Soho, with Green and Kelly taking their turn as chairmen.

In a secluded corner beside the vestry wall Hill was waiting for them with a horse. The body was taken from the chair and hoisted on to the horse's back. The legs had to be prised apart, and the others held the corpse upright until Hill had mounted behind to support it. He then set off for the fields to the north with Gerald, Kelly and Green walking alongside to lend hands. That had been the last Prance saw of them because he had turned back, apprehensive of being missed at home.

That was Prance's tale, and he held to it doggedly under interrogation, swearing repeatedly to its truth and accuracy until ordered to be led away.

Asked his opinion by the king as soon as the Council sat alone, Sir William Coventry pointed out that this version of events differed from Bedloe's in a number of respects. The scene of the murder was different. So too were the manner, the time and the motive. Even the murderers were not the same. Yet in other important respects the two accounts converged. Both identified Somerset House as the place where the crime was committed, and both witnesses testified that they had seen Sir Edmund's body in a room at the palace at approximately the same time on the night of Monday, October the fourteenth.

Sir William expressed his regret that the Irish priests, Gerald and Kelly, had eluded capture and disappeared, presumably smuggled abroad by the Venetians through the negligence of the navy. But he reported with satisfaction that Green, Hill and Berry were safely under lock and key.

In their subsequent deliberations members of the Council were inclined to ignore the discrepancy in details and accept this new evidence as the truth. There was general relief and delight that they now had papists to hang for the murder of the Protestant martyr.

The Duke of Monmouth was the most delighted of all. The Duke of York dissented violently. The king said nothing but looked, as always, sceptical. He announced that proceedings were concluded and, as the others were bowing themselves out of the room, signed to his son to remain.

'So, Jemmie! Do you really suppose that the mystery is solved, or do you entertain some secret doubts?'

'None, sire.' The elated heir presumptuous now felt able to press for the exile of both his uncle and the queen. 'His Royal Highness may choose to deny it for the sake of his religion, but Somerset House has long been known as a hive of traitors and criminals harboured by Her Majesty – unwittingly, we must suppose,' he added hastily, warned by his father's frown.

'You do not find the motive weak?' the king inquired gently. 'My memory must be failing me, for I do not remember Sir Edmund as a scourge of the Catholics. Was he not, rather, noted for his leniency towards them? Pray remind me, do.'

'This wretch may have been misinformed as to the motive, but his story was too circumstantial to be disbelieved. The whole Council was convinced, as Your Majesty saw for yourself. Except, of course, for my uncle.' The duke was making no concessions to his father's blandness.

'The Council expressed itself as convinced; which is somewhat different. But you may be right nonetheless. Men are apt to believe what they wish to believe. I have caught myself at it from time to time; it makes life more agreeable.' The king was now hiding behind cynicism to conceal the depth of his alarm at the turn of events.

'As to the plausibility of Master Prance's circumstantial tale, however,' he continued, 'we should bear in mind, should we not, that his work for the queen's household will have acquainted him with the byways running through that labyrinth?'

'That is of little account,' argued the duke. 'He could never have concocted such an invention for himself, and if Captain Bedloe had coached him it would have corresponded with the captain's account instead of contradicting it.'

'I have the advantage of you there, Jemmie,' replied the king. 'My spies report that Prance was taken from Newgate yesterday for a private interrogation by your friend, the Earl of Shaftesbury. Perhaps you should inquire of him how the conversation between them ran. It has come to my ears, too, that a paper was delivered to Prance's dungeon this morning containing some guidance for him. I am told that it urged him to mention, amongst other matters, the threat of an uprising by some Catholic peers who are the earl's antagonists. So I was not surprised at that revelation by the prisoner, although its relevance to the good Godfrey's murder escaped me.'

'What matters its relevance if it be true?' the duke demanded. 'What matters it if Prance is lying about his own involvement? Shaftesbury, like Your Majesty, has secret channels of intelligence. You would scarcely treat threats to your life and realm so lightly if I were to divulge to you all I learn through the earl's kindness.'

'As you value your life, beware that man. He twists like an eel. Yesterday he was my friend and faithful minister; today he is my implacable foe. Today he is your ally – a king-maker who will put you on the throne when I am dead. Tomorrow, when he finds that he cannot carry the country with him, he will fawn on your uncle instead. When you no longer serve his purpose he will cast you off without compunction. I speak plainly because I love you dearly.'

The king spoke earnestly, and when his son did not condescend to reply, the crust of his reserve broke. They were standing, warming themselves in front of the fire, and a tear splashed on the hearth.

'It is for you I fear, Jemmie, not for myself,' he said, wiping his eyes with a lace cuff. 'If I do not pretend to believe in this plot, Shaftesbury's fanatics may rise against me in your name. But they will be defeated, and what will become of you then?'

'What would you have me do?' the duke asked sulkily. If only his father would stop snivelling in private and show some real affection by openly acknowledging a secret marriage with his mother instead of denying it!

Guessing his thoughts, the king spoke bluntly and severely. 'Curb your follies and excesses. Keep better company. Think for yourself. When the Almighty blessed you with more beauty than any other man, He cannot have forgotten to include a brain. Suspect flattery. Be no man's puppet.'

'How does Your Majesty suggest that I begin?' The duke was choking with rage, and the words were spoken with an ill grace.

'Start by imagining how Mr Justice Godfrey's body could have been carried in and out and up and down Somerset House without being noticed by servants and tradesmen coming and going. Ask yourself why it was kept there for almost a week while the hunt for it was on. Ask yourself how you would have disposed of it had you been one of the assassins. Why, for instance, was it not taken the short distance to the water-gate and thrown into the river? A weighted body cast overboard in midstream would be lost for ever. And why, if it had to be carried out, was it taken three miles to Primrose Hill when there are fields in plenty north of the Oxford road within a mile? Consider a man supporting a corpse on horse-back and three accomplices stumbling along beside him for an extra two miles when a single challenge of Who Goes There might have brought them all to the gallows.'

The duke hung his head, but not in submission. 'What, pray, are Your Majesty's own answers?' he demanded coldly.

'You shall not have them until I have yours,' the king replied. 'You will go this evening to Somerset House. Nine o'clock will be the most suitable hour. You will take with you the rascal Bedloe and order him to guide you to the room where he swears that he saw Godfrey's body. You will check every item in his testimony on the spot. You will be done by ten o'clock, when I shall have Prance delivered to you, and you will then follow his itinerary, taking especial note of the places where he alleged the body lay.'

'I am not the best person –' the duke began, but his protest was overruled.

'I am inquisitive and would go myself,' said the king, 'were it not improper for me to be seen burrowing in the queen's warren. Mr Secretary Coventry will make all the necessary arrangements and will accompany you, but it will be your conclusions and reasons I shall require, not his. Which of the witnesses is telling the truth, or are both of them lying? Those are the questions.'

'Why should both of them be lying?'

'Bedloe for £500; Prance to save his skin.'

'That does not explain their agreement on Somerset House.'

'The reason for that may be that they have both been in communication with that earl whom we mentioned earlier. I would wager my crown that the queen's residence is where he would most desire the scene of Sir Edmund's demise to be set. Go and see for yourself whether you can discover any grounds for exonerating your little lord and master from my suspicions.'

It dawned upon the duke that his father was setting a trap for him. If either Prance's or Bedloe's confession were true and murder by Catholics proved, the way would be paved for the Duke of York's exclusion from the succession and his own recognition as heir to the throne. But, since the king held that both were lying, he must be inviting the person for whom he professed a deep love to destroy his own prospects or become a party to perjury.

'I bow to Your Majesty's commands,' he answered stiffly; 'although my task is hardly necessary, since there is no other explanation for the murder.'

'Think harder,' the king urged, 'and several may occur to you. A stern Justice of the Peace makes many enemies in the underworld. One may have taken his revenge.'

'And left a fortune in his victim's pocket?'

'A small sum to a prosperous rogue. But if you mislike that supposition, try asking yourself who has gained from the crime. Has it not made Oates a hero again just when his star was waning? If any man possesses the visage and malice of a murderer, it is assuredly the learned Doctor Oates.'

Monmouth laughed in ridicule. 'One staunch Protestant murdering another!' he exclaimed. 'You will be accusing my lord of Shaftesbury next.'

Charles shook his head. 'The eel-earl is an instigator, not a perpetrator. But if we give him and, if you choose, Oates and the underworld too the benefit of the doubt, there still remains the possibility of suicide, ingeniously disguised as murder disguised as suicide. His estate was large enough to warrant some ingenuity on the part of his heirs.'

The now scowling duke was preparing to remonstrate when a discreet knock heralded the appearance of Chiffinch, who stood impassively in the doorway, needing to make no further sound or sign for his message to be understood.

'Until tomorrow then, my dearest Jemmie,' said the king, striding towards the door. 'I shall hear your report in the morning. For now you must excuse me. Her grace of Portsmouth, the fairest of the fair, awaits my pleasure and, as I truly believe, her own.'

— 15 —

TRIAL FOR MURDER

On the first Wednesday in February Robert Green, Henry Berry and Lawrence Hill, labourers, late of the parish of St Mary le Strand in the county of Middlesex, were taken from His Majesty's jail of Newgate and brought to the bar of the court of King's Bench, where they were arraigned for the murder of Sir Edmund Berry Godfrey.

The clerk read out the charge in a dispassionate monotone: 'You, Green, with a linen handkerchief of the value of six pence did choke and strangle your victim till he did die, and you, Berry and Hill, feloniously, voluntarily and of your malice aforethought were present aiding, abetting, comforting and maintaining the aforesaid Robert Green.'

'Culprit, how wilt thou be tried?' each was asked in turn. 'By God and my country,' they responded, but only after some prompting. All then pleaded not guilty, and the trial was appointed to be held on the following Monday.

When Monday came, it saw one of the spectacles of the century. The crowd was as large as the one which had thronged Westminster Hall to jeer and cheer at the trial of the Gunpowder Plotters during the reign of the late King James.

Not one to miss a momentous event, Mr Pepys was an early arrival, privileged to enter the hall before the admission of the mob. The verdict was not, he supposed, in doubt: the accused seemed condemned in advance. But Mr Pepys himself was not convinced that Miles Prance's evidence could be relied upon. Within a week of making his confession the wretch had requested a private audience with the king; and there, free from intimidation, with nobody else present except William Chiffinch and

Captain Richardson, he had confessed that every word of his deposition to the Council had been a lie and prayed abjectly for pardon and forgiveness.

'Upon your salvation, is this so?' the king had demanded.

'Upon my salvation the whole accusation is false,' Prance had replied. 'I most wickedly devised an horrid story. I feigned myself a party to the murder, the better to gain credit for my damnable forgery. With unspeakable grief I solemnly and sincerely declare that whatever I deposed upon oath is, in the whole and every part thereof, a falsehood.' He ended by thrusting into the king's hands a paper on which those words were written and signed. All this Mr Pepys had learned from the good Chiffinch for a small consideration.

The next day Prance had repeated his retraction before the Council, who immediately ordered him back into leg irons, consigned him once more to Little Ease and sentenced him to be deprived of all light and heat until such time as he chose to sing a different tune. The severity of this punishment soon persuaded him to withdraw his recantation; yet he reaffirmed it within a few hours. Little Ease had then all but crippled him and the freezing chill of January brought him to the point of death before he finally agreed to abide by his original statement incriminating the accused.

In the time-honoured tradition of English justice, the jury was packed. To deliver a verdict on the three labourers, two baronets, two knights and eight reputable esquires were selected and empanelled. While the oath was being administered to them, the hall buzzed with excitement at the appearance of the Duke of Monmouth, splendid in a white silk cloak and scarlet hose. The presiding judges, headed by the Lord Chief Justice, rose to their feet and bowed respectfully, inviting the duke and his company to be seated beside them.

Mr Pepys eyed the party with distaste. The plain, foreign lady in the low-cut gown was Louise de Keroualle's sister, the Countess of Pembroke, and behind her towered her husband, who had last appeared at a murder trial in this very hall in the role of guilty felon. But it was the man unobtrusively taking his seat on the duke's other side who attracted most attention.

Drab in dress by comparison with Monmouth and insignificant in size beside the Earl of Pembroke, this little creeping, misbegotten creature was, nonetheless, the puppet-master who manipulated them both and half the country besides. But for the ambitions and intrigues of Anthony Ashley Cooper, Earl of Shaftesbury, Mr Pepys told himself, Sam Atkins, today's accused, the broken Prance and hundreds of imprisoned Catholic priests and laymen would all be at liberty and going about their normal business without hurt or threat from or to any fellow human being.

The prisoners in the dock looked drawn and defeated, all too conscious that the dice were loaded against them. Forbidden the services of lawyers to present their case, they faced a team of prosecutors led by the Attorney-General (Sir William Jones), the Solicitor-General (Sir Francis Winnington) and the Recorder (Sir George Jefferies).

It was Mr Attorney-General who opened for the Crown. 'Murder,' he said, 'is a crime of so deep a stain that nothing can wash it away but the blood of the offender. The murder which is now to be tried before your lordship is the most heinous and most barbarous that ever was committed. It was a murder upon a gentleman, upon a magistrate, and upon a Protestant magistrate.'

The prosecution case was then unfolded. Priests and Jesuits had designed at several consultations to take away the life of Sir Edmund Berry Godfrey in order to prevent the discovery of their Popish Plot. They were men who did not stick at shedding blood but rather accounted it meritorious. They sent people to spy upon him, to dog him into the fields, to follow him into dark alleys and other unfrequented places and there to despatch him. More than one attempt was made before they succeeded. Six offenders had been indicted for the crime, two or three of whom were priests: Father Gerald, Father Kelly and one Vernatt, either priest or Catholic layman, who was reported to have been present at the scene of the crime.

'These priests,' said the Attorney-General, 'are always the first to contrive mischief; likewise always the first to fly punishment. They have run away, leaving their blind followers, the prisoners at the bar, to answer for their bloody act.'

The court then heard an account of the day of the murder until seven or eight o'clock in the evening when, passing St Clement's church on his way home, the magistrate was lured into Somerset

House on the pretext of breaking up an idle scuffle, and there set upon and done to death by the accused.

The first witness was Titus Oates, the hero of many in the hall. His rolling eyes swept the chamber for hidden traitors. Speaking in a deep, steady voice, he recounted how he had gone to Sir Edmund with depositions. Afterwards, a week before he was missed, Sir Edmund had come to him, he said, to complain of threats from some popish lords and of being dogged. 'I shall name their names when the time comes,' he promised ominously.

Miles Prance then took the stand. He described meetings at the Plough ale-house two or three weeks before the murder, when two priests enticed him into becoming an accomplice. They had told him it would be no sin but a charitable act. He then testified to the murder itself and the subsequent to-ings and fro-ings in Somerset House. Well rehearsed and secure in his pardon from the king, he appeared confident, if shifty-eyed.

Although not one of the party who took the body as far as Primrose Hill, he affirmed that Gerald, Kelly and Hill had told him how they had run the magistrate's body through with his own sword, thrown it into a ditch and laid his gloves and other accoutrements on a near-by bank. A week or two later, he said, he had joined the priests and the others in celebrating their success over a barrel of oysters and a stew of fishes in the Queen's Head at Bow.

According to what Mr Pepys had learned from Chiffinch, Prance's subsequent visit to Somerset House in the company of the Duke of Monmouth had not served to confirm much of his story. The witness had lamentably failed to identify the corpse's alleged itinerary. At the chaplain's house the duke had been told that Lawrence Hill was no longer employed there and had not been on the premises for several months. Yet the prosecution now boasted how Prance had led the duke directly and positively to the places he had described.

As soon as the prisoners were permitted to address the court, Hill took the stand. Tall, black-bearded and defiant, he vigorously protested his innocence and prayed that Prance's evidence might not stand against him, as being perjured by his own confession.

'How?' demanded the Lord Chief Justice at his fiercest.

'I suppose, my lord, it is not unknown to you that he made a confession before the king.'

'Look you, sir, I tell you I know not that ever he made a confession to contradict what he hath said on oath.'

Listening to this exchange, Mr Pepys wondered how even a lickspittle like Sir William Scroggs could demean himself to lie so brazenly in open court.

'He was on his oath, my lord,' Hill insisted, but the judge chose to misunderstand him.

'Yes,' he replied, 'he accused you upon oath, but afterwards, you say, he confessed that it was not true. That confession was not upon oath. How then can he be guilty of perjury?'

'My lord,' Hill protested, 'if a man swear a thing and afterwards deny it, he is certainly perjured.'

'If a man go back from what he had before discovered upon oath, you cannot say that man is perjured if he did not forswear it; and nobody did believe his denial because his first discovery was so particular.'

Captain Richardson was summoned to bear witness that, although in the king's closet Prance had fallen to his knees and said that he was innocent and they were all innocent, as soon as they were back at Newgate he had begged the keeper to go to the king and tell him that what he had said was false, what he had sworn was true: he had recanted because he believed his life would not be safe and he would lose his trade among the Catholics.

Mr Pepys groaned to himself. Every one knew that, even if Prance's private statement to the king had not been made on oath, he had certainly sworn to it when brought before the Council the next day. Yet that could not be proved in court if, under Shaftesbury's watchful eye, the Lord Chief Justice and the keeper of Newgate were forced to quibble and lie or risk being driven from office.

Hill was beaten, but would not give up. He was the youngest of the prisoners, the one with most life to lose and the first to show fight. 'All that Mr Prance says is false,' he declared emphatically. 'I deny every word of it. I have a great number of witnesses who can prove that I was not out of my house on that evening.'

But first, amid stamping and cheering almost equal to the applause which had greeted Oates, the prosecution called upon

William Bedloe, who proved disappointingly subdued. Thanks to Chiffinch, Mr Pepys knew the reason: Bedloe's visit to Somerset House with Monmouth had gone even less well than Prance's. The place he identified as the scene of the crime bore little relationship to the description in his deposition or to the place identified by Prance.

The captain's function in court was therefore reduced to implicating priests in the murder and swearing that he had recognised Prance among those standing round the body. He had not, he said, noticed any of the three prisoners. He could not swear they were there. Nor, though, could he say they were not.

The next witness was Mr Brown, the constable from St Giles's, who stated that the two discoverers of the body were Catholics and, although not charged with the accused, were being held in prison on suspicion of involvement in the murder. He testified to the finding of the body; to there being no blood on it or in the ditch; to the broken neck and bruising on the chest; and to the quantity of gold and silver in the pocket of the coat.

'Ay, ay,' put in the Lord Chief Justice at mention of the money. 'Catholics count theft a sin, but not murder. They left the coins to make us believe that the man murdered himself.'

The surgeons who had examined the body then confirmed that the broken neck, not the sword wound, was the cause of death. Mr Skillard reiterated his finding that death had occurred four or five days earlier. 'When we ripped him up, he began to putrefy,' added Mr Cambridge in confirmation.

At the appearance of the next witness a flicker of lechery warmed Mr Pepys's loins. It was the young girl he had invited to join his household after Godfrey's inquest: the wench on whom young Sam had cast a lustful eye. Blushing with embarrassment, she was introduced by the Attorney-General.

'Mr Prance did say that the men on trial had been several times at Sir Edmund's house inquiring for him. We now call his maid to say what she knows about that. Elizabeth Curtis, look upon the prisoners and tell my lord and the jury whether you know any of them or no.'

'This man that I now hear called Green was at my master's a fortnight before he died. He asked for my master and spake with him.' Her voice was hesitant and almost a whisper.

'Upon my soul,' interjected Green, stung into speech, 'I swear I never saw the man in all my life.'

'He was wearing a dark-coloured periwig and spent about a quarter of an hour with Sir Edmund.' The wench was trembling, stumbling over the words – an inexperienced liar, Mr Pepys could tell.

'Are you certain that this was the man?' The Attorney-General put the question sternly.

There was a momentary hush while she seemed to be remembering her lines. 'Yes,' she then replied; 'and that other man, Hill – he was there on the Saturday morning when my master disappeared. He did speak with him before he went out.'

At this, Hill too cried an outraged denial. The Lord Chief Justice silenced him and demanded of the witness how she knew that he was there.

'I was in the parlour at the time, making up the fire. He was wearing the same clothes as he is wearing now.' Her answer was prepared; it came without hesitation.

Hill was unable to control his anger. 'When she was brought to identify me in Newgate,' he shouted, 'she said that she had never seen me in her life. I have witnesses of my own – witnesses who do not lie on oath – who can prove where I was that morning.'

Elizabeth's blush deepened. Her eyes were downcast. She would not look the men she was accusing in the face. Mr Pepys's heart ached for her. He could guess at the bribes and threats which must have been employed to induce this guileless young innocent to commit perjury. Opposite him Shaftesbury's face betrayed nothing, but Pembroke was grinning like an ape and ogling the poor beauty as she was hurried away to avoid any further interrogation.

'We have done with our evidence.'

The Attorney-General bowed to the Lord Chief Justice, who refreshed himself from a flask of spirits before addressing the accused. 'Come now, what have you to say for yourselves? You shall have all the freedom you desire,' he promised magnanimously, confident that the verdict was already assured.

Lawrence Hill called four witnesses to prove that he had been in his lodgings on the Saturday and Wednesday nights in question and had not stirred outside. They swore that he was always indoors by eight o'clock. The prosecution objected, however, that none of them was to be believed, because they were all Catholics.

Robert Green, the elderly Irishman who did menial work in the queen's chapel, appeared resigned to his fate, too dazed by the calamity which had befallen him to offer a defence. But his landlord testified on his behalf that he had come home from a game of bowls at dusk on the Wednesday in question and remained in the house the whole evening until midnight, when he went to bed. The landlord, however, was another Catholic.

Henry Berry, the gate-keeper, insisted that he was no Catholic but a true Protestant. He had friends among the sentries who guarded the queen's palace. The corporal of the guard, the sentinel at the Strand gate and three other soldiers of the watch on duty on October the sixteenth were his witnesses. The sentry told the court that he had never left his post, and all swore that no sedan chair had left the palace that evening, nor could have without their noticing it. All were Protestants, but the Lord Chief Justice warned the jury that even honest men could be mistaken about a date.

Hill's wife, a respectable woman driven to despair, then took up the cudgels on his behalf. She desired Prance to swear to the reason why he confessed to the king that he had lied. He answered that it was for fear of losing his employment with the queen and other Catholics, which was most of his business.

She next desired him to swear whether or not he was tortured to make him recant his confession and revert to what he had previously sworn. 'Captain Richardson hath used me as civilly as any man in England,' he replied sweetly.

'It was reported all over town that Mr Prance was tortured,' she insisted, appealing to the Lord Chief Justice, who responded with the quip that it must have been only the witness's conscience which was tortured.

'There are several about this court that heard him cry out,' she persevered. 'And he well knows all these things that he has sworn are false. His perjury is common knowledge. The world will see it confessed again hereafter, but then it will be too late.' She broke down in tears.

'Madam,' the Lord Chief Justice rebuked her, 'would you have the court believe that Mr Prance would swear three men out of their lives for nothing? How is it possible to entertain such a wicked thought?' He had been applying himself liberally to his flask during the cross-examination and now, without waiting for replies, ordered counsel to bring proceedings to a conclusion without more ado.

The Attorney-General obediently took this cue and told the jury that his address to them would be exceeding brief, because the king's evidence was so strong and the prisoners' defence so much weaker than could have been foreseen.

'It is impossible,' he argued, 'that Mr Prance, a man of mean intelligence, should invent a story with so many circumstances all so consistent, if there were not truth at the bottom of it. Never was evidence better fortified with circumstances. This was a crime committed through zeal for a false religion, and I take leave to say that there was never such a barbarous murder committed in England since the people of this realm were freed from the tyranny of the Bishop of Rome.'

The Lord Chief Justice nodded his agreement, drained his flask, fixed the jury with a solemn and somewhat glazed stare, and proceeded with his peroration, pointing them in the direction where their duty lay.

'If all this were a chimera and not really so, then Prance must be one of the most notable inventors in the world; and it must be the mightiest chance in the world that Mr Bedloe and he should agree so in all things; that the maid should swear that Hill was at the victim's house that morning; and that the constable should find the body just as the accused had told Prance that they left it.'

'How then was the body taken out of the palace when there were sentinels placed at every gate?' This interruption came from Berry who, before he was quietened by ushers, cried out that, as God was his witness, Mr Justice Godfrey was a gentleman he had never met in all his life.

'The court is aware that you must say and believe as your priest tells you,' replied Sir William, unruffled. 'All men know that you must act as your priests instruct you, and as the Devil instructs your priests. They preach freedom of the will but allow you none. You papists are not permitted to be quiet in your own religion unless you disturb ours. I wonder that any man should be of your persuasion and yet keep his reason.'

His duty was done, and the jury soon did theirs. Their verdict of 'Guilty' was welcomed by congratulations from the bench and a great storm of applause from the whole assembly, Mr Pepys alone abstaining. He scurried back to his office in a state of considerable agitation, his stomach in pain and his heart palpitating as the verdict and sentence of hanging rang in his ears. There, but for the grace of God, he too might stand condemned.

Once safely home, he ordered physic and a bowl of punch to soothe his nerves and summoned Will Hewer to conference.

'I have never before seen three such palpably innocent men so abused by a drunken judge; nor the words of a tortured witness and two utter rogues given such credence,' he spluttered in a passion. 'Prance must lie or die, and Oates and Bedloe are a pair of insolent, insufferable good-for-nothings who will do or say anything for money. And,' he added for good measure, 'they have a kindred soul in Sir William Scroggs, the Lord Chief Injustice of England.'

Will pursed his lips in disgust. 'Yes,' he agreed. 'Those who should curb their excesses encourage them. They grow wilder and wilder. Every day I hear new reports of Bedloe's debauchery, and this morning one of Lord Danby's men told me how Oates yesterday made an abominable attempt, not fit to be named, upon one of his own menservants. Where will it all end? Will Sam go to the gallows on the word of Sodomites? I cannot sleep at nights for imagining what may become of him.'

When they had explored the darkness of the future and returned to the events of that day, Mr Pepys's account of the trial was long and bitter.

It must have been apparent to all, he said, that Miles Prance had been subjected to torture and that he and Elizabeth Curtis were perjuring themselves from terror. It was as clear as daylight that the similarities between Prance's and Bedloe's evidence were because they had both been fed the same story. The prosecution had spoken the truth for once when the jury was told that Prance was incapable of inventing it for himself. He had been picked upon because he was familiar with Somerset House from doing business there. As for Bedloe, Mr Pepys declared himself willing to hazard a hundred pounds to a penny piece that the villain had never set foot in the palace until he was ordered there by the king.

When he had finished, they sat for several minutes in an unhappy silence. Mr Pepys took alternate sips of punch and medicine, while Will brooded despondently on how the hanging of these three innocents would affect Sam's fate.

'The spider spinning this tale for others to recite is, of course, your old foe, Lord Shaftesbury,' he said. 'But we have to assume that his responsibility will never be proved. He moves too secretly and subtly for that.'

'His lordship remains a republican at heart and is set upon becoming a second Cromwell,' declared Mr Pepys. 'Once he has the Duke of York discredited and barred from the succession, he will round on the king himself as a secret papist guilty of treasonable correspondence with France. He will then make Monmouth a puppet king until he has gathered sufficient support to cast the half-wit aside. For him Sir Edmund's death is nothing more than an opportunity to be exploited for his own advancement.'

'Where then lies the truth? Do you hold to your belief that Sir Edmund took his own life?'

'With less certainty,' Mr Pepys confessed. 'I am sure only that Sir Edmund's body was never at Somerset House at all.'

— 16 —

ANOTHER TRIAL

Sam was taken to Westminster Hall the next morning, in time to hear the death sentence on the condemned men formally pronounced. They were told that they were to return to the place whence they were brought and thence to the place of execution; and there to be hanged by the neck until they were dead. This was to be their punishment for barbarously murdering a worthy gentleman and committing a desperate act of villainy in the Romish cause.

All reaffirmed their innocence. Henry Berry reiterated that he was not a Roman Catholic, as alleged, and knew nothing whatever of the matter. Lawrence Hill declared that he had nothing to say but that Almighty God knew him to be guiltless. Robert Green swore by his Saviour that he was as innocent as a child in its mother's womb.

'All who heard your trial are satisfied that every one of you is guilty,' retorted the Lord Chief Justice, 'and I for my part am satisfied most of all.' With a dismissive gesture he consigned them to the mercy of their Roman God and ordered the Clerk of the Court to proceed with Sam's case.

'How sayest thou, Samuel Atkins, art thou guilty as accessory to the said felony and murder whereof thou standest indicted, or not guilty?'

'Not guilty.' The firmness of Sam's response belied his pallor. His spirit was unbroken still.

'Culprit, how wilt thou be tried?'

'By God and my country.'

'God send you a good deliverance.'

The ritual of this exchange was no more than a preamble to the trial for which Sam had been waiting impatiently and the date fo. which had still to be set.

'Are you a papist, Master Atkins?' inquired the Lord Chief Justice.

'No, my lord, I am not and never was.' Sam did not pause to draw breath on the heels of this denial, but continued before he could be interrupted: 'When is it that your lordship pleaseth to have me tried, for I have lain these sixteen weeks in prison and do earnestly desire my trial?'

'You shall be tried as soon as we can,' Sir William promised: 'tomorrow, if Mr Attorney-General thinketh fit.'

Sam was dismissed and spent that day and most of the next sleepless in his cell, picturing the three labourers on the scaffold and preparing himself for his own ordeal. But when in the late afternoon he was brought before the bench once more, it was not for trial but to be asked whether he had bail ready.

'No, my lord,' he protested, utterly downcast at the prospect of yet more delay. 'I am prepared for my trial, but not for bail.'

'It is the latter end of term, and we cannot put aside all other business for yours.' It was the close of a busy day for the Lord Chief Justice and he was testy; but Sam was desperate.

'My life lies at stake,' he pleaded, 'and I humbly pray that I may be tried. I have many witnesses who have stayed in town on purpose to give evidence for me. They have been kept waiting since the last term. I am aware how precious is your lordship's time and how greatly in demand, but I hope and believe that my trial will be a brief one.'

'How, pray, can you suppose that it will be quickly done with if you propose to call so many witnesses?'

'Although I have many ready, I trust that I shall have occasion to use only a few,' Sam replied.

Sir William Scroggs summoned Sir William Jones, the Attorney-General, to the bench, and the two Sir Williams put their heads together. 'We cannot do it,' he ruled at the end of the whispered consultation. 'The prisoner must be content to wait his turn. He shall be tried at the sessions in three weeks' time, or thereabouts.'

'My lord,' a voice called out, 'I am a witness on behalf of this gentleman and cannot be in England three weeks hence.'

'My lord,' said Sam, 'this is the captain of one of the king's ships. He is under sailing orders on His Majesty's service, and this is so with several other of my witnesses.'

This time there was a conference between all the judges and lawyers for the Crown, and it lasted for several minutes. The argument appeared to sway to and fro, until the Lord Chief Justice was pleased to overrule the Attorney-General's objections. 'Very well,' he told Sam; 'if what you say is so in truth, you shall be tried tomorrow. Captain Richardson, you are charged to bring the prisoner up very early.'

The morrow was a grey, misty, uninviting February day, but Mr Pepys, too, rose very early from his unshared bed (Susan had still not been replaced). Sam's defence had been his main preoccupation for the last four months. He had quite neglected his duties at the Navy Office to sit through all the legal proceedings and ensure the constant presence of the team of witnesses which he was holding ready for whatever day the trial might be ordered. In Sam's interest – and his own – he was retaining them week in week out, regardless of the exigencies of the king's service.

Mr Pepys believed, with all his heart and soul, that in protecting Sam and himself he was protecting the English navy – the sole defence of the realm – and the very throne itself. It was he who had prompted Captain Vittells's intervention in court. If that had not proved successful, affairs would have reached a parlous state when the Admiralty board met later that week. Some members were Shaftesbury's henchmen. The rest were too dull to foresee the train of events which would lead inexorably from Sam's conviction to a republican England under Protector Shaftesbury.

He arrived at Westminster Hall wet and apprehensive: ill-tempered but clear-headed.

In the light of the evidence given by Prance at the previous trial, Sam had been discharged from the indictment of being a principal in the murder. It was no longer alleged that, in company with others, he did choke and strangle Sir Edmund Berry Godfrey with a certain linen cravat. Instead, he was indicted as one that was privy, knowing, consulting and abetting to the commission of the murder, and that after the murder was committed he did receive, harbour, comfort and maintain the murderers.

Mr Pepys cursed all lawyers under his breath. The jury would find the charge more plausible, and the penalty was the same. It seemed that, instead of being satisfied with the conviction of the others, the prosecution was more determined than ever to hang one of his clerks.

Opening the case for the Crown, the Attorney-General told the jury how the prisoner had complained to a witness, Charles Atkins (no relation), that Sir Edmund ought not to be allowed to live and had inquired of him about the courage and resolution of one, Child, whom he then ordered to be sent to him. He had desired the witness to join him as an accomplice in the killing and offered him a reward. When Sir Edmund was murdered on October the twelfth last, another witness, William Bedloe, had identified the prisoner as one of those standing around the corpse.

Mr Pepys could scarcely contain himself when Captain Atkins unfolded his bundle of lies with such an artless demeanour. Because he was a son of the Governor of Barbados, the disgraced scoundrel was treated with a respect merited neither by his naval career nor by his venal testimony.

It was (the captain wanted his lordship to believe) a cause of much sorrow to him to be forced to give evidence against one for whom he had such a high regard, and he was doing so only on the king's account. He and Child were drinking companions at the Three Tobacco-Pipes near Holborn Fields, and it was thither he repaired when the prisoner had asked for Child to be sent, not to the prisoner himself, but (and he desired to make this clear, in all honesty) to the prisoner's master.

At this the Lord Chief Justice directed a searching look at the ranks of the gentlefolk among the spectators. When it alighted on Mr Pepys's irate countenance, he allowed himself a thin smile. 'Pray what is the name of Mr Atkins's master?' he inquired.

'Mr Pepys, my lord.'

'Mr Pepys of the Navy Office? Speak up, Captain Atkins. The court must hear what you have to say.'

'Mr Samuel Pepys, the Navy Secretary. Yes, my lord.'

'So the prisoner feared that Sir Edmund would ruin his master – this Mr Pepys – by a revelation about the Popish Plot?'

'So I understood, my lord. Later Child told me that he had been and talked with Mr Pepys. He did not say what that gentleman had asked him to do, but when we met at the Three Tobacco-Pipes afterwards he endeavoured to engage me in the murder of a man, whom he did not name. When I refused, he offered me £100 o hold my tongue. He threatened that, should I inform on him and reveal the crime, I would not outlive it. He then left me and I have not seen him since.'

After delivering this statement with feigned reluctance, Captain Atkins stood down and quickly made himself scarce among the crowd. In his place a nervous lad, aged about fifteen, was led into the hall and thrust forward in front of the bench.

'Now, my lord,' said the Attorney-General, 'because it seems a strange thing that Mr Atkins, who says he is a Protestant, should be engaged in this business, we have a witness here to prove that he hath been seen often at Somerset House at mass.'

The boy shrank when all eyes were turned upon him and the Lord Chief Justice warned him that he must tell the truth. He was about to be sworn when Sam, who was standing unidentified among officers of the court, called out: 'Do you know me?'

Before he could be stopped, the boy, surprised and flustered, replied: 'No, sir.'

Above the ensuing hubbub the Lord Chief Justice could be heard shouting for the witness to be sworn. Another judge was furiously rebuking Sam for his boldness and impropriety. The Attorney-General was holding an agitated consultation with his colleagues for the prosecution, trying to agree how best to retrieve the situation.

'My lord,' he said when he could make himself heard, 'this witness is not in my brief. I desire, before he is sworn, that he tell the court plainly whether or not he knows the prisoner.'

'If that be him, no; I do not,' replied the boy when Sam stepped forward.

'My lord, I perceive there has been a mistake.'

The apology came grudgingly. As he made it, the Attorney-General glanced at one of his colleagues to indicate the culprit and absolve himself from responsibility. He passed the interrogation of the next witness to the Solicitor-General with an icy bow which suggested that he was washing his hands of a bungled case.

Mr Pepys sat rubbing his hands with delight and pride at Sam's sharpness. If, as he suspected, the real purpose of the trial had been the mention of his own name in open court, now that that had been accomplished there was new hope for Sam if he continued to keep his wits about him.

The next witness was an even less reputable captain thar Charles Atkins. William Bedloe took the stand with the king's reward of £500 already in his pocket and the wary look of a man who did not intend to spoil his good fortune by being caught committing perjury. Sam's discrediting of the previous witness had put him on his guard.

When sworn, he recounted how he had been told that one of those who would be removing Sir Edmund's body from Somerset House was a Mr Atkins. He had supposed this to be Mr Charles Atkins, but had been unable to recognise him among the company around the body on the night in question, Monday the fourteenth of October. So he had asked one of the young gentlemen whether his name was Atkins and he had replied that it was. He had then asked whether he was Mr Pepys's clerk and the answer had again been 'yes'.

'Is this the gentleman?' The Solicitor-General stabbed a finger directly at Sam, defying this witness too to deny it.

Scenting danger in either 'yes' or 'no', Bedloe prevaricated. 'There was very little light, so that it is hard for me to swear that this is he,' he pleaded. 'I do not remember that he was such a person as the prisoner is. If I recollect correctly, he had a more manly face. And,' he added as though suddenly struck by the thought, 'as I verily believe, a beard,'

'So you rather think that it was not he?' The Lord Chief Justice cast a contemptuous glare in the direction of the phalanx of prosecuting counsel as he intervened.

'I cannot say that it was he, my lord,' Bedloe blustered. 'It might have been someone that did assume his person.'

'You do well to be cautious, Mr Bedloe,' the Lord Chief Justice told him curtly and called upon the prisoner to present his defence.

'Captain Atkins is a man that I have kept from perishing,' Sam told the court. 'I have petitioned for him, solicited for him and been instrumental in getting him released from prison. He has repaid me with malice and invention. I never had the conversation with him that he has reported. I am not surprised that Child has chosen to disappear rather than corroborate a deceit. And I swear to this court and Heaven above that, so far from seeing Sir Edmund's body there, I was never inside Somerset House in all my life.'

'Then call witnesses to prove where you were that night and you need trouble yourself and the court no further.'

'Captain Vittells of His Majesty's navy is here with his men, my lord, awaiting your lordship's pleasure.'

'If any of them can say where you were on the fourteenth of October last, a couple will suffice.'

It was now apparent to all that, since the Attorney-General had lost heart and there seemed no escape from the disgrace of an acquittal, the Lord Chief Justice was impatient to be done with the case. Captain Vittells, however, was determined to give his testimony in full and establish Sam's innocence beyond all doubt. He had been kept waiting long enough.

On the sixth day of October (he said) he had returned from carrying some officers to the king's garrison at Antwerp. It was (he reminded his lordship) a Sunday. He had come ashore the next day to report to Mr Pepys at the Navy Office, and had then been instructed to return to his ship and await further orders. On the following Friday he had reported again and been told to come back after the week-end because Mr Pepys had gone to Newmarket at the king's command.

On the Monday, which was the fourteenth of October, the captain had called at the office once more at eleven o'clock in the morning, only to find that Mr Secretary's return to Whitehall had been delayed. He had therefore spoken to Mr Samuel Atkins, whom he had known, man and boy, for fourteen years; whom he could vouch for as a steadfast member of the Church of England since childhood (as he felt sure his lordship would be reassured to learn); and to whose honesty and general good conduct over the years he could confidently bear witness without fear of contradiction. To anyone familiar with the prisoner and his devotion to the truth it was, in the opinion of the master of the *Catherine*, unthinkable that –

'We are inquiring into the events of one day, Captain Vittells,' interrupted the Lord Chief Justice. 'You are not here to enlighten us on what you may believe to be thinkable or unthinkable. This court has other important business to conduct; so pray do us the favour of proceeding at what I understand the sea-going fraternity is accustomed to calling a higher rate of knots.'

A jest from Sir William Scroggs was a rare occurrence, and Mr Pepys caught Sam's eye in a gleam of triumph. The other judges and counsel laughed dutifully, while the witness made haste to proceed with his evidence.

'Mr Atkins informed me that two ladies were desirous of visiting one of the king's ships that day, and I immediately returned to make arrangements for their reception. He came aboard with them at half an hour past four. The ladies inspected the vessel and made some inquiries about its armament and speed. When they grew tired we repaired to my cabin, where I uncorked some wine newly arrived from Madeira. We talked about life at sea and our engagements with the enemy and drank pretty freely. It was half after ten when I put the three of them in the ship's boat to be rowed ashore. The ladies were very merry and Mr Atkins, who is wont to be abstemious, had – I regret having to inform your lordship – all but lost the use of his voice and legs.'

On hearing this, the Lord Chief Justice ordered Bedloe to be recalled and required him to state without equivocation at what hour of night he had been at Somerset House.

'Betwixt nine and ten o'clock,' Bedloe affirmed.

'The man you spoke with there – he was sober, was he not?'

'Yes indeed; very sober.' Bedloe had no doubt about it.

'Then call just one of your men, Captain Vittells, and we have done.'

The name of Boatswain Tribbett was called. He was sworn and spoke confidently in a deep West Country burr, telling how he and his oarsmen had rowed the party up river that night as far as Billingsgate, where they had arrived about half an hour past eleven and the young gentleman had had to be helped ashore.

The Attorney-General was then called upon to address the court. 'My lord,' he said, 'it is vain to contest in a matter that is plain. But because some will perhaps make ill use of it, I desire that they would please take notice that here is no disproving the king's evidence. For Captain Bedloe did not at first, nor doth he now, charge the prisoner directly and positively to be the man he saw. Every word that Captain Atkins and he said may be true, yet the prisoner be innocent.'

The Lord Chief Justice thereupon advised the jury that 'Mr Atkins doth appear to be a very innocent man in this matter', and after a brief consultation at the bar the jury obliged with a verdict of 'Not Guilty.'

His lordship welcomed the acquittal of a Protestant; the cheers f Captain Vittells and his men shook the rafters; Mr Pepys congratulated himself on the successful conclusion of his campaign; and Sam smiled for the first time in sixteen weeks. He had reconciled himself to death but now, God willing, many years of life and liberty stretched ahead.

Mr Pepys was shaking his hand as though it were the handle of a pump, and he found himself kissing his master's cheek in gratitude, tears in both their eyes. 'Am I free to walk with you, sir?' he asked when he could speak.

'That cannot be, Master Atkins.' It was Captain Richardson, still standing by his side, who spoke. 'You are my prisoner until I receive an order of release from the Lords who ordered your confinement. That is the rule.'

Back to Newgate! Sam's spirits sank. 'How long?' he asked.

'As long as it takes for their lordships to be notified of the jury's verdict and issue the necessary instructions.'

'It will be but a day or two,' Mr Pepys consoled him, seeing Sam's dismay. 'Rest assured that I shall press for the order to be expedited. In the meantime the Navy Office and their lordships of the Admiralty will expect your keeper to make your remaining stay in custody as comfortable as may be.'

'You have my word on that, Mr Secretary,' Captain Richardson promised respectfully and led his prisoner away.

Mr Pepys threaded his way through the crowd and out into the rain-swept passageways of Whitehall, deep in thought. Sam was not the only one for whom the triumph of the day was tarnished. The slander that he himself was implicated in the murder and therefore in the plot had been publicly aired in criminal proceedings. That had been more important to his enemies than Sam's conviction.

Mr Pepys was not impulsive by nature, but once his mind was made up, he was accustomed to act decisively and without procrastination. It was time to make a direct approach to the king.

— 17 —

MR PEPYS AND THE KING

Avoiding the clusters of office-seekers and favour-mongers in the corridors and public audience chamber, Mr Pepys crossed the palace garden and sought audience with William Chiffinch, whose door, half-hidden at the end of a narrow passage, was never closed to the rich and the influential.

The closet-keeper's manner was, as always, ingratiating, but he expressed himself as most unsure whether the king would be willing to grant a private audience at such short notice, even to somebody of such consequence and distinction as the Secretary to the Navy. His Majesty was not well, Chiffinch confided: the turbulence of the times had overstretched him; and, he inquired courteously, was not the Admiralty Board Mr Secretary's proper and usual channel of communication?

Judging that these objections were not insuperable if a high enough price was paid, Mr Pepys refused to be deterred. He explained that he did not come on naval business and insisted on the seriousness of his mission in the king's own interest. This, when accompanied by coin in the palm and the promise of more, sufficed to overcome Chiffinch's resistance. An appointment was made for the same evening, unless word reached the Navy Office that the king had withheld his consent.

No message having arrived, Mr Pepys donned his finest clothing and crowned himself with his periwig curled in the very latest fashion and his beaver hat with an ostrich feather. Surveying his appearance in the looking-glass, he flattered himself that few gentlemen, and none who had been born a tailor's son, could be seen to better advantage.

At nine o'clock precisely he was following Chiffinch up the

back stairs to the royal closet. Inside, the king lay sprawled on a sofa like an invalid. One of his toy spaniels on his lap was staring anxiously into his face, which was wan. Standing over him, as though in waiting for the crown, was Mr Pepys's former master and patron, James, Duke of York.

He bowed low to each of them. The duke, who was his usual robust self, greeted him warmly; while the king graciously expressed his pleasure at the sight of the man who had recorded for posterity the miracle of his escape from death thirty long years ago. At this welcome Mr Pepys stifled his agitation and glowed with pride and self-satisfaction. He had come far and, if he played his cards skilfully enough, would go further. A time of danger was a time of opportunity, and the knighthood which he coveted was overdue.

'So His Majesty's fleet is under attack again: is that your business?' asked the duke. 'It has kept the country safe from foreigners, but not from those dogs in Parliament, eh? They fear its loyalty to the king and intend to destroy it through the pretence that every naval officer is a secret Catholic and every Catholic a traitor. Whatever you have come to propose to His Majesty will have my support, Mr Secretary.'

Charles had sanctioned the interview out of curiosity, but he was now regretting the intrusion of this vulgar little functionary whom he saw preening himself and coming to pester his betters. He felt listless and wished to be left alone.

Mr Pepys sensed the aura of hostility and caught himself praying that the king would not recover from his illness – that he would die and die quickly, before the Whiggish Opposition in the Commons could force the passage of their Exclusion Bill through the Lords. With the duke on the throne, his own advancement and the dignity of 'Sir Samuel' would surely not be long delayed. His experience and record in the public service well qualified him to hold a ministerial post, and King James would, without doubt, stand in need of trusty advice and sound guidance.

'With respect,' he said, addressing the duke, 'the target of the Green Ribbon revolutionists is not so much the navy as Your Royal Highness himself. I and my colleagues at the Navy Office are but stepping stones on the path to your intended destruction. And,' he added pointedly, 'His Majesty's.'

There was a yelp as the king threw his lap-dog to the floor and bestirred himself. 'If you have come to tell us that, Mr Pepys,' he grumbled, 'you have come to tell us what we already knew and we do not thank you for disturbing us.'

'I come with news for Your Majesty – news of a delicate and dangerous nature,' Mr Pepys hastened to assure him. His mood too had changed, and he asked himself anxiously whether the king had guessed his thoughts, whether he had divined his secret contempt for this lazy, lecherous travesty of royalty – a contempt which he was at such pains to keep concealed beneath a show of obsequiousness. If so, his mission was a failure before he had even come to the point.

'If you have intelligence to impart in confidence, you may proceed. I have no secrets from my brother,' said the king, acknowledging the lie himself with a half-smile.

'At the trial of one of my clerks today, a visit by two ladies to one of Your Majesty's ships lying at Greenwich was mentioned in court. In evidence from the captain it was stated that they were inquisitive about the vessel and its speed. In preparing Mr Atkins's defence I took precautions to ensure that they were not called upon to give evidence; nor were their names revealed. Their identity is known only to myself and my head clerk, who is the most trustworthy of men.'

'It must be known also to the captain and the accused man.' The king spoke unconcernedly, but Mr Pepys was not deceived.

'They may have made a correct conjecture, but their mouths are closed. Both are discreet and have been cautioned.'

'Have you requested this audience so that you may reveal their names to me? Is that your purpose?' The king had been taken by surprise and was suspicious. As an excuse to turn his back on his visitor, he strolled across the room and adjusted the timing of a handsome ormolu clock. He was unsteady on his feet, Mr Pepys noticed.

'Part of my purpose is to discover whether Your Majesty is aware of their names already.'

It was a bold response and, by the grace of God, not taken amiss. The king turned and stared Mr Pepys in the face. 'As I see that you have guessed,' he replied, 'the expedition was made with my knowledge and consent. You did well to broach this little affair with me directly. You are forthwith relieved of any responsibility in the matter.'

Mr Pepys bowed his thanks, but did not choose to take what might have been a hint that the audience was over. The king wearily threw himself back on the sofa, the duke was seated in a chair, but the low-born visitor was left to stand.

'It would seem,' he said, 'that Lord Shaftesbury is intent on indicting me as an accomplice in the murder of Mr Justice Godfrey (if murder it be) and on accusing me of involvement in a plot which he and his friends have invented. If these ladies are permitted to pursue their design at a time when the navy is under strict orders to prevent Catholics from leaving the country, I shall be blamed by Parliament and my fate will be sealed unless I can look to Your Majesty for my preservation.'

At the mention of Catholics the duke pricked up his ears. 'What business is this, pray?' he demanded.

'It is but some trifling feminine trickery,' drawled the king. 'My fair Louise believes that every papist in England is about to be massacred, and herself, with you, among the first. The hysteria is infectious and her sister Henriette too is afflicted. But in her case she believes that her husband will beat her to death before the assassins get to her. They are both demanding to be shipped home to Brittany.'

'Trifling indeed!' James was aghast. 'Your connivance in what Parliament deems a crime would raise a storm. The attack on the navy would gather force. No, no; I beg Your Majesty to be firm with the ladies and forbid the enterprise absolutely.'

The king's dog was troubled by a flea, and the king assisted by scratching its hindquarters while considering his reply.

'Tell me, brother,' he said after a short silence. 'Why should I not exile them for their own safety and the safety of the realm? If Parliament is sincere in believing the canard that Louise is a French spy, which its hired hacks are paid to scribble and publish to the nation, then Parliament must believe the realm to be safer without her.'

Mr Pepys coughed to signal his intervention in the royal duologue. 'Your Majesty may call it exile,' he said, 'but it will be dubbed an escape by the Commons. They will spread the libel that the ladies were guilty of assisting the plotters, and Your Majesty may then need to pay heed to your own safety.'

'Upon reflection I shall take your advice,' the king gravely assured them both. 'I see that you truly have my interests at heart, and I shall forbid it because I cannot do without my Louise. Castlemaine and Nellie together could not console me for her absence.'

Mr Pepys was shocked at this show of levity, and the duke snorted and begged his brother to be serious. 'Keeping the Duchess of Portsmouth against her will can hardly serve that purpose,' he said. 'If I know the hussy, she will sulk and turn her back on you.'

'So much the better,' replied the king with a leer, and Mr Pepys deemed it prudent to join in his laughter. 'Take note, then, that if she chooses to leave me it will be no doing of mine. She is wilful and cunning and has exceptional favours to grant to any man who aids her in eluding my guards. So she may succeed despite my best endeavours.'

Mr Pepys's laughter died abruptly. His finely tuned antennae at once picked up the king's meaning. He would attempt to dissuade her, but Louise was likely to have her way, and in that event the assurance which he had given only a few minutes earlier would be worthless. Mr Pepys would become the quarry of the resulting hue and cry.

'I am sensible of the honour of being taken into Your Majesty's confidence,' he said. 'A close watch for priests and other suspicious persons is already being maintained day and night at every port, but I will now issue a command to all captains to exercise particular vigilance to prevent the flight of female fugitives.'

This, as he well knew, was not what the king had in mind. A termagant mistress brought back by force would be unlikely to turn either front or back to him in bed.

'You must do your duty as you think fit,' replied the king coldly. His brief spell of good temper was at an end.

'I desire only to serve Your Majesty and Your Royal Highness.' This dutiful, if less than truthful, sentiment emerged as a plaintive cry. Mr Pepys was in despair at the course the interview was taking.

The king ignored him as now beneath notice and addressed the duke as though they were alone.

'You must be aware,' he said, 'how greatly it grieves me that I am no longer able to offer protection to even the most faithful of my servants, whether Catholic or Protestant. Should they suffer the misfortune of giving offence to Parliament, they must expect no help from me. The Commons grow ever more impudent, and the Lords, who were once properly subservient to the bidding of their sovereign, have a new master in Shaftesbury.'

'The fault is your own,' answered the duke bluntly. 'Your Majesty has permitted six loyal Catholic peers to be despatched to the Tower and has disabled the remainder. Those of their lordships who are free to attend and are not Shaftesbury's lackeys have become intimidated. Now that there is no curb on legislation from the Commons, I urge you to bring the Opposition to heel before they do irreparable mischief. Pray permit me to remind you that a member of my own household has been condemned as a traitor; yet he was as honest a man as ever lived. The queen's physician will soon follow him on a hurdle to Tyburn. This is but a beginning. Mr Pepys speaks truly. It is but a short step to my banishment and your own martyrdom. Remember our father.'

'You exaggerate,' scoffed the king with a sniff and a yawn. 'Coleman was a foolish fellow. He brought his fate on his own head. As for Dr Wakeman, I know him to be unjustly accused and shall do all I can to save him.'

'A pardon for every one of Oates's victims has lain within your power. Yet you have allowed men of God to be condemned by perjurors and butchered by atheists and republican sons of Satan.' The duke's choleric humour was off the leash, and he was now shouting at the Lord's anointed.

Unruffled, the king stifled a sneeze and pointed out that, with the nation in its present mood, granting pardons would have guaranteed his martyrdom.

'And your salvation, brother. Think of your soul.'

The argument was interrupted by the appearance of Chiffinch, who emerged out of the shadows in one corner of the room to shuffle into the candle-light and murmur in the king's ear.

'Very well,' Charles answered with the sigh of someone already martyred. 'You may bring him to me now. But, first, pray escort this gentleman down the stairs.'

Mr Pepys had been embarrassed to witness such a scene, but he had stood his ground. The moment was far from propitious, but he was determined to salvage something from the ruin of his expectations. A direct appeal was his last hope. Backing as if to depart, he paused at the door to beg two favours: one for Sam and the other for himself.

'Samuel Atkins is the name of my clerk who was on trial today for the murder of Mr Justice Godfrey. He is a loyal servant of Your Majesty; none more so. His innocence was proved and, thanks be to God, he was acquitted. I beg for his early release from prison, where he has already suffered undeserved hardship for many weeks.'

'Be assured that he shall be released in proper form and due time.' The king sank into a torpor, overcome either by his ailment or by boredom.

Mr Pepys could scarcely suppress his rage at this snub, but brought himself to signify a pretence of gratitude by inclining his head respectfully. 'Yet Mr Atkins's acquittal will not deter the Opposition,' he said. 'I am much in fear lest I become their next victim, and I humbly solicit Your Majesty's protection should that calamity befall me.' At last he had reached the crux of his visit.

'Alas! I no longer have the ability to protect any man, as you have just heard me informing the duke. No monarch in all the world has ever been so stripped and deprived. And I a Stuart, God's representative here on earth!' The king preferred indulging himself in self-commiseration to taking pity on this importunate suitor who did not have the good manners to leave when dismissed.

'Come, brother,' the duke remonstrated. 'You possess the power. What you lack in your present condition is the will. When you are yourself again, you will stand by all your loyal subjects. No man has deserved better of you than Mr Pepys.'

'How can I save Mr Pepys if I cannot save my chief minister?'

'Through the exercise of your royal prerogative.' The duke spoke sharply again, as though addressing a tiresome child.

'Then Parliament will abolish it, and I shall lose even the authority to save my heir from exclusion and exile.'

This threat reduced the duke to speechlessness.

Before taking his overdue leave, Mr Pepys threw a quick glance round the room, taking in the dimly-lit pictures and precious ornaments which he would never be privileged to see again. On the sofa the king was sneezing and snivelling and being comforted by his spaniel, which was licking his face affectionately. Was his sickness serious or exaggerated for reasons of state? Was it wholly in the body or mostly in the mind? There was no telling.

As they descended the winding staircase together, Mr Pepys tapped the closet-keeper on the shoulder. 'What did His Majesty's reference to his chief minister mean?' he whispered.

Chiffinch's response was to turn and put a finger to his lips. In the darkness at the bottom of the stairs a man was standing, stamping his feet against the cold. A cloak was drawn over the lower half of the face, but before Chiffinch could hustle him past Mr Pepys recognised the Earl of Danby.

'Heaven help us!' he muttered to himself outside in the courtyard. 'Have matters come to such a pass that this is the hour and means whereby the Lord Treasurer of England must seek audience of the king?'

The Opposition, as Mr Pepys well knew, was pressing ever harder for the earl's impeachment. His mother was a Catholic, and for weeks they had been accusing him of a treasonable lack of resolve in bringing the plotters to justice. Now the ambassador in Paris had returned after a quarrel with him and disclosed his secret correspondence with French ministers.

The rain had passed, but a frosty northern breeze in the night air was a sign of the times. It almost nipped the nose from Mr Secretary's face. Clouds blanketed the sky and covered the stars. In the pitch blackness his journey back to Derby House on foot was a perilous one, but his thoughts were not on unseen obstacles and lurking footpads.

If the king allowed Danby to be thrown to the wolves, nothing would stand between himself and Shaftesbury's malice. He would be dismissed, arrested, and charged, not with murder, but with high treason. He must now urgently look to his own defence as effectively as he had looked to Sam's.

With his mind feverishly preoccupied, Mr Pepys stepped into a puddle and hastily out of it to strike his shin against a kerb. His pomponed shoes and finest silk hose were ruined. It was an ill omen.

— 18 —

RELEASE

Faced with the king's indifference and the stubborn ill-will of Sir Philip Howard, whose scheme to win £500 for his nephew had been frustrated by Sam's acquittal, it took Mr Pepys more than six weeks to obtain the release of his innocent clerk.

So it was early in April, on a raw spring morning, when Sam at last received his long-awaited farewell handshake from Captain Richardson and stepped out into the street. There he was greeted in the murk of dawn by Tom Walbank, who had been sent to wait beside the gate and fetch him safely home in a hackney-coach. When he embraced his fellow clerk, Sam could not restrain himself from bursting into tears of relief. Never had he been so glad to see a friend or so grateful to breathe the poisoned air of a London haze.

They carried with them to Derby House two other prisoners whose release Mr Pepys's importunity had secured at the same time. Bromwell and Walters were the unfortunate baker and blacksmith who had chanced upon the magistrate's body. Their honesty in reporting it and refraining from robbing the corpse had been rewarded by five months in Newgate, where they had been held on suspicion of being hired by the plotters to make the discovery. Because he desired the opportunity to interrogate them before they rejoined their families, Mr Pepys had sent a message inviting – or, rather, demanding – their company at his celebration of Sam's return.

Tom's great news was that Mr Pepys had become a Member of Parliament at the recent elections and was busier and more self-important than ever. But Tom warned that he was no longer his old self. Their master, he said, had lost his hitherto irrepressible zest for life – whether for business or pleasure, politicking or wenching, music or learning. All his staff were distressed about his health and well-being.

When he had been welcomed into his master's arms and they stood back to appraise each other's looks, Sam could detect new furrows on a face which had aged beyond its years. Mr Pepys saw a jaded youth, but also tempered steel. In Sam's eye shone an undimmed glint of determination that the sufferings of the innocent were not to be in vain; wickedness must not triumph; justice must be done. It was the rash look of one who would not learn from experience and would soon be in trouble again.

That day, however, was an occasion for unclouded merriment. The cares of office, the threats of foes, the deep shadows hanging over the future were all banished. The stern disciplinarian melted into a genial host. Playing Master of Ceremonies with all the considerable relish at his command, Mr Pepys entertained his entire household to a celebratory breakfast. He presided at the head of the table as though every one was a cherished member of his family. In the absence of a mistress of the house, Will Hewer was assigned the seat at the other end and the toasting role of Mr Vice.

A barrel of oysters was soon emptied, and it was followed by dishes of anchovies, neats' tongues and botargo – a sausage made from eggs and blood of sea mullet which was Sam's special favourite. To help these delicacies vanish, they were washed down with great draughts of Northdown ale and wines choicer than the clerks had ever tasted before.

To sustain Sam during his last weeks in Newgate, Will Hewer had arranged for him to receive fresh food and strong ale at the Navy Office's expense. Even so, the difference between the present feast and prison fare was – so Sam informed the company – as wide as the Atlantic ocean.

No celebration at Derby House was complete without a speech from Mr Pepys. Fortified with wine, he rained extravagant praises on Sam's modestly bowed head for a full ten minutes. All previous misdemeanours and backsliding had been forgotten, at least for the day.

'No youth of his straitness of fortune,' he concluded, 'has ever withstood such temptation to become a villain. With his young life at stake, yet defying menaces and devilish blandishments alike, he utterly refused to depart from the truth by a single syllable. May our good and faithful friend, Samuel Atkins, henceforth enjoy the fullness of God's grace and blessing and all the comforts of life here and hereafter! We may be sure that his reward awaits him in Heaven, but may he first enjoy earthly happiness for as many years as Methuselah! Mr Vice, I give you Master Atkins!'

'Gentlemen, pray charge your glasses and rise,' responded Will. 'The toast is: Sam!'

They all stood with glasses raised and drank to Sam's health and long life. His response was brief, but it came directly from the heart. He was near to collapse from faintness at so much talk and revelry after months of silence and solitude, but before he sat down he had unburdened himself of what had been uppermost in his mind throughout his imprisonment.

'Life without justice is an affront to our Maker,' he said, 'and I have no desire to live to old age in an unjust world. Innocent victims of the law cannot be brought back to life, but the real plotters and perpetrators of Sir Edmund's murder can be found and must be punished.'

The feast was at an end. Bromwell and Walters were borne away for a private talk with Mr Pepys. The others returned to their duties, leaving Sam alone with Will Hewer, the man who had become a father to him since the death of his own.

'It is good to have you among us again, Sam. The navy has not been faring well without you.' Will gave one of his lop-sided smiles and poured him a glass of brandy.

It was typical of Will to notice what he needed. Unlike Mr Pepys, Will was undemonstrative. Unlike Mr Pepys, he was unobtrusive, never taking the centre of the stage. Business was managed by him without fuss. In all the Navy Office's affairs his had been, for nearly twenty years, the unnoticed hand steadying the tiller. It was Will, not Mr Pepys, who would decide a junior clerk's future. Sam took a long gulp from the glass and prepared to listen.

'You will need to know what has been happening during your absence from the world,' said Will. 'First let me tell you that our ambassador in Paris has betrayed the king and Danby by disclosing to the Commons that His Majesty has been receiving secret largesse from Louis to make him independent of Parliament. The Commons have chosen to retaliate by starving the navy of funds. They argue that the king can afford to pay for his own ships. Debts of nearly £40,000 have been owed to victuallers since the beginning of the year. All building and repair work is at a standstill. Mr Pepys is at his wits' end.'

Sam was aghast. 'How then can the fleets be kept at sea?'

'They cannot be. The Home Fleet is confined to port, and a complete withdrawal from the Mediterranean has been ordered.'

'A victory for the French without a gun fired!' Sam felt sick for his country. 'Who then are the traitors?' he asked bitterly.

'It is said that Louis has been lining Shaftesbury's and other pockets besides the king's,' Will replied cautiously. 'But the earl's friends in the Commons blame the king and Danby and seek to evade responsibility by alleging extravagance in the Navy Office. Anyone in the service who confronts them with denials, as Mr Pepys has been bold enough to do, is tarred with charges of treason and popery.'

'But surely the king is taking steps to bring them to heel?'

Will sighed. 'His Majesty is sick, perhaps gravely so. He has given up the struggle. As so often before, he attempted to silence the Opposition by proroguing Parliament. In these days of plot and murder, however, it provoked such an uproar that he was persuaded that rebellion was imminent. He took fright and bowed to the clamour for dissolution and a new Parliament.'

'Tom told me that Mr Pepys was one of those elected.'

'Yes; he stood at Harwich, where the voters are staunch for the Crown. Portsmouth too would have chosen him – and any other port, I dare say. But elsewhere Shaftesbury's men roused the country with their lies that Godfrey's murder proved the existence of a Popish Plot. You could not walk the street without meeting a man wearing a green ribbon with "No Popery" on it. They say that fifty thousand were distributed and more were called for. A tide of sedition swept the earl's candidates to victory. Now the Commons are more mulish and fanatical than at any time since the Restoration.'

The glasses were refilled, and the brandy conquered Sam's weariness. He was alert and all ears. 'There must be other loyalists in Parliament besides Mr Pepys,' he said.

Will shook his head sadly. 'It may be, but few in the new House will speak for the king now that he has been unmasked as a pensioner of the French; and the lower His Majesty sinks, the higher his enemies ride. He has even been forced to order the heir to his throne into exile – for the duke's own safety.'

His master's patron – the king's own brother – banished! Sam was too bewildered for words.

'The duke is blamed for everything,' Will continued, 'and it cannot be denied that the papists have been waxing busier and bolder ever since he forbore to attend services at the king's chapel and boasted openly that he was one of them and his conscience would not permit him to deny or conceal it. Now he is in Brussels, whence he is reported to be chewing the carpets in his rage. And that is not all.'

Will held up a hand to stop the question on Sam's lips.

'Danby has been despatched to the Tower for his pains in carrying out the king's commands. It is expected that, within a few days, Shaftesbury – yes, Shaftesbury – will be at the head of a new administration. There can be little doubt that he will lose no time in dismissing some of the Admiralty Commissioners and making new appointments to the Board. Mr Pepys is convinced that he will then be turned out of the office of Secretary and sent to join Danby in the Tower.'

'But on what charge? Has Mr Pepys not done his duty as faithfully and dependably as any servant of the Crown?'

'Have you not yet learned, my dear, innocent Sam, that one cannot do one's duty without making enemies? You must understand that Mr Pepys is still regarded as one of the duke's chief lieutenants, just as Mr Coleman was. The same fate as Coleman's threatens him, and he makes matters worse by not flinching from defending the duke in the Commons whilst others keep their silence.'

'Is defending the heir to the throne a crime for which a Member of Parliament can be arrested?' Sam demanded in dismay.

'The accusation against Mr Pepys is that he has betrayed his country by selling secret information about the navy to the French, in order that the duke may return with Louis' assistance to usurp the throne and bring in popery. It is yet another palpable invention, and Mr Pepys is well prepared with his rebuttal, but we fear that nothing will save him from disgrace and imprisonment once Shaftesbury becomes President of a Council of republican liars and rogues.'

'What proof of such an allegation can there possibly be?' Even as he voiced the question, Sam reminded himself ruefully of the ease with which it could be forged.

'We must expect a perjuror – a new Oates, another Bedloe, a second Prance. The reward for false evidence is high. There will be no shortage of applicants.'

'What is to be done, then? Had it not been for Mr Pepys, I would be a dead man. I am willing to undertake any mission to repay him.' Sam leaned across the table and offered himself to Will.

The head clerk nodded his grateful acceptance. This, it became clear to Sam, had been no idle chatter, but discourse with a purpose. A plan had been hatched.

'First,' said Will, 'you must regain your health and strength. Go to your uncle and aunt in the City and lodge with them until you are fully recovered. I have the wages owed to you, and you will continue to be paid for as long as it is within my power. At present there is little work to be done in the clerks' office. We have to twiddle our thumbs until Parliament comes to its senses. So you need feel no guilt at being absent from your normal duties. You have earned a holiday.'

'I have been idle long enough,' Sam protested. 'I desire no more leisure, and my uncle will be unwilling. In the City I shall be a public spectacle like the lions at the Tower. My acquittal will count for nothing. I shall be bad for trade, and my aunt will be ashamed to have me in the house.'

'If you truly desire to serve Mr Pepys, the navy and your country,' Will replied, 'I have that to propose which will occupy your time, but you must not be seen in the office until the assignment is completed. I spoke with your uncle and your aunt yesterday and won their consent to your lodging there. Your aunt's sole condition, to which you will not object, is that you accompany them to church next Sunday and take the holy sacrament to demonstrate your devotion to the Protestant religion before all the parish.'

'But this is my home. I have spent days and nights longing to be here again with you and Mr Pepys and Tom and the others.'

Tears were welling in Sam's eyes, and he could not hold them back.

Will took his hand and squeezed it. 'I understand,' he said gently; 'but you will do well to put some distance between yourself and Whitehall for a while. As I recollect, you used not to be averse from an occasional absence from your desk.'

They smiled together, and Sam raised his arms in a sign of surrender. Will then revealed what was expected of him.

'You did speak, did you not, of your desire to bring Mr Justice Godfrey's murderers to book? His killing is the cause and kernel of our present discontent. Mr Pepys has been inclined to believe it suicide dressed up as murder, but his opinion is now the same as my own: that it was a murder, and one of the most wicked committed in the whole long history of crime. We are agreed that it was not the handiwork of the wretches who were hanged for it. We suspect that the real culprits are Protestants, not Catholics, and if it can be shown that Lord Shaftesbury was privy to it . . .'

Will let his last sentence hang in the air between them, and Sam leaped to finish it: '. . . then he will be discredited and lose power, and Mr Pepys will be safe. The earl is my especial enemy too, and nothing would delight me more –'

'Not so fast!' It was Will's turn to interrupt. 'Mr Pepys is convinced that the crime was not committed at Somerset House. Where then was the deed done? First bring us the answer to that question. It will lead us to our quarry. You must proceed with caution and take only one step at a time. That is necessary both for the success of the inquiry and in your own interest, for the danger is very great.'

'It will be God's work. He will protect me, never fear. But tell me: where shall I begin?' Sam was eager but puzzled.

'You have been to my home?'

Sam nodded. A head clerk could afford to live in a house of his own. Will's was in Buckingham Street, one of the quiet byways running down from the Strand to the river bank, like Hartshorn Lane. The other clerks were sometimes sent there on errands.

'Go to your uncle's now and rest. In a week or so, when you feel accustomed to walking and talking, take this letter to Colonel Welden. He is a neighbour of mine. He has given evidence in court, but has more to tell if he chooses. He nurses a secret which he claims to have been the cause of Godfrey's death. Press him hard, and remember: the letter must be destroyed in your presence as soon as he has read it.'

They embraced with tenderness. Not only was Will the father Sam had lost; Sam was the son Will had never had, and he vowed not to disappoint him.

— 19 —

BUCKINGHAM STREET

Three days later Sam walked down the Strand, revelling in his liberty. The rude bustle of horse and foot to-ing and fro-ing between the City and Westminster – even the stench of the filth in the gutters – gladdened him. Squeezed between the palaces of the nobility which lined the street were shops and hostelries doing a busy trade. This was life, the life for which he had returned from the grave.

York Buildings stood at the foot of Buckingham Street, overlooking a water-gate and the river beyond. There he introduced himself to Colonel George Welden, a tall, bony, rheumy-eyed veteran, direct in manner and speech. 'Lord! I had thought you were a hanged man!' was his greeting.

'My neck is not yet broken, as you see, sir,' was Sam's rejoinder. 'Nor is my spirit. My trial was a rare victory for justice, thanks to my master, Mr Pepys. Mr Coleman was less fortunate.'

They were seated in the parlour, where the colonel read Will Hewer's letter and returned it to Sam, who threw it in the fire, as instructed.

'I am told that Mr Coleman was known to you.' Sam broke the silence while his host was still staring at him appraisingly.

The colonel cleared his throat as though reaching a decision to speak. 'That is correct,' he said. 'I first met Edward Coleman at Cambridge, where we studied together at Trinity. He was the most brilliant undergraduate of the day and the leader of a set of which I was proud to be a member. "Lo, a damned crew," the wags used to jeer at us. It was an anagram of his name, don't you see? We made wagers amongst ourselves whether he would become Lord Chancellor, Lord Treasurer or President of the

Council. But religious fanaticism quite undid him. He caught the disease whilst visiting Paris one vacation. Yet I fear his real reason for converting to Rome was spite against his father, a clergyman with a living in Suffolk whom I once met and found excessively bigoted and quarrelsome.'

'I believe you were familiar with Mr Justice Godfrey too?'

'It is his coal warming you now. Hartshorn Lane is but a short stroll hence and our paths often crossed. My friendship with Edward Coleman was not extinguished by a difference of religious faith. He was witty and amusing, and he and Godfrey enjoyed each other's company in private here. They could not afford to be seen associating with each other in public. Godfrey would have been suspected of popery, and Coleman did not wish to cause him embarrassment or have an end put to their conversations. They grew close, gossiped freely and valued an exchange of intelligence.'

'Mr Hewer supposes that an indiscretion by Mr Coleman in this house made Sir Edmund the master of a dangerous secret. He says that he is not privy to its nature, but is of the opinion that, whatever it may have been, it was the cause of Sir Edmund's death.' Sam looked expectantly at his host.

'Mr Hewer is a good neighbour, you have an honest face, and you are both in the king's service. The killers must be caught, so I will trust you,' said the colonel after a pause for reflection. 'These two friends met here on the evening of Saturday, September the twenty-eighth: the day when Godfrey took Oates's second deposition alleging a plot. Coleman had learned of Oates's accusations and was impatient to see the evidence and learn the details.'

'So the meeting was not by accident?'

'No: we had made an arrangement that whenever Coleman desired to meet Godfrey I would send a servant to Hartshorn Lane with a message that one Clarke would speak with him. On that day Godfrey came immediately, bringing the deposition with him, and they put their heads together over it in this room for two or three hours. When Coleman was fully apprised of the threat against his life, he went home to destroy his papers. Had he not forgotten where he hid some of his foolish correspondence with the French king's confessor, he would be alive today.'

'But how, pray, was Mr Coleman responsible for what happened to Sir Edmund?'

'Do you swear to being a true adherent of the Church of England, abhorring all Roman beliefs and practices?' The colonel looked fiercely at him and spoke in a parade-ground voice.

'I do,' Sam hastened to reassure him.

'Mr Hewer, so he tells me, imagines that Godfrey was murdered by Protestants and not by Catholics and has employed you to track them down on Mr Pepys's behalf. He is misguided, and I have to warn you against an error which might prove fatal. You must take it from me that the murder was in truth committed by Catholics.'

Sam was not to be bullied and did not disguise his disagreement. 'Saving your grace, Colonel Welden, I find it impossible to suppose that Berry, Green and Hill were justly convicted.'

'I assert no such thing. Those hapless men were the victims of a second Popish Plot – a plot to shield the guilty by sacrificing the innocent. Miles Prance was suborned by the Jesuits to lay a false trail so that the real criminals should escape justice. I will wager you any odds that it is those masters of deceit who are behind the rumour that the murderers were Protestants intent on inflaming the mob against papists.'

'Such is indeed my own understanding,' Sam confessed.

'Then permit me to enlighten you. The secret I hold was not one conveyed by Godfrey to Coleman. It was let slip by Coleman in the presence of Godfrey and myself. The core of Oates's deposition – that which gave it credibility – was the statement that he had been present at a congregation of Jesuits of the English province, held on April the twenty-fourth last year at the White Horse tavern in the Strand, where the plot to assassinate the king and return England to Rome was proposed and agreed. "Here is proof positive that the dog is perjured!" Coleman cried out when he read that passage. "That meeting was never held at the White Horse," he said. Whereupon Godfrey inquired the true location, and Coleman could not resist telling him the truth.'

At this point the colonel's narrative was brought to a halt by a fit of coughing. Sam held his breath and tongue, willing him to continue, while the colonel called for a glass of water and drank it slowly before resuming.

'According to Coleman's account, the gathering did take place on the day stated by Oates, but there was nothing untoward about it. It was a regular meeting, known as a consult, held to discuss internal matters affecting the Order. The only unusual aspect was that Coleman had arranged for it to take place, not at the inn as stated by Oates (who was, of course, not present), but at St James's Palace.'

Sam grasped the implication of this at once. St James's was the residence of the Duke of York. If the real venue became known and the rest of Oates's testimony were believed, the duke would be open to a charge of treason. His powerful enemies would press for his impeachment and execution. Nothing would suit Shaftesbury and his fanatics better than this revelation.

'I was on the other side of the hearth while they were whispering together,' continued the colonel, 'and I pretended not to hear. Godfrey betrayed instant alarm. Again I pretended not to notice, but I was not surprised. If he did not disclose what his friend had told him in confidence, he would himself become a party to treason and be liable to the same traitor's death as the duke. As a magistrate, too, he had always insisted on obedience to the law. When he left, he was flustered and Coleman may have guessed what was in his mind.'

Sam began to ask a question, but was sharply ordered to be silent. The colonel's hesitancy had passed. He now wanted to be done with unburdening himself.

'I saw Godfrey several times during the remaining two weeks of his life,' he said. 'His countenance had altered; plainly, his mind was depressed. I guessed that he must be wrestling with this terrible dilemma: a choice between friendship and justice on the one side and duty and injustice on the other. But when he came here again, on a Friday evening after a vestry meeting at St Martin's, he appeared in a cheerful mood. It was the day before his disappearance and he was settling his affairs. My conscience is clear, he told me.'

'So he had decided to prefer duty to friendship. Was that your understanding of his meaning?'

'It was; and I inferred too that he perfectly understood the consequences. Sitting where you are sitting now, he said that I would soon hear of the death of someone – the name he refused to divulge, but again his meaning was plain. When I invited him to dine with me at midday the next day, he would not give me a yea or nay, but answered that he could not tell. I am convinced that he was about to disclose what Coleman had revealed and was reconciled to not knowing whether or no he would be alive to eat another dinner.'

'Pray forgive me,' Sam interrupted, 'but if he was killed to prevent the disclosure, someone else must have learned of his intention. Or do you suppose that Coleman would have told of his suspicions?'

'Coleman was still under house arrest at the time. His papers were being examined, and he had not yet been despatched to Newgate. I suspect that Godfrey, with his strong sense of honour, was foolhardy enough to send his friend a warning in the hope that it might spur him to make an escape to France. Coleman must have warned the Jesuits, and they must have decided that Godfrey had to be silenced. The Duke of York has been the pivot of all their scheming, and Sir Edmund's death was their only means of rescuing him.'

'So Sir Edmund was enticed into Somerset House and murdered there by Catholics, as Prance and Bedloe alleged, but not by the men convicted for the crime. Is that your belief, sir?' Sam did his best not to look doubtful.

'I know the ways of Jesuits, Master Atkins. They either do their own killing or hire seasoned desperadoes. They would not entrust such work to household servants.'

'Mr Pepys doubts whether the deed was done in Somerset House,' Sam ventured to observe.

'Then you may tell Mr Pepys from me that the proof of it lies in the white wax stains found on the dead man's clothes. Like you and I and all the world save the high and mighty, Sir Edmund used tallow for candle-light in his house. It is in Roman Catholic churches that bees-wax candles are burned. The Catholic queen's palace is a nest of Jesuit vipers, and her chapel was a fitting choice for the scene of a devilish crime.' Colonel Welden's face grew purple at the thought.

'I have fought in the Protestant cause in Flanders,' he continued, working himself into a rage. 'England and Protestantism, truth and liberty – the four are indivisible. I have hazarded my life for them and would do so a hundred times again. Have I misjudged you, Master Atkins? Are you not a loyal Englishman? Do you not value the truth and enjoy your freedom? Very well then. Promise me that you will do nothing to give credence to the deception that the culprits in this affair are Protestants who turned on their own. In so doing you would be playing the pope's and Satan's game.'

'If what you believe so sincerely is indeed the truth, then I trust to God to guide me accordingly.' Sam spoke appeasingly, performed his deepest and most respectful bow, and made a quick departure before a promise could be extracted from him which he might not feel able to keep.

'Remember his shoes,' the colonel called after him at the door. 'When the body was found on Primrose Hill, the bottoms of the soles were as clean as if he had just come out of his own chamber. It is sure evidence that he was never killed on that spot. He was carried thither from the palace, as witnesses at the trial testified.'

Carried thither certainly, but from Somerset House by no means certainly, Sam said to himself as he took a path leading from the bottom of the street to marshy ground by the water's edge. Colonel Welden was blinded by the anti-popery which afflicted all military men; yet his familiarity with Coleman had survived the latter's conversion to Rome. Was that not strange? An explanation began to stir inside Sam's head.

He tested his strength by picking up a stone and throwing it as far as it would go, startling kites and ravens scavenging among the sedge. Commonsense told him that the colonel could not be right about the religion of the perpetrators of a murder which had proved to be what any man could have foreseen: a calamity for Catholics and a Godsend to Protestant trouble-makers. Suspicion whispered in his ear that Colonel George Welden was a Green Ribbon man who had informed on his friend Coleman and confided in Sam for the purpose of misleading him.

He left the path and stepped knee-high through a tangle of reeds and loosestrife growing among rubbish dumped or washed on to the river bank. In the mist hanging over the water he could distinguish dredgers and skiffs plying their trade. The air was foul and fetid, but a thousand times less so than Newgate's. Outwardly nothing had changed since his last visit to Hartshorn Lane, which lay but a few yards ahead. It was time to find out what had happened to the members of the magistrate's household and what they might be able to tell him.

He stopped at the door of the familiar brick house next to the wharf. An unknown maid answered his knock and told him that Elizabeth Curtis no longer lived there. His request to speak with

Judith Pamphlin met with the same reply. Henry Moor was his last hope. Yes; Mr Moor still lived there. But no; he could not be spoken with because he was not at home.

Sam was leaving disappointed when he espied a figure approaching down the lane and gave a shout of recognition. It was a more bent figure than he had known only a few months ago, but it was unmistakably Mr Justice Godfrey's clerk.

At his cry the old man stopped short, then quickened his pace to greet him uncertainly, as though welcoming the ghost of a former friend. 'I never thought to see you alive again,' he said, echoing Colonel Welden's words and laying a hand on Sam's arm to satisfy himself that the apparition was real.

Sam embraced him heartily. 'Where is Elizabeth?' he asked.

Henry shook his head gloomily. 'You will not thank me for what I have to tell you, Master Atkins, and this is no place for confidences.'

He turned back to the Strand and led the way to an inn. 'The landlord here serves the best ale in London,' he said when Sam appeared reluctant to follow.

But it was not the quality of the drink which concerned Sam; it was the sign hanging above the door. For this was the White Horse tavern which Oates had chosen to identify as the Jesuits' meeting place. He looked around him curiously. 'Is this house not reputed to be a haunt of papists?' he inquired.

'I have been drinking here for thirty years and not noticed it,' Mr Moor replied. 'Titus Oates has bestowed that reputation upon it, but the landlord denies being a Catholic or in sympathy with that religion. He asserts that Oates is actuated by malice because he was refused free ale. Those of us who drink here are inclined to think Oates the greater liar. It is common knowledge that he is not accustomed to paying for what he buys and takes revenge on any who will not yield to him.'

Solicitous for Sam's welfare, he asked many questions about his imprisonment and trial. But even while making his answers, Sam's mind was occupied with this explanation for Oates's location of the Jesuit consult at this inn. Was it not confirmation that the real meeting place lay elsewhere, and did that not lend plausibility to at least part of Colonel Welden's evidence? Now Sam did not know what to think.

When Mr Moor was done with his interrogation it was Sam's

turn to buy the ale and put the questions; although this, he thought, was a worse place for confidences than Hartshorn Lane. There would be private chambers upstairs for hire, but here in the crowded public rooms which ran round the bar all the booths were occupied – for the most part by men with whom Sam would not have cared to mingle. He had therefore pushed his way into a corner where he could stand and watch for eavesdroppers over Henry Moor's head.

It was a pitiful tale the old man had to tell. After the second visit by Oates and Tonge, Sir Edmund had grown daily more sad and pensive. He told his clerk that he was like to be knocked on the head at any hour; yet continued to walk the streets without a servant to protect him, saying that it was a hindrance to a man. Within a few days he became ill and took to his bed, where he lived on a diet of jelly and whey. A surgeon was summoned to open a vein, but blood-letting could not cure his melancholy; which was hereditary, although aggravated by fear.

Some of this Sam remembered hearing when he had called three days after the disappearance, and he now repeated a question he remembered asking then: Of whom was this once fearless magistrate afraid?

Mr Moor was emphatic that he did not know. All he could say was that the anxiety which had at first worried his master almost to the grave concerned his concealment of Oates's accusations against innocent persons. In the end, in a state of grievous distress, he had risen from his sick-bed, gone to Westminster and handed the deposition to Lord Chief Justice Scroggs, thus fulfilling his duty to report alleged acts of treason. That had occurred on October the fifth, or perhaps the sixth, and thereafter he had become cheerful and his old self again until the evening of Thursday the tenth, two days before he vanished. On that day he returned home depressed and as sorely troubled in his mind as before. 'Mark my words,' he had told his clerk: 'I shall be the first martyr.'

Henry Moor's account was long and full, but, beyond this reference to martyrdom, he had no firm answer to the question: Did Mr Justice Godfrey believe his life to be in danger from Catholics or Protestants?

Sam replenished their jug of ale for a second time, determined to loosen the old man's tongue further. Whether or not the White

Horse's liquor was the best in London, his own head was beginning to bear witness that it might claim be among the strongest.

Mr Moor had sorrows to drown and drank readily. He swallowed a large draught, wiped his mouth with his sleeve and continued his narrative without more urging.

It had been on the very next day, Friday the eleventh, that a messenger brought the letter which was a prelude to the murder. It was handed to Elizabeth at the door. She took it to Sir Edmund in his parlour, where he read it. She then returned to tell him that the messenger would not go away: he had been ordered to wait for an answer. According to Elizabeth, her master had flown into a temper and said that he did not know what to make of the letter. He refused to give her an answer, and she persuaded the man to leave without one. She had never seen him before, and Sir Edmund disclosed neither the letter's contents nor the name of the sender.

Sam's eyes widened. Surely, he thought, this had to be the death warrant! The writer must have been the murderer or an accessory. But how could he be so careless or carefree as to send a messenger who might be recognised or identified later? Sam felt triumph at the prospect of Elizabeth giving him a description as soon as he could find her. Solving the mystery together would seal a bond between them.

Meanwhile Mr Moor had still not finished, and Sam was becoming drowsy. He had to fight the effect of the ale to make sure of catching every word.

After receiving the letter Sir Edmund had gone out to a vestry meeting and then called at Colonel Welden's house. On his return he said nothing about his plans but appeared resolved to settle all his outstanding affairs that evening. He examined Mr Moor's ledgers and accounts and gave instructions about the conduct of the business. Before going to bed he collected bundles of papers from the drawers in his office and trunks upstairs and called Elizabeth to help him burn them in the hearth. While they were being burnt, he took a letter from his pocket and threw that too into the fire. It was *the* letter: Elizabeth had said there could be no mistake. She was certain that she recognised the ribbon with which it was tied.

In the morning Mr Moor had performed his usual duty of helping his master put on his coat. Sir Edmund chose his new one at first, but changed his mind and asked for an old one instead, saying that that would serve the day well enough. What he meant by that, Mr Moor could not tell. At the gate he had stopped and seemed about to say some last words, which might have given a clue to his destination. But once again he changed his mind. Mr Moor had watched him stride up the lane until he was out of sight – and never saw him alive again.

At the end of his tale the old man collapsed on Sam's shoulder, overcome by emotion and ale. They were being stared at with more than idle curiosity, and Sam grew frightened lest they be seized on suspicion of plotting. He felt in need of support himself, but made a determined effort. 'Come, Mr Moor,' he said and assisted him into the street. He had no wish for another spell of Captain Richardson's hospitality.

'I pray you tell me where I may find the maid Elizabeth,' he implored when they reached the seclusion of the lane, where the briskness of the air revived his companion. The inquiries which he had made for her in the City had come to nothing.

'She has vanished, and good riddance! When she dies, she will roast in Hell for sending innocent men to the gallows. Doting on that perjured wench ill becomes you, Master Atkins. Let her be or, if you cannot, search the whorehouses in Whetstone Park. Those are the only fitting habitations for the likes of Mistress Curtis.'

Mild Mr Moor spoke with the vehemence of the fuddled, but when he saw Sam's anger and dejection, he was at once contrite. First peering around him for spies and informers, he whispered consolingly: 'But I have one secret to impart.'

'If it will assist the cause of justice, I will listen to it most gladly,' Sam answered, tearing his thoughts from the fate of the girl on whom his heart was still set.

'Its relevance to Sir Edmund's death will be for others to determine, Master Atkins, and you must on no account name me as the source of your information. He came, like yourself, from Puritan stock, as you may know. His father was a Member of Parliament in opposition to the Crown during the reign of the late king. Although otherwise outwardly a loyal and faithful subject of His Majesty, Sir Edmund himself, you will remember, once challenged the royal prerogative and was arrested for it.'

'Outwardly only, do you mean? What then was his secret, Master Moor?'

'He was most particular never to mention it, and to the best of my belief it was known to no one amongst his acquaintances save myself, but Sir Edmund was a secret member of the Green Ribbon Club.'

— 20 —

HERTFORDSHIRE

It was May and the sun was shining again after a hard winter, but not for Mr Pepys. After the triumph of republican and Protestant extremists in the February elections, the king had decided to protect himself by dismissing his ministers. He had recovered from his illness but not from the threat to his throne. As Mr Pepys and Will Hewer had feared, Shaftesbury's opposition party was now the party of government and a new Navy Board had been appointed, packed with the Secretary's enemies.

In the House of Commons Mr Pepys was defiant. He denied that there was a single Catholic serving on any of His Majesty's ships and defended the exiled Duke of York, while deploring his religion. There had, he shouted above a hubbub of dissent, never been a greater Lord High Admiral than the duke. The response to this provocation was an official inquiry into 'the Miscarriages of the Navy'.

Personal accusations of popery, piracy and treason were levelled against Mr Secretary himself, and without the support of king or Board he had no hope of riding out the storm. His forced resignation from office was not sufficient to appease the now all-powerful earl. Treason was the most serious of the charges against him, and to provide the necessary evidence, a perjuror as barefaced as Dr Oates and Captains Bedloe and Atkins was coached and groomed.

'Colonel' Scott, the son of a miller in Kent, had emigrated to New England, where his first recorded crime was a land swindle on Long Island. He had been jailed for theft in Connecticut and almost hanged for murder in St Kitts. He then joined the army, was court-martialled for cowardice, and fled back across the

Atlantic to Holland. There he lied about his military rank, was given command of a regiment and absconded with its funds. As a last resort he had offered his services to the republican underworld, where there were always clandestine operations to be undertaken by men without honour or scruple.

On the word of this informer, Mr Pepys's arrest was ordered by the Commons on a charge of selling naval secrets to the French. Loss of office had entailed eviction from Derby House; so it was from Will Hewer's home in Buckingham Street that he prepared to depart for the Tower – in his own coach and a state of high indignation.

He kept the two officers sent to arrest him waiting while he finished writing letters vigorously protesting his innocence. Will was instructed to have copies delivered to the king in Whitehall, the Speaker of the Commons in Westminster and the Duke of York in the Spanish Netherlands. While he wrote, Sam loaded the coach with bags full of papers from which he intended to prepare a defence capable of defeating even the most corrupt of witnesses and most unjust of legal systems.

There were sad farewell embraces in the street, and Sam returned to the house red-eyed and low in spirits. It was almost six weeks since his conversation with Henry Moor in the White Horse tavern – weeks during which he had covered much ground in his investigations, but made little progress towards a solution. It had become his routine to perform the duties required of him in the Navy Office in the mornings and pursue the trail of Mr Justice Godfrey's murderers during the remainder of the day, under Will Hewer's supervision.

He had imagined that Mr Pepys's downfall would precipitate Will's and his own, but in the event it had served to make the head clerk and his underlings indispensable. The new Secretary was an ignorant placeman who busied himself currying favour with the Board and transmitting their commands, gladly leaving the work of administration in experienced hands.

Will, seated now in his own parlour vacated by Mr Pepys, looked surprisingly cheerful. 'Not only is the Tower more comfortable than Newgate,' he assured Sam, 'but release is easier if the king will bring himself to command it. His Majesty's present retreat is tactical. I see him hovering over the little earl like a hawk, waiting for him to expose and overreach himself. Then he will swoop, and it will be all change at the Tower. Danby and Pepys will come out and Shaftesbury will go in again.'

'Give me leave to abandon the investigation and do nothing but work for our master's release,' Sam begged. He was frustrated and restless.

Will tutted reprovingly. 'You disappoint me, Sam,' he chided. 'Have you not understood that the best service we can render Mr Pepys is to demonstrate to all the world that the Earl of Shaftesbury was the instigator of Mr Justice Godfrey's murder? It must be he, for he has thrived upon it. It is this murder which has won him the election and carried him to power. Colonel Welden is certainly deceiving himself if he truly believes that the Catholics could be so foolish as to bring such odium upon themselves.'

'Yet, if we are to trust the word of Mr Moor, Sir Edmund was a member of the earl's party,' Sam objected.

Together they pondered on what Sam had uncovered. Henry Moor had taken fright at having spoken rashly in his cups. He had refused a second meeting. One of Sir Edmund's brothers and his wife had moved into the magistrate's house, and Sam was told that he was not welcome unless he came on Navy Office business. So Will had armed him with an order for timber, and this had gained him admittance and another instalment of information.

'Let us rehearse what you have learned of Sir Edmund's movements after his clerk's last sight of him,' said Will.

As Mr Moor had remembered, it was between nine and ten o'clock when the magistrate left the house on the morning of his disappearance, and past noon when a servant arrived from Colonel Welden to inquire why he had not come to dine. 'My master believes that papists have been watching for him these last days and have caught him at last,' the servant had said; at which Mr Moor had expressed surprise that Catholics should wish to harm him, because he had never been an enemy to them.

'Never *openly* an enemy would be nearer the truth if he belonged to the Green Ribbon Club,' Will commented and signed to Sam to continue.

Before the day was out, the rumour that Sir Edmund had been done to death by papists was all over town, but spread by whom? By Green Ribboners? By his brothers? By Colonel Welden or his servants?

Early next morning, which was a Sunday, Henry Moor went to Hammersmith where the magistrate's mother lived, but he was not there and she knew nothing of his whereabouts. The clerk then went to the City to report the absence to Sir Edmund's brother Michael, who instructed him to keep it a close secret. He returned home in time for morning service at St Martin's with the rest of the household. There, so he told Sam, 'it was in all people's mouths' that the magistrate had been murdered by papists in Somerset House.

Will interrupted again to note the early mention of Somerset House. If that was not the real scene of the crime, did this not suggest that all the rumours were started by the murderers themselves in accordance with a prepared plan of deception?

At dawn on the Monday Mr Moor set out to explore the fields and woods where his master was wont to take exercise in the fresh air and wander undisturbed. He scoured the country around Marylebone and Paddington, including Primrose Hill. He questioned everyone he met and his hunt lasted until darkness fell. While he was away, the brothers conducted their own search in town, but that too proved fruitless.

The disappearance was publicly announced the next day, and the rumours which then circulated were of suicide. Perhaps they were spread by papists out of desperation, Sam surmised. There was also talk of an attack by thieves; of a hurried escape abroad to avoid creditors; of a secret elopement with a rich widow. Various sightings were reported, but none could be confirmed.

When Sam stopped, Will asked for his explanation of two strange incidents: one at a barber's shop, the other at a bookseller's.

While the barber was shaving a customer, a man had put his head into the shop and called out that Sir Edmund had taken his own life and his remains had been found on Primrose Hill. That was on the Tuesday, two days before the discovery of the body.

'Neither the barber nor the man he was shaving can describe the appearance of the stranger, who was but fleetingly seen,' said Sam. 'But both are sure of his words and the date. I have spoken to them several times, but cannot shake their testimony.'

'A premature disclosure containing two facts, one right and the other wrong!' mused Will. 'The answer can only be that the body was already there on that day and first discovered by an innocent passer-by who took care not to fall under suspicion. Bromwell and Walters would have done well to be as prudent.'

Sam disagreed. 'According to evidence given at the inquest by a man out hunting in the fields, there was no sign of the body there on the Tuesday or Wednesday. And the gentlemen at the bookseller's were told a different tale.'

Two clergymen browsing in a bookshop in St Paul's churchyard had reported being asked by a stranger whether they had heard the news that the missing magistrate's body had been found in Leicester Fields, run through with his own sword. Their informant was described as a well-spoken young man wearing grey clothing, but all Sam's explorations had failed to trace him.

'The town is full of madmen and pranksters,' sighed Will. 'Some delight in conveying false intelligence.'

'It is another premature disclosure with one correct fact,' Sam pointed out. 'This news that Sir Edmund was stuck with his own sword was reported at one o'clock on Thursday, a full hour before Bromwell and Walters stumbled across the body.'

'So we have a mystery beyond solution,' said Will, rising to his feet. 'You have done your best to retrace the murdered man's movements on the last day when he was seen alive. You have inquired of all those who reported seeing him. You have questioned the landlords at all the hostelries mentioned in evidence by Oates, Bedloe, Prance and your namesake. You have interrogated all the guards and servants at Somerset House who will speak with you. You have sought out the relatives of the men wrongfully condemned. You must be weary of tramping the streets of London. What more can be done?'

Sam rose too. 'Mr Hewer,' he said solemnly, 'I was born and bred here. I have spent weeks in prison longing to be allowed to walk the streets. It is a joy and no hardship, I do assure you. I love London as I love the truth and as I love –'

His throat closed and would not let the next words pass. 'Besides,' he continued when he could, 'I owe it to Mr Pepys and yourself to succeed. Pray grant me more time.'

Ever kind and sympathetic, Will understood. 'You have not yet found Elizabeth Curtis,' he said, taking the name from Sam's lips. 'Sir Edmund's pretty maid who has stolen your heart has disgraced herself and Mr Moor will not talk of her. She has gone to ground, but whether with friends or in a whorehouse or a graveyard we do not know.'

Sam flushed. 'I believe Elizabeth lies hidden against her will; otherwise she would have discovered herself to me. The mystery may be resolved if I have your permission to ride out to Hertfordshire. I would be gone in an hour and return on the morrow.'

'What information have you that the wench is hiding her shame in that direction?' Will was taken by surprise.

Sam explained that Mr Moor had persisted in affirming that he had no knowledge of the girl, nor wished for any. But yesterday they had met in the street and the old man had said that he was tired of being badgered and told him where he might find Sir Edmund's housekeeper. Mistress Pamphlin's services were no longer required in Hartshorn Lane, and she had retired to live with her sister in a village near St Albans. It was she who had employed the maid. If anyone could direct him towards Elizabeth's hiding place, Mr Moor said, it would be Judith Pamphlin.

Will Hewer considered the proposal and gave his consent, and within the promised hour Sam had hired a horse and set off.

In the fine spring weather the road to the north was almost as thronged with wayfarers as the Strand or Cheapside itself. Coachmen in haste jostled with slow-moving waggoners, and both cursed horsemen obstructing their path. All three shouted abuse at those afoot who presumed to stray from the verge. Around them the country was green and burgeoning, but most were townsmen impervious to the beauty of the wild. Sam's mind was occupied with his mission and visions of his lost love.

After a night at an inn overshadowed by the abbey church he rode on for some six miles through narrow twisting lanes until the village identified by Mr Moor came into view. Beside the green he dismounted and questioned a boy, who pointed to one of the houses. It was little more than a cottage, and Sam, remembering the proud mistress of Mr Justice Godfrey's household, wondered at how low she had sunk.

The door was opened at his knock, and there she stood, as erect and gaunt and stern as ever. 'Master Atkins!' she exclaimed, her look of astonishment quickly changing to suspicion. She would not allow him to enter the house, but he could tell that she was eager for news from London and persuaded her to put on her cloak and bonnet and walk with him in the sunshine outside.

They strolled around the pond on the green, while she asked at first about Henry Moor and the new occupants of the house in Hartshorn Lane, and then about the new administration and the fate of Dr Wakeman and others awaiting trial for plotting.

'Now, Mistress Pamphlin,' he said at last, 'I have obliged you this past half-hour. Pray return the favour and oblige me. I seek the maid Elizabeth, who has vanished. There was, as I recollect, a bond of affection between her and yourself, and I think she will not have concealed her whereabouts from you.'

'I am as ignorant as yourself, Master Atkins,' she protested. The look of suspicion had returned and she would say no more except to inquire how else she might oblige him.

'You must believe that my desire is to help Elizabeth, not for her to be harmed in any way,' Sam persisted. He was finding the other's suspicion infectious and wondering whether there might not be some reason other than shame at her reduced circumstances why he had not been invited indoors. Turning on her without warning, he cried accusingly: 'She is here!'

'I would that she were, but she is not. My sister is sick, but you may search the house if you doubt my word.'

She spoke sincerely and he believed her. 'Must I return to London empty-handed?' he demanded. 'Surely you are not averse from assisting me to solve the riddle of your old master's death? Would you not have the real culprits punished?'

'I will assist you in so far as it lies within my power and in so far as it brings me no more grief,' she replied.

'Then tell me, I pray you, whether Mr Moor speaks truly when he says that Sir Edmund was a member of the Green Ribbon Club. He has confided in me that he alone knew this secret, but you too must have been aware of it if it be true.'

She inclined her head in confirmation. 'Because he was reluctant to enforce the law against Catholics, he was sent a message from Lord Shaftesbury demanding that he join the club to prove his loyalty to the Protestant cause. Otherwise he was threatened with denunciation as a covert papist; which he never was. Sir Edmund was as antipapist as the next man, but he bore individual Catholics no ill will. If they were born to that religion, that was not a crime but their misfortune, he used to say. The persons he detested were the vile earl and his minions.' Mistress Pamphlin sniffed her own disapproval.

'Yet he joined them?'

'Not at once, nor willingly. But I believe he saw it as an opportunity to keep watch on their misdoings.'

'When, pray, did this occur?' Sam asked.

'It was two years ago this month. I remember the date well because in all my thirty years' service in his house I never, until his last days, saw Sir Edmund so downcast. The threat made him ill and he took himself off to France. He must have realised the danger in which he stood. Believe me, Master Atkins, it was no accident that Tonge and Oates chose him to swear before. His loyalty was being tested again, and this time he chose not to submit. He went straight to warn his friend, Mr Coleman, heedless of the consequences to himself.'

Sam drew her into the village church: at first to the chancel, where they knelt together in prayer, and then to a high box pew out of the sight of prying eyes. 'So you feel sure that Sir Edmund was killed by Protestants?' he asked.

'As surely as I know that there is a God in Heaven,' she replied. 'Those three poor Catholic labourers were as innocent as babes. I would be suffering the torments of Hell had I sworn against them.'

Her reserve had ebbed, her resistance was over, and he judged that no further prompting was necessary. They sat in a communion of silence until she chose to speak again.

'Mr Moor, Elizabeth and myself – we were all taken to Newgate to inspect the three prisoners charged with Sir Edmund's murder. We were to identify one of them as a man who was said to have called at the house between nine and ten o'clock on the morning of the day when he was last seen alive. When they were paraded in front of us, Mr Moor excused himself on the grounds that he was out of the house at the time searching for his master. Elizabeth and I both swore that we had never seen any of them before in our lives.'

'Did Elizabeth not identify Hill as the man?'

'Not on the first occasion; nor on the second. They were all taken away and brought back shaven, and we were again urged to recognise one of their faces. I repeated that they were all unknown to me, and that I had no knowledge of any man calling that morning to inquire in what direction the magistrate had gone and for what purpose. Elizabeth agreed with me at first, but took fright when pressed hard and said she could not tell.'

At his own remembrance of Newgate and the thought of the ordeal which the two women had suffered, Sam shuddered and ventured to squeeze Mistress Pamphlin's bony hand in sympathy.

'The next day,' she continued, 'a brute of a man came to the house and at the sight of him Elizabeth fainted clean away. I bade him be gone but he would not. When the girl recovered her senses, he told her that he had an order for her arrest in his pocket. He said that she knew full well that Hill was the man who had called at the house that Saturday morning, and that if she did not promise to stop lying and tell the truth she would be taken to prison and indicted as an accessory to the murder. When I intervened, he threatened me with violence.'

'Then we must not blame her too harshly for perjuring herself in court,' said Sam. 'Mr Moor is unforgiving, but I pity her. It made no difference to Hill. He was a dead man with or without her evidence. She had cause to reproach herself, but not to hide in shame from her friends.'

Judith Pamphlin shed a tear. 'I loved her as I would a child of my own,' she cried, 'and I can tell you what terrified her. She recognised the brute who was sent to threaten us. It was the man who had brought the letter to Sir Edmund on the eve of his disappearance. *He* was a real accessory to the murder, and he saw that she knew it. After the trial she was snatched from the house while Mr Moor and I were out, and that must be the reason. She would never have left of her own free will without a word to me.'

Sam, venturing further, put an arm around her shoulder and spoke in her ear: 'Have you truly heard nothing at all from her? Have you made all possible inquiries without avail?'

He waited on tenterhooks until she had regained her composure. 'There has been one report,' she said at last, 'and one alone. But it gives me hope that my Elizabeth is still alive. A servant from a house across the lane told me that he had caught a glimpse of her when out on an errand one day. It was in the neighbourhood of Leicester Fields.'

Sam echoed those last two words. Was that not the very place where Sir Edmund's body was first reported to have been discovered? God had not been slow to answer his prayer.

— 21 —

LEICESTER FIELDS

Leicester Fields lay to the north-west of St Martin's church, on the far side of the parish from Hartshorn Lane and the Strand. Formerly lammas land, the ground had been bought by the Earl of Leicester during the late king's reign. He had laid it out as a square and built a mansion which occupied the whole of its north side. Town houses of other members of the nobility had filled the remaining sides, and these fashionable inhabitants were now dignifying the recently tamed fields with the more genteel name of Leicester Square.

Since his return from Hertfordshire Sam had spent every day crouched in the bushes which formed a garden in the centre. Secluded from traffic, the square was deathly quiet and seemed as many miles from the clamour of the Strand as Mistress Pamphlin's village. To the north, past Leicester House, there were still open fields leading to the villages of Hampstead and Highgate – and to Primrose Hill.

Sometimes a servant or tradesman would appear, and occasionally the silence was broken by the clatter of a coach arriving or departing. At other times Sam was alone with his fears, and a full week passed before his vigil was rewarded.

It was hard to watch all four sides without betraying his presence, and he nearly missed her. But all of a sudden there she was, only a few yards from where he lay hidden. His dearest one looked jaded. She walked with dragging steps and downcast eyes, closely escorted by an evil-looking ruffian. They must have emerged from one of the houses while his back was turned – no doubt from the one he most suspected.

Her guardian was peering about him and Sam decided that

pursuit would not be worth the risk of discovery. Instead he stayed where he was and prayed that they were making but a short expedition and would soon return. An hour later his patience was rewarded. Beauty and the beast came into view again, laden with provisions. His heart thumping, he watched them enter one of the mansions by a side door. It was *the* mansion. All his forebodings were realised.

Leaping through the bushes and vaulting the railings, he ran to the door. It was unlocked. He pushed it open, stumbled down some steps and was at once plunged into a dark passageway. As he hesitated, the dim outline of a female figure became discernible ahead of him. 'Elizabeth!' he called softly. She swung round in alarm and uttered a half-stifled scream.

They ran towards each other and he pulled her, hugger-mugger, into the nearest room. 'Speak quickly before we are discovered,' he urged. 'Are you kept prisoner here?'

'Yes,' she whispered. 'They will never let me go.' Her eyes filled with tears, and he longed to kiss them dry.

'Do they hold you because you know who killed your master?'

'The murderer is here – in this house. He . . .' She broke down, shuddering with terror, sobbing to him to take her away.

'Speak,' he begged her. 'Speak or it will be too late.' He threw a glance around him. Their refuge was a narrow, unlit pantry. With luck they would be safe for a few more minutes.

'There was a letter which Sir Edmund tore up and flung into the fire. When I cleaned the hearth the next morning I noticed a fragment which had fallen out and not been burned. It bore the signature.' Her voice was so low that he had to strain to hear what she said.

'Why did you not tell Mistress Pamphlin or Mr Moor? Why did you lie at the trial if you knew the truth?' He spoke more roughly than he intended and shook the words out of her so that they fell from her lips in a flood as though suddenly undammed.

'Because the name scared me nigh to death,' she whispered, 'and when the servant came back to make me swear that I recognised Mr Hill and I told him that I knew who his master was, he said that I would be killed. So I promised not to reveal it and to swear what they wanted if only they would leave me alone. But they broke their word and keep me here against my will. Dear, kind Sam, pray take me away with you now, at once, this very instant, or neither of us will ever leave this – *his* house – alive.'

He drew back the door cautiously and looked outside. There was no sound and no one in sight. He seized her hand and together they tiptoed to the end of the passage. Only the steps to the street lay between them and freedom when all at once the way was blocked. The ruffian whom Sam had seen with her in the square sprang out and barred their path.

'That is the murderer's man!' Elizabeth cried. 'That is the messenger who brought the letter!' She shrank away from him against the wall.

He was a porter and had been on duty waiting for them, Sam realised as they grappled with each other. Sam had been taken by surprise, but his opponent was armed with a stave and well prepared. Beaten to his knees, he shouted to Elizabeth to run for her life, but the noise had brought other servants hotfoot. Sam was knocked to the ground and Elizabeth pinioned to the wall. On the porter's orders, they were dragged back inside the house and locked in the pantry.

Lying dazed and blinded by his own blood, Sam called urgently to Elizabeth to escape through the window, to run to Buckingham Street and tell Will Hewer where he was to be found.

'There is no window, Sam,' she told him, kneeling to cradle his head and wipe the blood from his face. 'We shall die here together.'

He stirred himself to give her courage. 'If they meant to kill you, Elizabeth,' he said, 'they would surely have done so already. But, by the grace of God, even the most wicked may scruple to molest a woman.' She was so young, so innocent, so fragile; harming her was unthinkable. At the word 'molest' she flinched as though he had hit her.

His eyes were clear now and through the gloom he could distinguish the misery on her face. His words, he saw, had not brought comfort, but pain and a flush of shame. The reason struck him like another blow from the porter's stave. 'Have you been forced to lie with him?'

No words from her were needed. They were written on her face. A perjuror and now a whore! He groaned for her honour, for her peace of mind and his own, and vowed revenge.

They lay in each other's arms and lost count of time. Whore or no, she was the sweetest of creatures and he loved her still: the wrong she had done was not of her own volition.

She whispered to him of her childhood: how after the death of her parents from the plague she had been caught stealing food to save herself from starvation, and how Justice Godfrey had pardoned her and taken her into his own house out of the kindness of his heart because she had no home and nowhere else to go. In return Sam spoke of his mother, the only other woman he had ever loved. She had died giving birth to his sister, leaving a void in his heart not filled until he met Elizabeth.

A key grated in the lock. The porter entered with two footmen, who pulled them to their feet without ceremony and led them out of the servants' quarters, across a marble hall and up a broad flight of carpeted stairs. At the top they were taken into a bare panelled chamber. The footmen stood on guard either side of the door, while the grim-faced porter disappeared to fetch his master.

Soon heavy footsteps approached. 'Close the door and leave us,' commanded a voice which Sam remembered all too well. It was the Mighty Giant himself. He was wearing a black velvet coat and a scarlet silk waistcoat with a countryman's thick boots and the grin of a drunken madman bent on mischief. His size was as menacing as his glazed look. He towered over them, muscular and broad-shouldered like a prize pugilist, swaying gently so that his wig brushed the ceiling.

'Samuel Atkins of the Navy Office at your service, my lord,' Sam boldly introduced himself, keeping Elizabeth behind him and backing towards the window in trepidation even as he bowed. 'I am acquainted with your lordship through seeing you convicted of the manslaughter of Nathaniel Coney in Westminster Hall last year. I believe that to be not the only homicide for which your lordship is responsible.' Inwardly he was quaking at his own rashness.

'You, sir, have had the effrontery to enter my house uninvited,' said the earl in a slurred, measured tone: 'a lecherous cur sniffing after that pretty little bitch you are trying to conceal from me. Pray be informed that you have arrived too late for her maidenhead. The slut has lost it and become part-worn. She has been in need of greater protection than a low-born creature like yourself can afford her and your heroics can do nothing for her now. I shall not stoop to take notice of your insults, but before I teach you a lesson in killing, it would interest me to learn what other homicide you have in mind.'

Sam pondered desperately on his next words and actions. When Will Hewer heard of Judith Pamphlin's mention of Leicester Fields, he had had inquiries made about the ownership of all the houses in the square. As soon as he and Sam saw the name of Philip, 7th Earl of Pembroke and Montgomery, they felt sure that they had found their man. Nathaniel Coney had not been his only victim. His lordship had gained notoriety for a long record of violent assaults, mostly unprovoked and committed in his cups. Coffee-house gossip went so far as to credit him with no fewer than twenty-six brutal murders.

Here then, looming over Sam, was a man too high, too rich and too powerful to be subjected to the law. The witnesses to his crimes were too intimidated to report them or to appear and give evidence if they came to court. Thanks to Sir Edmund's determination to have the law upheld without fear or favour, he had been brought to justice on one further occasion after the Coney affair and this time convicted of murder. But so far from being hanged, as promised by the Lord High Steward after his conviction for killing Coney, he had escaped all punishment. The king had graciously granted him a pardon at the instance of the Earl of Shaftesbury.

'I refer to the murder of Sir Edmund Berry Godfrey,' said Sam, casting all caution to the winds.

'All the world knows that Mr Justice Godfrey died a martyr to the Protestant cause. He was done to death by vile papists who have justly suffered for it. Can you be so ignorant as to be unaware of my devotion to the Church of England and the party of the Green Ribbon? May God rest the martyr's soul, say I.' To Sam's amazement the Mighty Giant was showing no anger at the accusation. He was proud of what he had done and laughed with a chilling, high-pitched giggle.

Sam stood frozen with fear. The man was a maniac beyond doubt and reason, and his breath was strongly flavoured with the smell of brandy. Even more alarmingly, he was shaking his head from side to side and squaring his shoulders to throw off his sluggishness and brace himself for action.

Talking until the torpor returned – and with it, God willing, stupefaction – seemed to Sam his only hope.

'Sir Edmund's body was bruised on the chest and stomach as Mr Coney's was,' he said. 'Sir Edmund was beaten, strangled and stabbed, as I am led to understand that other of your victims have been. Few men kill another not once only, but in three different ways.'

'That is because few are man enough to show the delight in killing which all men feel. It is a sweeter pleasure than bedding a young virgin.' The earl leered. His confession was a boast. Without taking his eyes from Sam's face, he moved across the room, picked up a heavy candlestick from the mantel and tossed the candle to the floor. It was wax, not tallow!

'Traitors must be punished,' he said. 'That is a universal law in civilised societies, be they realms or parties or clubs. I offered your precious Godfrey the choice of being knocked on the head in the street or coming here to explain his conduct. He chose to obey my summons. I allowed him two or three days locked up without food to repent of his treachery. Then he was brought to this chamber, where he had the impudence to remonstrate with me. Whereupon I enjoyed the pleasure of sending him into the next world to account for himself there. Now I shall satisfy your curiosity to the full, Master Atkins, by demonstrating how it was done. Pray stand to one side and let me get to that shivering draggle-tail behind you. She is no longer of any use to either of us, I do assure you.'

Sam carried no weapon, but he stood firm in front of the terrified girl. 'Will your lordship be kind enough to satisfy my curiosity on another point first?' he asked in desperation. 'I beg you to inform me who chose you to be the executioner.'

'No man commands the Earl of Pembroke,' his lordship replied. 'There was a score to be settled between Sir Edmund and myself. He lacked respect for his betters and a proper sense of duty. Last year he was instrumental in having me, a nobleman, indicted for murder. Come now,' he added brusquely, 'let us have done with this prevarication, Master Atkins. For the last time I bid you: stand aside. Your turn will come next, I do promise you. But first you must watch her die. It will not take long.'

While he was speaking, Sam had continued to edge backwards towards the window with a trembling Elizabeth still clutching his coat tails. He had glimpsed a balcony from which she might call for help or jump to safety. To cover her escape, he had to keep taunting the lunatic and encouraging him to brag. 'Are our bodies, too, to be found on Primrose Hill?' he asked.

The earl curled his lip in a sneer. 'I would not trouble my servants to carry them thus far. They will be thrown on the nearest dung-heap like Godfrey's – and any other dead dog's.'

'But we have no swords with which to be stabbed in a pretence of suicide. Have a care and spare time for thought, my lord, or you will be hanged at last.' Behind his back, as he spoke, Sam pushed Elizabeth to one side and contrived to prise the window open a few inches.

The earl's response was an ominous narrowing of the eyes and another giggle. 'We are sometimes attainted and beheaded for treason,' he said. 'But noblemen are not to be hanged for ridding the world of base fellows and their strumpets.' The candlestick, held high, was now being brandished like a mace, ready to descend at any moment and crack Sam's skull like an eggshell.

'Who moved Sir Edmund's body, and for what reason?' Even in the hour of death, with his eye fixed on the weapon poised above him, Sam was desperate for the truth.

'Others thought to move it to a place where he was wont to walk, near to a tavern frequented by papists. It proved a clever move, did it not?' The laughter became mocking.

'The order to move it was given by a clever man, I have no doubt,' Sam replied. 'So I must suppose the idea to have been the brainchild of your master, my lord of Shaftesbury.'

This was one provocation too many. Sam realised that he had spoken a truth never to be uttered. The laughter ceased abruptly. Warned just in time, he leaped to one side.

The blow from the candlestick missed his head by a hair's breadth and fell on his shoulder. Gritting his teeth against the pain, he closed with his assailant, pummelled him on the chest and then caught him round the waist to keep Elizabeth out of his grasp. Ill-matched in strength, he all too quickly found himself flung to the ground and felt the pounding of those heavy boots crushing his ribs.

The girl was half-way through the window when the earl broke away from Sam to seize her in his giant arms. She tumbled back into the room shrieking. He put both hands round her throat and with a gloating smile lifted her off her feet. She struggled in the air, dangling like a snared animal, until he squeezed so tightly that a bone in her neck snapped like a pistol shot and he let her crumpled body fall.

Sam staggered weakly to his feet and set about the murderer with all the force he could muster. It was not enough. He had retrieved the candlestick from the floor, but it was wrenched from his hands and a blow over the ear sent him reeling against the wall.

Within a few moments he was lying sprawled on his back on the floor again, losing consciousness and with it the will to live. All he could make out was the smirking face of the mad peer drooling over his next victim. He was about to be trampled to death, but could not bring himself to care, knowing that there was nothing to be done to save himself. Unbearable, though, were the knowledge of Elizabeth's fate and the thought that the secret of Mr Justice Godfrey's death would die with him.

He was struggling to rouse himself in a final effort to stay alive when the door burst open and he became aware of a frenzied figure catching the Mighty Giant by surprise and battering him with a club from behind until he toppled over like a felled tree. Sam's last memory was of the crash of the earl's head landing beside his own and the awful shudder of the wooden floor beneath them.

When consciousness returned, he was lying between silk sheets, surrounded by damask hangings, in the largest and softest bed he had ever known. Save for the throbbing in his head and the aching of his ribs, he might have arrived in Paradise. At his stirring the curtains were drawn apart and a woman's voice bade him not to be distressed, for the earl had been bundled into a coach and despatched to Wilton, where he kept all manner of beasts as wild as himself.

A firm hand prevented him from rising. 'You must stay and rest,' the voice continued. 'Am I not practised at caring for you in bed?'

He puzzled over the words and the foreign accent. Slowly the haze surrounding his memory dispersed and he remembered who it must be with a feeling of shame. She was the lady's maid of the Duchess of Portsmouth, the king's French mistress. She was the one who had accompanied the duchess on her incognito visit to the *Catherine* at Greenwich – the one he had woken from his drunken stupor the next morning to find himself in bed with. She had been by no means handsome, but, as he now recollected, excessive wantonness in the darkness had amply compensated for want of looks.

'How do you come to be in this house, Mistress Sarah?' he asked in astonishment.

'Mistress Sarah!' she repeated mockingly. 'So your mind is clear enough to remember my *nom de guerre* on the day of that little excursion down the river! My sister called herself Mistress Jane for the day, I think.'

Sam sat up with a start and groaned at the pain and his own stupidity. Of course he and Captain Vittells had recognised His Majesty's eye-catching Louise – who could have failed to guess the identity of such a beauty? But how could he have mistaken Henriette, Countess of Pembroke and Montgomery for one of her women? It was not in this room, but somewhere he had lain with the earl's wife! He had cuckolded the Mighty Giant!

'I humbly entreat your ladyship's pardon,' he corrected himself, sinking back in the bed and pulling the coverlet up to his chin in embarrassment. 'I owe my life to you, and I most earnestly trust to God that in saving mine you have not endangered your own.'

'Have no fears for my safety,' she told him. 'My plans are already laid. I leave for Brittany tomorrow.'

'But the ports will be closed to you,' he warned her. 'The navy and Lord Shaftesbury's men are on the watch for the queen and your sister and other Catholic ladies fleeing the country.'

She laughed. 'Let me whisper a secret in your ear, Master Sam. My sister and the little earl have become allies since he came to power. He pays her well for reports of His Majesty's prattling when their heads are together on the pillow. To oblige her, he has himself made the arrangements for my journey – without my husband's knowledge.

'Now you must go to sleep again,' she went on, smoothing the bedclothes and his forehead. 'This is my bed and I have one more night to spend in it, so you must be rested and fit by then.' She leaned over him again to cool his burning cheeks with rose-water and kiss him on the lips.

When he felt her tongue burrowing through his teeth, he

sprang from the bed as though brought suddenly back to life. His head whirled and he lost his balance and fell to the floor, but regained his feet before she could reach him. 'Your ladyship is too kind,' he mumbled unsteadily, 'but I shall be good for nothing for a seven-night or more and must drag myself home before an alarm is raised.'

She must have stripped him, for he was stark naked and oil had been rubbed into his bruises. Hastening to don his clothes, he felt her eyes running over his body. Modesty was not among her virtues, but she made no attempt to detain him. 'The maid Elizabeth,' he asked breathlessly when he was dressed: 'How is she?'

The countess took him by the hand and led him to the panelled room, where the girl's body still lay as he had seen it flung by the earl. The head was askew like a broken doll's – and the dead magistrate's. The icy chill of her hand froze his own. He knelt beside her, weeping, until the countess pulled him away.

'The wench shall have a Christian burial,' she promised. 'I will give the order before I leave. Do not seek to have the earl brought to justice; it is you who would suffer. But at least he shall pay for her funeral.'

Together they descended the grand staircase, her arm around his shoulder and her hand steadying him at every step. The two footmen bowed them impassively through the hall and opened the door for him with a flourish, not looking him in the face.

'They will say nothing,' she told him, 'nor will the porter. Do I have your promise of silence too?'

'Ask anything of me but that, my lady,' he implored, 'for it is a promise I cannot make. The world must know who really killed Mr Justice Godfrey. But you have my word that I will keep my silence until you have left the shores of England. Pray rest content with that.'

'You are a young fool, Master Atkins,' she called after him. 'You will be putting your life in hazard again for nothing, for you will not be believed. Where would your countrymen be without their Popish Plot?'

He staggered down the steps from the porch into the street and through the hushed square, out into the bustle of the road to Charing Cross. Passers-by stared at him as he went reeling like a drunkard, faint with pain, uncertain whether his battered body would carry him to Buckingham Street unaided.

But on the way he forced himself to turn aside into St Martin's church, where he had three solemn duties to perform.

First, he offered a prayer at the altar for the soul of Elizabeth Curtis, spinster, late of this parish. 'May all her sins be forgiven her, O merciful Lord!' he prayed. *'Requiescat in pace!'*

Next, faltering, swaying on his knees, he humbly thanked Him who had rescued Daniel from the lions' den for his own escape from Pembroke House and the preservation of his unworthy life.

Lastly, he summoned his remaining strength to swear before the Almighty and All-Seeing that he would never be party to the suppression of any truth, divine or human – most especially, the truth about the murder of Sir Edmund Berry Godfrey.

POSTSCRIPT

The king was taking his morning stroll through St James's Park, outwardly unconcerned at the political and religious turmoil afflicting his realm. His attention seemed fully engaged in inciting his spaniels to chase the ducks.

His mood was one of secret self-congratulation. He had thrown off his sickness and languor and called an abrupt halt to Shaftesbury's mischief by proroguing the new Parliament. Lords and Commons had been sent scuttling indignantly out of town before they could present him with any further instalments of the seditious legislation which they were so zealously debating. They had thought it a game he could no longer afford to play, but if Louis continued to pay what he had promised – and who could doubt the word of a king? – it would be a long time before what he privately dubbed 'that regicidal rabble' received a royal summons to reassemble.

Sam was resplendent in a smart new suit of clothes and a hat and periwig of the latest style, all supplied by courtesy of Will Hewer. Thus attired, and twirling one of Mr Pepys's silver-knobbed canes, he treated the sentries at the gate to a blade's supercilious stare and gained entry to the park as though of right. At the court of King Charles the clothes were the man.

A week had passed since his escape from Pembroke House, but he was still in pain. His bruises were tender, his back was stiff and two of his ribs were fractured. Concealing his trepidation beneath an air of nonchalance, he joined the fringe of the king's entourage, taking care to keep at a respectful distance while awaiting his opportunity.

This came when the king stepped forward to throw some

crusts to wildfowl in the canal. Before he could be stopped, Sam had dashed forward and was on his knees, begging for permission to convey confidential intelligence of the utmost importance.

When he understood that the young dandy was a mere clerk in the Navy Office, Charles smiled at his impudence. Welcoming the unexpected diversion, he ordered his guards to stand back, curious to learn what important secrets such a person might possess. Sam was commanded to rise and speak.

He was also bidden to hold the royal bread basket, so that the fowl would not go hungry while he told his tale. But no sooner had his revelations begun than His Majesty's attention was caught and held and the birds went unfed. By the end the king stood transfixed, amusement and indifference banished. He said nothing and, by long practice, his face was expressionless, so that his thoughts could not be read.

The absence of response unsettled Sam. 'Your Majesty must believe me,' he urged. 'I swear in the name of God that every word which has crossed my lips is gospel true.'

'Truth is a dangerous commodity, Master Atkins,' the king replied gravely. 'It has to be handled with care, like gunpowder, or it may explode in one's face. Discretion is much to be preferred.'

'Does Your Majesty not mean to have the Earl of Pembroke put on trial and the injustice of the previous trials for Mr Justice Godfrey's murder publicly acknowledged?' Sam's question was more respectful than his feelings.

'You have no cause for complaint: you were acquitted. The others cannot be brought back to life. My lord of Pembroke has already faced trial for murder twice to no effect, and no good will come of a repetition. His friends will see to that.'

The king's calm voice of experience and commonsense stung Sam into a heated rejoinder. 'But justice –' he began.

'If you value your life, pay heed to my words, Master Atkins,' Charles interrupted him. 'Justice and the law are often strangers in these topsy-turvy times, for the law is an instrument of government, which is no longer in the hands of the sovereign, where it rightfully belongs. So if you are insistent on pressing these charges, it will be my duty to refer you to my lord of Shaftesbury.'

Sam was scandalised. 'But, as I have just informed Your Majesty, the Earl of Shaftesbury –'

'– is my chief minister and therefore the proper person to advise me on your allegations. If you do not favour another interrogation by his lordship and further imprisonment at his lordship's pleasure, you would do well to say no more about this unfortunate affair. Casting doubt on our famous Popish Plot will not make you the nation's hero, and I would lay odds that on this occasion the charge would be treason and you would not escape so easily. I speak now for your own good, Master Atkins.'

'Does Your Majesty advise or command my silence?' Sam put the question defiantly. When he read on the king's face that it was a command, he added boldly: 'Then I crave a favour in return.'

'Oh ho!' the king exclaimed, feigning anger. 'Subjects do not bargain with their sovereigns, as you would soon learn if you honoured us by coming to court more often. But tell me, pray, what favour do you have in mind?'

'I humbly petition Your Majesty for the release from custody of your loyal servant and my respected master, Mr Samuel Pepys, formerly of the Navy Office.'

Charles resumed his leisurely walk and signed to Sam to stay by his side while he considered the request.

'Very well,' he said at length. 'I shall mention to my lord of Shaftesbury rumours of his involvement in Godfrey's death and suggest that I consider them too far-fetched to warrant investigation. At the same time I shall inform him of my wish that all proceedings against Mr Pepys be brought to an end without delay. He will not be slow to discern a connection between the two. Your name will not be mentioned. There! Is that to your satisfaction?'

'I am deeply grateful to Your Majesty,' Sam replied with the humblest of bows. 'But, come what may, the truth must be told before I die. My silence cannot be commanded for ever.'

'Lord!' tutted the king. 'What a hard man you are to please! I see that I can do nothing to save you. Your wilfulness and this unhealthy obsession with truth will certainly be the death of you.'

'But surely Your Majesty would at least agree that the truth should not be concealed from those who come after us,' Sam pleaded doggedly. 'History –'

But the king had finally lost patience with him. 'History and the truth!' he sneered. 'They are as strange bedfellows as justice and the law. History, Master Atkins, is what men wish to think about the past, and they will always choose to believe in the Popish Plot and the martyrdom of Mr Justice Godfrey by Roman Catholics.'

This from the man whose account of his adventures after the royalist defeat at Worcester Sam had been ordered to write in his fairest hand so as to be sure that posterity would know the truth! Sam could not trust himself to say another word.

'You are young and will outlive me if you have the good sense to curb your tongue,' the king continued. 'After I am dead you may speak as you please, but do not expect to be believed until the two faiths have learned to live together like Christians.'

The bread basket was retrieved and Sam dismissed.

He returned disconsolate to Buckingham Street, where he learned that the danger to his life was imminent. A band of the Earl of Pembroke's men had been to the house searching for him and said they would return. He had scarcely crossed the threshold before a pale Will Hewer despatched him in great secrecy to the house of a cousin of Mr Pepys near Huntingdon.

There he lay undiscovered for six months, recovering from the hardship of Newgate, the mad earl's assault, the loss of his Elizabeth and disappointment at the king's refusal to act.

News of the great world reached him sparsely and late. With the rest of the household he rejoiced and hurried across the fields to the parish church to give thanks to God, when they heard that Mr Pepys had been set free.

Next came a report that Sir George Wakeman, the queen's Catholic physician, was at last brought to trial to answer Oates's accusation that he had plotted with the Jesuits to poison the king. This was followed by another the next day, bringing news of his acquittal, which Sam did not at first believe.

It was reported that the king had threatened the Lord Chief Justice with his gravest displeasure should a person so close to the queen be condemned, and that Sir William Scroggs had duly conducted the trial in obedience to his sovereign's wishes. Violence had broken out in Westminster Hall when the verdict was announced, and Sir William and the jury were lucky to get away with their lives. Overnight, the man who had become a hero by feeding the mob's appetite for popish victims became instead the most unpopular man in London.

With this mood prevailing, what was to be done with Sam?

When he had regained his health and strength, Mr Pepys and Will Hewer held a conference to decide. Mr Pepys then paid him a visit and offered a loan of £20 to buy himself a commission in the regiment which was stationed in Tangier, where he would be beyond the reach of his enemies.

Mr Pepys explained that, although all the charges against himself had been dropped, he was not yet restored to favour or reinstated in the Navy Office. He was, therefore, powerless to protect Sam if he chose to remain in England. Fortunately, though, Will Hewer had succeeded him as Treasurer of Tangier and could promise a berth in a troop-ship which was due to sail the following week.

'It will sadden us both beyond measure to part with you,' Mr Pepys assured him, 'but your life will be safer among marauding Mussulmen and Barbary pirates than left to the Christian mercy of my lords of Shaftesbury and Pembroke.'

Sam was still numbed by misfortune and accepted with gratitude. Ten days later, equipped as a military officer, his pen exchanged for a sword, he left England for the first time in his life.

His period of soldiering in North Africa lasted for four long, hot years, until Will arrived one day bearing secret instructions from the king to evacuate the garrison and abandon the town, which had become too expensive for the Treasury to maintain. The regiment was posted to Flanders, where Sam then served his country and the Protestant cause for a further six years before returning home. No armed enemy, either in Africa or in Europe, succeeded in wounding him as severely as had the Earl of Pembroke with candlestick and boots.

During his absence both the evil earls had died: Pembroke of drink and Shaftesbury in disgrace and exile. The king too had met his Maker, although whether as a Protestant or a covert Catholic, He alone knew. The Duke of York had succeeded to the throne as James II and brushed aside the challenge of the Protestant extremists, led to disaster by the Duke of Monmouth.

Mr Pepys had been reappointed to his old post. Titus Oates, convicted of perjury, had been pilloried, whipped by the common hangman from Aldgate to Tyburn, and imprisoned for life. Bedloe had died unrepentant before he could be punished, but Miles Prance had pleaded guilty to an indictment of wilful perjury and confessed that every word he had spoken on oath at the trial of Berry, Green and Hill had been a falsehood.

Sam's home-coming was occasioned by King James's blundering bigotry, which turned the country against him. Now Captain Samuel Atkins, he was a company commander in the army under William of Orange which drove the Catholic king into exile.

More than ten years had then passed since the killing of Mr Justice Godfrey, but still the real facts were not known. With Protestantism triumphant, antipopery was as rampant as on the day when Oates first called on the magistrate with his lying testimony. So, when Sam resolutely proclaimed what he knew, all ears were deaf to his words. Mr Pepys and Will Hewer shook their heads over his foolishness.

Undeterred, Sam persisted year after year, but all in vain. An effigy of the martyred Godfrey continued to head an annual pope-burning procession through the streets of the City, dispelling all disbelief in Catholic wickedness and burying the unwanted truth beneath a growing mound of myth.

At an annual ceremony of his own, in St Martin's churchyard on the anniversary of her death, he strewed Elizabeth's grave with rosemary for remembrance and rue for sorrow. True to her memory, he never married.

In old age he used to remember how on every Lord's day in Tangier he had sat with a heathen holy man and discussed Christianity and Islam, life and death, right and wrong in an endless search for truth. Most of all, he remembered one of the holy man's sayings which, unlike King Charles, Mr Pepys and even Will Hewer, he could never, never bring himself to accept or approve: 'It is good to know the truth and speak it' (so the Sufi taught in his wisdom), 'but often it is better to know the truth and speak of palm trees.'